LIES OF CONVENIENCE

A Route 66 Mystery

Lies of Convenience

M.M. Gornell

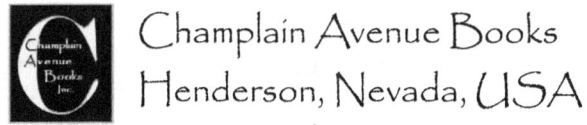

Champlain Avenue Books
Henderson, Nevada, USA

Published by Champlain Avenue Books, Inc.
Quality Fiction

Copyright © 2012 by M.M. Gornell

International Standard Book Number
ISBN-13: 978-0-9855008-0-1

Cover by LAWRENCE

FIRST EDITION - 2012

Printed in the United States of America

Dedication

John Thomas Jones

Acknowledgements

As always, my gratitude goes to my excellent editors--Mike Foley and Virginia Moody--and to my marvelous agent and editor, Kitty Kladstrup. This story would not be published without them.

To my relatives and friends, Frank Jones, Mary Hollis, Judi Moran, Barbara Ryan, Diane Gornell, Denise Jones, Abner Boles, Colleen Walsh Fong, Marjorie and Sig Hess, Gail and Jay Dobberthien, Pamela Pope, Katherine Newsom, Len Tufo, Joan Truesdell, Kathie Brown, Janice Maloney, Mary McGee, DeAnn West, and Marilyn and Jerry Phipps—thanks for your continuing words of encouragement.

I'm also most grateful to my Route 66 and Public Safety Writers Association (PSWA) friends and business owners who so graciously provided information on animals, politics, law-enforcement, and local lore. In particular, thank you Paula and Paul Deel, Vonnie and Kevin Kranz, Sandi Brittian, Wayne Weierbach, Mark Stauter, Tim Dees, Quintin Peterson, and Guy Painter. And to Barbara and Thomas Hines—who I continually pepper with questions about trucks, truckers, and all things "Mojave."

And to my cousins Marie and Harry Griffin, who have the most wonderful view of Chicago's lake front—*a view that was the starting spark for this tale*—THANK YOU for sharing your lives, constant encouragement, and most importantly—your love.

As always, thank you Larry for being there.

Preface

The world of this author's mind is populated with a multitude of places and characters—many composites, and many imaginary. Occasionally, some of these people and places escape—intermingle with reality—and become backdrops and inspiration for tales of mystery.

Situated on Route 66 as it crosses California's Mojave Desert, NewTown is a fictional place, but its inspiration is drawn from the many "small dots" spreading themselves along The Mother Road. This particular NewTown tale—even though populated with imaginary characters involved in fictional events—is nonetheless, triggered by the realities of High Desert terrain, weather, and the fortitude of its very real inhabitants.

CHICAGO, on the other hand, more than halfway across the country from NewTown, and at the start of Route 66, is on a capital-letters-scale, a world-renowned, sophisticated, and larger-than-life city. Indeed, to experience Lake Michigan's unparalleled waterfront, especially under the magical shroud of night, with city lights a-sparkling—is to be bedazzled, awed, and visually imprinted for life.

Besides their shared Route 66 heritage, how do these places and people—real and imaginary—intersect? *Therein lies the story…*

Primum Non Nocere

First, Do No Harm

How Margot Madison-Cross Became Involved

The night was clear, the stars twinkling diamonds in a cloudless ink-colored sky—and Graham Madison was a happy man.

He cherished his home and its location on the outskirts of Palm Springs. But when it came to his pearl-black Audi S5 Cabriolet, *now that was a love affair*. And sitting behind the wheel tonight, he was anticipating the feel of his sports car handling the curves ahead with great joy.

His convertible's top was up, but both windows were down so he could taste dry air and hear his tires embrace asphalt. Graham released a sigh of contentment that he had moments like this, a car like this, and a wonderful winding road as a driveway.

What could possibly go wrong? It was a perfect night.

For sure, he considered himself extremely lucky to be able to experience the exhilaration of driving his two-seater every time he came home. *Well, yes, lucky indeed—but part was his thoughtful planning.* Then there was his willingness not to settle for less. Money, time, and strength of character had finally all come together in this perfect place—a place he and Meredith had chosen together. But after their divorce, and even after her death—he'd stayed on.

For a moment, the pain of no longer having Meredith to share times like tonight surfaced—but Graham quickly refused his mind access to those emotions. *No,* he would enjoy the winding uphill stretch back to his home without troubling memories.

After leaving his favorite restaurant in Palm Springs, Graham had slipped on his hand-woven wool Scottish driving-cap, his *Fratelli Orsini* Italian-leather driving gloves, and of course, his well worn *Ferragamo* driving loafers. German car, highland's cap, and Italian gloves and shoes—his high-speed fantasy world was complete. Now, from the comfort of his body-hugging leather seats, and with his handy electronic device, Graham opened the automatic gate. The massive two-piece wrought iron panels swung open smoothly.

"What an evening," he said, and pulled through. A glance in his rear-view mirror told him his personally-designed homage to Orson Welles closed smoothly behind him.

He smiled, then made a right turn onto his nameless one-lane road that wound its way up his plateau—a minor hilltop on the edge of the San Jacinto wilderness—regally claimed by his, and only two other sprawling haciendas.

The stretch from the main road up to his home was about five miles, with several lovely curves to navigate. He enjoyed every nuance of the road as he and his machine leaned into the turns. Indeed, he grinned as he fancied he could hear air flowing over the surface of his aerodynamically designed fenders.

"Ahhh," he told the world, and wished that at least his sister Marg was enjoying this with him. Why did she insist on living in Chicago? They'd done "The Mother Road" together in their father's old Mustang—one hot summer of adventure for her twenty-first birthday. He'd been a year too young, but she'd had her first legal drink on that trip. Chicago to California—what a time they'd had.

We've both changed, he thought. *A lot.*

Caught unawares for a second, he gasped slightly as he glimpsed the barefoot trespasser again from the corner of his eye. *The second time in two weeks.* Tonight, he saw him from the rear, as the interloper's shadowy figure bobbed his way through creosote and sagebrush down to the road. Strangely, even though dusk had completely swallowed the landscape, Graham could still make out his silhouette.

That's odd, he thought. But without warning, and before Graham could speculate further or get angry at the intruder's repeated audacity—a mule deer leapt directly in front of him—the animal suddenly staring back at him in the illumination of his xenon headlights.

Graham slammed on the brakes and whipped his steering wheel to the right.

His S5 easily swung onto the shoulder away from the startled deer without skidding—but he felt his front wheels hit the roadside ditch. Still, his car obeyed him until sideswiping a boulder that seemed to come from nowhere—causing man and car to roll, hit a second boulder, then roll again.

Graham remained conscious as car and man eventually landed right-side up—partly off the ground in a broad and stubby stand of mesquite. Amazingly, the Audi's motor still purred, though the car's wheels were spinning amongst mesquite branches, sending rhythmic and eerie flapping sounds into a previously silent night.

What an amazing car, was his first thought. *Saved my life.* Then Graham tasted blood in the corner of his mouth, and felt the pressure of airbags on his chest and shoulders. *Airbags saved my life*, was his next thought. He wanted to bring his hands up to check his face, but he couldn't move. Pain told him there was a gash across his forehead, but he wasn't sure. Thank God he hadn't gone through the windshield, or smashed into the steering column.

"I could have died," he half mumbled, half cried. "I could have died." Inanely, he wondered where his hat was, and if his driving gloves were bloody?

He tried inhaling a deep breath, and sharp pains shot across his chest. Salt stung his eyes. *Must be sweating from fear. Crushed ribs, maybe?* He prayed he wouldn't succumb to shock—and in that instant—his world, and how he viewed his life, changed. One mule deer crossing the road at the wrong time. Now everything was different.

In his painful semi-conscious fog, his older sister Margot's face again came to him. She was staring at him, her grey-green eyes peering into his own, and beyond—*right through to my very being.* She'd always looked at him like that. He still remembered, even when he was a young child, she'd stared through the bars of his early childhood bed, looking into what was then his innocent soul. *But why envision Marg now?*

The answer was obvious. Before he died, the truth had to be told.

He'd kept his mouth shut until now, not wanting to cause any further harm. And for a moment, he next thought about his brother-in-law Harvey. Always going on about, "First, do no harm." Pretentious and arrogant—that was Harvey alright. Making sure everyone knew he was a doctor.

His chest was starting to hurt like hell, and he could hear his breathing, rough and labored. He tried to speak again—proof he was still alive. His words, "I need to tell my sister the truth," affirmed his resolve and still-living status.

First, he'd tell Margot, then *she* would have to tell Camille. "It's not right my sister and daughter don't know."

Why doesn't the trespasser come help me? Could he be that callous? As Graham's eyes closed and consciousness waned, he thought he heard a ring tone. *Or am I just imagining it?* He next heard, "Mr. Madison, Mr. Madison." He couldn't force his lips to respond to the strange voice saying his name. "Mr. Madison, this is On-Star." Understanding came, and he wanted to tell the female guardian-angel-voice what had happened, ask her to send help—but couldn't. "Mr. Madison, I'm sending emergency vehicles immediately," the voice informed him.

Oddly, Graham's fading thought was—*what a lucky man I am.*

Part One

All in the View

Chapter One

Friday Evening

Margot Madison-Cross was where she wanted to be, sitting in her oversized mauve wingchair, positioned *just so* to take in her cherished one-hundred-eighty degree view of Chicago's lakefront.

"Always changing," she said, while the fingers of her left hand unconsciously fidgeted with the ruby ring perched on her index finger. "Yet always the same." The quiet of her spacious living room gave her words a cavernous echo-like quality.

She couldn't imagine being anywhere else. Here she was comfortable, protected, and safe. Silence and calm reigned—almost. *Something was amiss tonight.*

Indeed, realizing she was not only talking out loud, but also rolling her grandmother's heirloom ring, she looked down at her long thin fingers and clasped them together in her lap with a nostalgic little sigh. The ring was deep burgundy, and clear. Thelma Edison-Hall, her long deceased grandmother, had been a guiding light for both her mother Martha, and herself. The ring was much cherished, and symbolic of generational values and culture. For a moment, her mind's eye brought back her mother's smile when she'd passed the ring on. The night before her cotillion. She would never feel what her mother had experienced that night—the mother-daughter bond—and Margot almost sighed again, but didn't. Tonight was a lovely evening—not a time to dwell on past regrets.

Such a long time ago.

Still, in many respects her perspective on current day Chicago was much the same as when she was a debutante. The ring was beautiful and special, but Chicago always was, and still remained the bejeweled center of her universe.

Taking in her city tonight—despite her enviable view, cherished memories, and a desire to stay upbeat, Margot was worried about her niece, Camille Metoyer-Madison. *Why*, was the question. Indeed, her concern was vague and hard to pinpoint. She knew her niece was independent and quite self sufficient. Was this a premonition of something unusual about to happen?

Rubbish.

But thoughts of her niece wouldn't go away, and she envisioned her habitually warm smile. Camille was like her father Graham in that he'd raised her to be positive and cheerful. *Nurture at its finest.* Camille's features might be on the weak side, like her own, but her smile and expressive eyes brought attractiveness, charm, and warmth to her face.

Margot tried refocusing her attention on Chicago's waterfront. Her twenty-second floor Michigan Avenue penthouse panorama was extensive, and brought her great pleasure. Especially at night, when darkness blanketed her beloved city and transformed the lakefront into a jewel. The incandescent sparkling of thousands of lights dotting her near-Southside vista was like a living painting—and immensely comforting.

All was well in her Chicago universe.

And in Camille's California world? Again, her thoughts returned to her dear one, and despite her living room being a perfect seventy-two degrees—she shivered.

I'm just being silly.

She heard the house phone ring in the rear of her penthouse, and knew her butler George would be coming any second with her hot chocolate. If the call were important, he would come and tell her. *Odd though, a call this late in the evening.* Now, a slight queasiness fluttered in her stomach.

She stood, then walked over to her wall of picture windows and touched the ultra-thick pane in front of her. As always, in all seasons, it was cold. She heard doors open behind her—then George's footfalls.

Looking out at her city as she awaited his approach, she couldn't ignore how much had changed in her little slice of Chicago's lake front. Always new construction it seemed, followed by an almost instant new high-rise. Fortunately, the Outer Drive which spanned her view, was like an old friend. And to the north, Navy Pier held a treasure trove of memories, while to the south, the Shedd Aquarium and Field Museum were landmarks in her mind. Not only of Chicago, but also of cherished childhood adventures.

And though she was loathe to admit it, lately on her rare excursions out and about—usually only as far as the Magnificent Mile—the sounds and crush of city life were occasionally annoying. Some kind of changing from within? *No*, she wouldn't go that far, but *something*.

"Madame," George said from across the room in his stock-in-trade Oxbridge accent. "Your evening drink."

She smiled hearing his voice and affected posh accent—*he does it so well*. As was another of her habits, Margot ran her long fingered hands down the front of her thighs—tonight clad in silken lounge-pants.

Then she waved George closer without turning completely, and he ended up behind her, close enough she could hear his breathing, catch his movements in her peripheral vision—smell his cologne. Burberry Brit, he'd told her. She wasn't fond of men's fragrances, but she didn't expect or require him to change. Indeed, she'd eventually accepted her deceased husband Harvey's cologne, Stetson Black, and she'd thought it awful for thirty years. Not that the fragrance was bad—more that it was an incongruous choice for a man who seldom wore a hat of any sort, and had never visited the West in his whole life. An annoying mismatch.

She assumed George had silently placed on the table next to her chair, a silver tray laden with her usual—a porcelain pot of hot chocolate, a matching cup and saucer, and two chocolate tipped butter cookies. Her cook, Phillip, made *Feines Buttergebaeck* weekly, using a recipe he claimed came from Germany, brought over by a distant refugee relative after World War II. Since Cook Phillip had what she guessed was a Cuban accent, Margot remained curious, but too polite to inquire further.

"And you have a call, Madame." George took a cordless handset out of his tweed hacking jacket pocket and waited for her to completely turn from the window. "Your brother Graham," he said, and handed her the phone.

What could possibly be prompting Graham to call tonight? And despite the lovely aroma of chocolate floating her way, her stomach lurched in earnest.

"Gray," she said, using her lifelong nickname for her younger brother. "Is something wrong?"

"Why can't you answer your own damned phone?" His tone was irritable. "I have to wait almost half an hour to speak to you."

Margot considered occasional irascibility part of her brother's charm. But tonight, there was something else she detected. *Fear?*

"What is it, Gray? Are you alright?"

She heard him inhale a sharp breath. "Had an accident last week, almost died. Time for some truth telling."

Her throat constricted, and for a moment, she couldn't speak.

When Margot didn't answer immediately, he said, "We're all living a lie."

Outside in Grant Park, the Buckingham Fountain light show began—usually a bedazzling, almost mesmerizing experience for Margot. She barely noticed.

There was no reason to be apprehensive.

In fact, a warm evening breeze brushing Camille's cheeks felt lovely, almost like a caress. Especially in contrast to the sand-permeated winds that had blasted through NewTown for days.

I should be enjoying this evening.

Doctor Camille Metoyer-Madison had gotten out of her minivan and was leaning against the driver's door, looking toward the horizon. She wanted a moment "to feel" the sunset—and maybe strengthen her waning determination.

With improved weather conditions, tonight's departure of the sun—composed of vibrant orange, red, and gold, all layered together by delicate pastels—was beyond eye-catching. Nonetheless, to her right, up two steps, and across a veranda, the faux saloon doors of Velma's bar held her attention.

Anxiety laced with fear had driven her to arrive early, and in the few minutes she'd spent waiting for Police Chief Parker Reed, her mind had elevated the bar's swinging double-doors to the level of Stargate-evoking portals, and tonight's grand sunset was doing little to change how she felt. Once she stepped through those doors, Camille was sure her world would alter, and there would be no return.

"Good grief," she whispered. *By now you'd think I'd be beyond all this.* She was a grown woman, not an insecure teenager. She shook herself like a ragdoll—hoping for an exorcism of irrationality.

For a moment, she forced herself to think about her aunt Margot in her penthouse in Chicago—with her calm personality. She wished for her at her side, holding her hand.

Unconsciously Camille rubbed the front of her faded jeans along her thighs, then pulled down on her Route-66 T-shirt. Her shirt and jeans-jacket—a present from a grateful patient—were the best she could do to evoke a country-western look. She had, however, brushed her short-cropped brown hair into semi-submission and carefully applied a light-red lipstick, hoping to make her weak lip-line more appealing. Though her large brown eyes had looked tired in her bathroom mirror, she knew the effects of back-to-back patients all day could not be vanquished with cosmetics.

Again she thought of her aunt—*Auntie Marg*. This time, visualizing her classic features and leggy stylishness—so nicely enhanced by a steady assuredness she'd always envied. In contrast, Camille felt she'd taken after her short, chunky, and rather scattered-looking mother, Meredith Metoyer. Fortunately, her dear Uncle Harvey had been similar to her in looks, and oddly, seemed to understand her better than Meredith.

She snuck another quick glance at the intimidating doors. Nothing had changed.

It's just a bar. Heck, the owners were patients, and the building certainly wasn't ominous. Built in the fifties she guessed, and styled like an old-time saloon, it was painted bright purple and sat back from the road on the south side of Route 66, down the road from Deel's Plumbing Supply. She sometimes grabbed a Coke at Velma's, but that was during daytime hours. Not at night, and not on a "date."

Bright halogen spotlights switched on. It was officially evening, and everything was different. *Worse.* Under the primeval spell of darkness, the main cause of her anxiety paradoxically became clearer.

Yes, it was memories of her mother Meredith that were in control this Friday evening. As vivid as on the day it happened—*she again saw* her father Graham charging into the country club bar, his face contorted in anger, yelling at her mother and chastising the bartender. *She again felt* him grab her six-year-old hand, pulling and hurrying her through the dining area out into the club's foyer where her Auntie Marg waited.

But it was silly and ungrateful being mad at Meredith. "She did her best," she murmured aloud. Indeed, her mother had told her in a flood of tears before she died—how many years it had taken to have a child, and how lucky she felt to have Camille.

In the way of the world, her life-hurdles were slight. She thought of her patient, Anthony Watson, whose angiogram results arrived from his cardiologist just this morning. He'd patiently endured both heart and carotid angiograms. His carotid arteries weren't in worse shape than what would be expected in a seventy-five year old man, but plaque buildup with a sixty percent artery narrowing was presenting itself in his heart.

An operation might be possible. But at his age, with high-blood-pressure and borderline diabetes, risk factors were a big consideration. She planned on doing some online medical research this weekend, and reviewing his family medical history again Monday morning. She'd also scheduled a consult with his cardiologist.

Anthony's condition—now that was a *real* problem. And all he'd said when she called this afternoon, was, "I'm not surprised." His voice had been calm, strong, brave. "Shoot, Doc, a life without problems and risks, ain't much of a life. Now is it?"

And here I am, agonizing over entering a bar because my mother had been an alcoholic.

Two Harleys were parked near Velma's entry steps. Next to them was a Volvo wagon. The evening was young, the clientele most likely agreeable. If she could just go in—wait for Parker at one of the small tables she remembered near the pool table. She'd sat at one of those very tables one afternoon, watching a group of European Roadies passing around snap shots. Faces, memories, to keep and share with new friends along the route.

"You been waiting long?" Parker Reed appeared at her side from seemingly nowhere.

"No," she lied, trying not to sound startled. Camille didn't look at him, but felt the warmth of his breath on her face. He didn't touch her in greeting, no hug, no arm around the shoulder, no hand discreetly caressed. Just the same, she felt a flush—only for a second—but unmistakable.

"I think you better follow me in your own car." He was in uniform, and his tone was somber.

Parker wasn't making sense. Their date, if you could call it that, was for drinks at Velma's. "Follow you where?"

"To your clinic."

She met his gaze. "Why?"

"Your precious Doc Lewis wants you there." His heavy-browed, almost black eyes stared back at her, curious. "Seems he asked for *you*, before calling his wife."

"Asked for me?" Camille's voice was almost a whisper. "What's happened?"

13

"Faye-Anne Miller has been murdered." He waited.

Camille didn't know what to say. *Nurse Miller dead?*

"Her body was found in Lewis's private office. A couple Sheriff's deputies are on their way—or are already there. But I'm the 'it' guy for the moment."

Murder had taken center stage.

Outside, the Buckingham Fountain light show was over, and in her living room with the lingering aroma of chocolate surrounding her, Margot savored the dregs of her second pot of cocoa. She was sitting in her wingchair again, George having dimmed the overhead cam-lights to ensure her view of Grant Park was unmarred by window reflections before taking his leave.

Something in the taste of the few remaining drops of chocolate was most poignant, and took her back to a childhood moment in Corpus Christi Church's rectory. Eating Danish and drinking cocoa the nuns had made—her brother Graham and Father Joseph in deep discussion. Even as a child, Gray was introspective and thoughtful. She smiled for a moment—remembering—relishing those times anew.

She forced her mind back to the present and wondered what Camille was doing—*it was two hours earlier there*. Once again her stomach fluttered—even though Gray hadn't mentioned Camille in his summons.

Margot turned to tell George how good her cocoa was before remembering he'd left to watch television in his quarters. She, however, was still reluctant to retire. Cook Phillip often baked late into the night, and the aroma of yeast also tantalized her from the back of her penthouse.

She tried to enjoy the moment, and without thought reached down to pet a German Shepherd that was no longer there. Faustus had left this world two years earlier, but was still with her in mind and heart. Quickly, she brought her hand back to her lap, and her mind back to her current predicament.

Why Graham preferred living across the country was still something she couldn't understand. Even Meredith had moved back to Chicago when they'd split up—*before she died*. Margot inhaled deeply, forcing back the pain of losing her sister-in-law, then having to deal with the aftermath of her messy life. Meredith's alcoholism had not made for smooth sailing, and clearing up her debts and promises—*few known to Gray*—had been difficult even with Margot's acumen and wealth.

She sighed and said, "Oh well."

Why had Gray been so darned cryptic? Insisting she fly out immediately. "It's a matter of life or death," he'd pleaded. "Please come. I can't tell you over the phone. Who knows what ears are listening."

Margot had almost laughed at his recurring phobia about nosey domestics. He'd persuaded her though, and she'd promised to come as bidden.

She'd bother George once more tonight to make her airplane reservation. He was a marvel doing things like that on the Internet.

It was getting late and nurse Deirdre Lorrie was tired; she just wanted to go home. Usually she loved being at the clinic. Tonight, however, after what had happened, her home-away-from-home felt different, like it was out of sorts. *Silly thought.* Buildings definitely do not feel. But "things" had changed, that was for sure.

On top of that, the strobe lights on the vehicles out front pulsed rhythmically through the clinic's front window in a way she found most disconcerting. In fact, they were making her a tad queasy. *Faye-Anne was dead.* What difference did the lights make now?

Deirdre was sitting stiffly in the first of three plaid upholstered chairs in NewTown Medical Clinic's reception area—waiting. Next to her was the clinic's modest magazine rack, sparsely populated with an eclectic assortment of reading material. Her practical mind said, *I need to bring in some new magazines—plenty at home.*

She was sitting exactly where the young deputy said to, and didn't feel she had a choice to leave or move around. Her usual areas, behind the front desk, and in their joint back office were off limits.

Dead bodies, she was realizing, changed everything.

Until tonight, she had thought herself quite clever in the way she'd set up their public work area. In fact, Deirdre had been very proud of arranging her and Faye-Anne's desks and computers so she could spy on the vain woman. *I don't feel so proud now.* Faye-Anne really couldn't help she was the office star. *While I can't help being the steady, in-the-middle staff member.*

"Thank God," she murmured to herself, "Faye-Anne was killed in Doc Lewis's office, not out here." Immediately, Deirdre regretted her thought and whispered words. *Okay,* she hadn't been fond of Faye-Anne, but the woman was dead. How could she possibly be happy about where it happened? She'd only been in the restroom a couple minutes—how had she missed seeing Faye-Anne leave their area?

Deirdre let her head fall forward, then put her hands over her eyes. She imagined she might be rocking, but wasn't sure. *Shock?* And she must look like hell. Frankly aware her "plain Jane" every-woman countenance did not hold up well under crying, she was sure her eyes, even though deep set, were swollen and red. Worse, her already chubby cheeks probably looked like tennis balls.

Jeez. She needed to compose herself—and with that thought, Deirdre straightened her back and shoulders. She was a professional, now wasn't she? And needed to comport herself accordingly.

Sitting where she was in the waiting area, Deirdre's view of the clinic was the same as one a patient would have. Limited—and as she now saw—not that pleasing. *Maybe I should spruce the area up a bit.* Thank goodness, Doc Lewis was a stickler for seeing his patients on time. And after Doctor Metoyer-Madison joined them six months ago, wait times had become even shorter.

Deirdre shook her head, and said softly, "Metoyer-Madison." *Silly thing, hyphenating your name.* In fact, because of the doctor's ostentatious last name, it had taken Deirdre awhile to warm up to her. The patients didn't use her full name anyway, most just called her Doc Madison. Thank goodness her mother hadn't saddled her with two last names. *Ignoring me had been enough.*

Her thoughts returned to Faye-Anne. Besides the front area, they'd also shared a private cubbyhole down the hall where paper records were filed. Both areas were now taped off. Could her murderer been hiding out in there? She shivered just considering the possibility.

But out here was where they spent most of their working hours, and the last place she saw Faye-Anne. For two years she'd successfully been able to watch the LPN's every action unobserved. But tonight, of all nights, she'd missed seeing her leave the reception area.

How could she possibly be so easily tricked? And for sure, there was a trick involved, and given time, she would figure it out. Not tonight, though. Tonight her head hurt and she felt tired and befuddled. Deirdre rubbed her forehead, as if to fix her mental fuzziness, and found her skin oily and damp. *I must look horrible.*

She wished Parker would arrive soon. The deputies were okay, especially the baby-faced one standing by the front door. He was sort of cute—but so immature. Not like Doc Lewis or Chief Reed. Now they were *real* men, and made her feel reassured—safe.

She also didn't think either deputy believed her. Heck, what had just happened seemed fantastic even to her. *But it's true.* Faye-Anne's dead body was testimony a murder had been committed. How could she possibly expect to be respected when she'd let a murder happen right under her nose?

* * * * *

Driving her minivan, Camille followed Parker's pickup truck through NewTown Medical Clinic's compressed-dirt parking lot. Two police vehicles and a medic van were parked in front. One cruiser, its side-door open and interior lights on, was occupied by a deputy on the radio; the second cruiser's interior was dark and empty. The medic van was pulled up to the front door with its back panel doors open.

She noticed all three vehicle sirens were silent, but their red and blue strobes were pulsing light into what was turning out to be a starless night. *Clouds hiding the desert nightlights?*

Mojave night skies and vistas were so different from the views she'd enjoyed from her aunt's Chicago penthouse. She could still remember those old moments of excitement—standing at her windows—looking out at a city alive with dancing lights. *How Auntie Marg and Uncle Harvey spoiled her back then.* Camille knew she was dredging up old and comforting pictures because she was scared of the one waiting for her inside. *Inside my clinic.*

As she continued to follow, Parker drove past the first-responders and around to the building's rear. The clinic—*her clinic*—was a one-story rectangle, not more than three or four-thousand feet in size. Tonight it seemed more isolated and forlorn than when she'd left it earlier in daylight. In the dark of night, and under the weight of a possible murder, its plain stucco façade now bore an aura of mystery—even danger. *Silly to think a building could elicit such thoughts and feelings.*

Nonetheless, just like with Velma's a few minutes earlier, nighttime's black shroud carried an effect. *I hate the darkness.*

Once parked next to Parker, she rubbed her face and eyes with both hands, hard. It wasn't a medically good thing to subject her eyes to such abuse, but she needed to be sharp and rational, not fanciful. *Faye-Anne was dead.* And Oscar wanted her help.

Parker opened the unlocked back door, held it, then followed her in.

As soon as she stepped inside, a muffled exchange reached her from down the hall near their first exam room. Only twenty-five feet or so away, the voices seemed to be coming to her from another world.

Everything has changed.

"Probably need to tape off the whole damn place before Forensics gets here," a man said.

A throaty female voice answered, "Yep. Picky lot. Better do this according to the book."

Camille composed herself and covered the few steps from the back door to the threshold of Oscar's office. It was the last room in the clinic, and inches outside his open door, she stopped and stood looking in—motionless for a moment—transfixed by the bright florescent-lit scene before her. For a tiny slice of time, a camera lens somewhere in her mind wanted to stay removed from any murder reality—only looking in, not a part of.

Parker stopped too— only a breath behind—and also mute and momentarily motionless.

Stage center was Faye-Anne's dead body, partly slumped in Oscar's oversized swivel-chair, and partly fallen forward across the desktop—face down. Her head was turned sideways, and unnaturally flat against a blood soaked desk-blotter. Blood also capped the back of her head and ran along the length of her thick black braid that hung limply against her back. *A hair piece,* she knew.

Camille instantly chided herself for thinking about Faye-Anne's hair vanity at a time like this. Knowledge of the hairpiece was a confidence her nurse had shared with her—one late evening before closing up. An intimacy that had helped bridge a discomfort between a new doctor and her experienced nurse. Camille fought back a lump of emotion that tried to rise in her throat.

The dead woman's arms hung lifeless at her side, and she was glad she couldn't see Faye-Anne's face from the doorway, preferring to remember the vibrant young woman as she'd seen her that morning. A little irritated, coquettish as always—but very much alive and healthy. With a life expectancy of eighty-plus years according to the Medical Journal she'd read yesterday morning—*an eternity ago.* And with that reflection, Camille was momentarily overcome by a sense of immense loss—quickly followed by anger at whomever had done this.

She caught her breath and tried to speak, but couldn't.

The other living participants in Faye-Anne's murder-scene also seemed to be trapped in a surrealistic hold-your-breath grip. A young male medical technician, stiff as a mannequin, was gazing down at Faye-Anne's body, while a sheriff's deputy stared at Camille and Parker.

Doctor Oscar Lewis, standing just inside the door, also seemed frozen—staring expectantly at Camille, his usually come-hither eyes scared, moist, and red in the corners. Both his demeanor and clothes seemed uncharacteristically limp and disheveled. Even his hair, dark and thick for his age, seemed dull.

"Help me, Camille," Oscar whispered through seemingly non-moving lips. Strangely, his plea did not break through whatever was holding them all trapped and immobile in the moment.

Suddenly the phone on Oscar's desk rang—shrill and loud—piercing the silence.

Behind Camille, Parker coughed—while in front of her, the deputy grunted and brought his gaze back to Faye-Anne's dead body. "Time" eased forward.

The medical technician said in a loud rough tone, "Perp bashed her head in good. Nothing I could do to revive her."

"Ass," Parker hissed loudly.

Camille took a deep breath, then a step forward. Someone needed to answer the phone. *Are they all deaf?* Oscar in particular. Why didn't he make a move to answer his own phone? Beyond his whisper for help, he'd remained stiff and still as a Madame Tussaud figure.

Parker stepped in front of her and went over to the deputy. *Doesn't he hear the phone, either?*

"Howdy," Parker said. "Don't think we've met." He didn't extend his hand. "Police Chief Reed. Local."

"I've been briefed about you," the deputy said enigmatically. "Deputy Jim Thompson."

Camille pushed past both men to get to the phone before it rang again. Looking back at Thompson, she thought his expression was apprehensive. Indeed, his khaki and drab-olive-green uniform looked straight-from-the-cleaners fresh, and emphasized his young, clean-cut, and inexperienced-looking features. *Probably his first murder case.*

Thankfully, her days as a student, then her residency, especially her first year as an intern were now memories. *Autopsies—government agency, school lab, hospital morgue—even a mortuary "field trip."* All suffered through, and never forgotten.

Once Camille could actually see Faye-Anne's face, her attention was irresistibly drawn to a small stream of dried white spittle in the corner of the poor girl's mouth. Besides the hairpiece, makeup had been a point of pride to Faye-Anne. At least her scarlet lipstick remained perfectly applied. *Faye-Anne's death mask,* she thought sadly, *will not embarrass her departed spirit.*

There had always been some little detail like that with the bodies in the morgue. Something that took-you-back to the person who had lived in the cold lifeless shell on the table or in the refrigeration-compartment. Camille forced her attention away from Faye-Anne's face and picked up the receiver just as it rang again.

"NewTown clinic," she said. "May I help you?"

Emma Kent's concerned voice was on the line. "Oh Doc Madison, thank God, you're there. I've been so worried."

Deputy Thompson demanded, "Hey," and reached to grab the phone. "You can't do that."

She took a step backward and said to Emma, "Mrs. Kent. Actually, we're closed. Is there a problem?" Nothing would stop her from addressing her patient's needs—neither an overzealous young deputy, nor a murder. The dead were past her help. But for Emma, she could still do something.

Camille easily envisioned Emma's warm and inviting oval face on the other end of their conversation. Born in the Philippines, raised in Orange County, married for thirty-years to an Iowa farm-boy turned Californian, mother to two marines stationed at

Twentynine Palms, and now retired in NewTown—Emma often brought homemade chocolate chip cookies to the clinic. She was also a Route 66 "Roadie," and seldom missed a local event.

"The pharmacy doesn't have a refill left on my prescription," Emma said. "I'll be out of pills after Monday. And Doc Lewis said how important it was to control my blood pressure." She took a quick breath. "And we're heading to a classic car show in Victorville at the Route 66 Museum tomorrow."

Deputy Thompson glared at Camille, while Parker smiled.

"Don't worry, Emma," Camille reassured her. "I'll call your prescription in for Teveteen first thing tomorrow morning. I don't think they're open now. You should be able to pick up your pills tomorrow afternoon if you're around, or Monday morning before you run out."

"I'm so glad you were in the office." She sounded relieved. "I'll bring you and Doc Lewis some cookies next week."

Emma's culinary delights were always warm, moist, and loaded with chocolate and pecans. Just like the ones Camille remembered her mother baking when sober. The cookie-occasions with Meredith had been few and far between, but like her residency time, never to be forgotten. Of course Auntie Marg's cook, Phillip, made light-as-air butter cookies with a foreign name she couldn't remember. Clearly, those memories of her mother were not about the excellence of her cookies.

And even with Faye-Anne's lifeless body only inches away, *and* Oscar stuck in zombie land; *and* Deputy Thompson ready to handcuff her; *and* Parker smirking through the whole horrible mess— Camille almost smiled mentally tasting fresh baked cookies like her mother used to make. She even felt a salivation response kick in—*at a murder scene*—with Faye-Anne's body only feet away. *How horrible,* she admonished herself.

Parker said to Deputy Thompson, "She's the other doctor here. And pushy."

"Prints," the deputy shouted, and again reached for the receiver in Camille's hand. "I don't care who she is. This is a crime scene. Are you both crazy?"

This time Camille took an avoiding step sideways—as if they were playing a game of tag.

All the while, Emma continued to talk into her ear. "You know I called Doc Lewis at home. When he didn't answer I was so worried. You don't have Saturday hours yet, do you?"

"Just started them last month." Oscar had agreed to a couple-month trial period. "What time did you call tonight?"

"Around six, I think."

Camille reassured Emma she'd call in her prescription, then hung up.

"Ma'am," the deputy said forcibly. "Forensics will be here any minute. Now they'll need your fingerprints to use when dusting that phone."

Camille took another step sideways. This time to remove Faye-Anne's face from her field of vision. "I'm in their databases."

In consort, Parker and Deputy Thompson lowered their heads and raised their eyebrows quizzically, reminding her of comic marionettes.

"Part of my California medical licensing requirements."

She redirected her attention to Oscar, the person who had brought her into this situation in the first place. The man she thought of as a mentor, her Uncle Harvey's old friend—still hadn't moved. From the look of his skin, his fixed expression, and the disconcerting look in his eyes, Camille immediately diagnosed shock. Maybe not physiological, but possibly psychological. She didn't think immediate medical attention was required, but wasn't yet sure. He wasn't acting dizzy, didn't look sweaty, and his breathing seemed normal—but from the dazed look in his eyes, she surmised his mind and body were struggling to cope.

Occasionally, when diagnosing a patient, especially when feeling a bit out of her depth, Camille thought of her deceased Uncle Harvey—her mentor before Oscar. He'd been her inspiration throughout medical school, and she sometimes symbolically reached across the void for his advice. This was one of those times, and she almost teared-up as his face flashed across her mind's eye.

She asked Oscar, "Are you alright?" She needed to know whether to send him to the hospital or not. *He needed to say something.*

Deirdre was sure she heard Chief Reed's voice out back. *Thank God.* Next she heard the phone ring and almost ran to her desk to answer, but stopped within seconds. Under the circumstances, the phone was not her responsibility.

Hopefully they'd talk to her soon, *then* she could go home and have a good cry. *Even RNs aren't made of stone.* She was also a little worried the police thought she had something to do with Faye-Anne's death. And even worse—that Doc Lewis was somehow involved.

She guessed they were all in the doc's office, and involuntarily shuddered visualizing Faye-Anne's body. But having to wait isolated in the reception area, flashing strobes disorientating her, and bombarded with her own thoughts—Deirdre didn't really know *who* was back there.

The doc probably hadn't arrived yet, *though they must have called him by now*; and hopefully his "ice-queen" wife hadn't appeared on the scene either. She shuddered yet again thinking about Ann.

Ann wasn't exactly what she called a perfect wife, but Doc Lewis certainly should have known better. Fooling around with Faye-Anne—*now really.* Everyone knew she was trouble. Still, Deirdre didn't really blame him. *Faye-Anne* could wrap any man around her finger.

She sighed and the young deputy stationed at the front desk gave her a quick glance.

How could I have missed her murder?

Where Deirdre was sitting in the waiting area, she couldn't see their desks, but, she'd been the one to suggest the desks should be turned so their backs were to each other, with their sides to the reception counter. The desk arrangement was perfect for Deirdre to watch Faye-Anne's every move in her computer monitor. *I should have seen something.*

She turned her head away from the deputy, and grimaced before starting to chew on her bottom lip. Next she brought her right hand to her mouth and nibbled on her thumb fingernail. *I'm acting too nervous.* She forced her hands to her lap, noticed they'd gone sweaty, and wanted to rub them on her lab smock—but didn't.

They can't possibly blame me. She'd checked the front and back doors were locked promptly at four. And she was sure there had been no one but her and Faye-Anne in the clinic when she'd so foolishly left her desk to go to the bathroom.

Forgetting the deputy's presence, she said out loud, "I couldn't have been gone more than five minutes." *Well, maybe ten.*

Nonetheless, in those few minutes, Faye-Anne had gone into Oscar's office and gotten her head bashed in. At least, that's what she thought happened. All she *really* knew was when she finally found Faye-Anne, she'd screamed, run back to her own desk for some reason—then called 911. She certainly could have used Doc Lewis's phone—but now in after thought—guessed she didn't want to go near Faye-Anne's body. *It was just too horrible.*

"Wish I hadn't screamed," she said. She was a *trained professional* for goodness' sake. Deirdre felt the deputy's eyes on her, then turned and gave him a weak little smile.

Must think I'm crazy. Or worse, a crazy murderer.

She slipped her right hand in her lab jacket and felt the folded piece of paper she'd pocketed earlier. *Can't forget,* she reminded herself. The call had come right before Faye-Anne's murder. She pulled the note out and reread it so she wouldn't forget to tell Doc Madison when she saw her. Maybe tonight? She'd scrawled the message fast, and now for a second, had a hard time reading her own writing. *Graham Madison,* she'd written down. *Doc Madison's father,* that part she was sure she'd gotten right. His message was for his daughter to call immediately. Something about a *Margot,* an aunt she thought he'd said—but had neglected to scribble on the note.

Then the name popped in her head, clear as a bell. Margot Madison-Cross—another three-dealer name. Doc Madison was supposed to call her Aunt Margot.

Forensic techs arrived and took over Oscar's office. They weren't wearing insignias she could easily see, so Camille had no idea where they came from—but with their arrival, Parker moved initial statement gathering to her office across the hall.

Camille was fond of the way she had decorated her office. The walls were freshly painted in a clean cream color, and several framed Asian bamboo and vine prints were strategically placed for her patients to see. She'd also spent considerable time picking a comfortable upholstered high-backed swivel desk chair, and three matching arm chairs. A Tiffany desk lamp, antique replica file cabinets, and one long mahogany Edwardian credenza were also her doing. Clean and fresh, but also "old world" inviting—so she had hoped.

Tonight her space felt emotionally cold and impersonal. *What a difference a murder makes.*

Instinctively, she didn't sit at her desk, choosing instead to drag a chair to the far wall opposite the corner Oscar now sat in. She planned on adopting a fly-on-the-wall approach. Watch, listen, and keep her mouth shut. Besides, her duty as a doctor came first, and she needed to keep her eye on Oscar. He seemed okay—responsive when forced—but still reticent.

Indeed, she was lucky Parker was letting her tag along at all, insinuating herself in the investigation. She really had no legal standing. Nonetheless, when initially deciding to move from Oscar's office to hers, she'd asked Parker to give Oscar a few moments before questioning, let his mind and body assimilate all that had happened. She still worried about shock, and considered it preferable he didn't go to the hospital unless absolutely required.

"Could you," she'd asked in a whisper, "start with Deirdre so she can go home?"

"So *he* has time to cook up an alibi?" Parker had grumbled. "Besides, how do you know Deirdre didn't kill Faye-Anne?" Still, after an exaggerated eye roll, he'd nodded.

Remembering their exchange, Camille stretched her shoulders, then rubbed her upper-arms. She expected to feel the soft cotton of a lab coat, and was surprised by the stiffness of her jeans-jacket. She'd forgotten tonight had started as a date. Ashamed of her personal fretting while Faye-Anne's dead body was slumped over Oscar's desk, she tsked and shook her head.

After bringing Deirdre back where they were, Parker sat down in Camille's chair, but turned it sideways and pulled up an armchair for Deirdre facing him. *Just the right distance*, Camille thought, not too close to be intimidating, but close enough to look directly into her eyes.

Thompson also stepped in, his body language stating he was taking a secondary position; she was sure the scowl on his face indicated he preferred otherwise. For the time being, it was Parker's show.

Deirdre was clearly nervous, twisting and turning a tissue in her hands. Camille watched with admiration as Parker got her to relax a bit—with very few words. *He's good at his job.*

Nonetheless, Deirdre was in the "hot seat"—and nervous or not, Camille knew her to be a competent nurse. And observant. You probably couldn't ask for a better witness than Deirdre. *Unless of course she's also a murderer.*

Camille stole a quick glance at Oscar in the corner where she'd instructed him to sit—almost behind her open office door. Initially she'd thought it a calming spot, out of harm's way until his turn. But now he looked more like a man in hiding.

He had called her for help—she needed to do what she could. At the same time, she also needed to be careful. *Do no harm* at the very least. Uncle Harvey had been fond of the phrase, and honoring him over the years, she'd internalized the Hippocratic admonishment and tried applying it to life in general—not just to the practice of medicine.

If he'd been having an affair with Faye-Anne, Oscar *was* a prime suspect. She sighed softly. Unfortunately, one time in the past she'd heard Deirdre and Patricia Miller discussing just such an affair. Arguing almost, if she remembered correctly.

In addition, Connie Ramirez, a rheumatoid arthritis-stricken patient and proclaimed butter lover with elevated cholesterol levels, had whispered to Camille during an exam, "I thought I saw Doc Lewis and Faye-Anne in the Upland's Trader Joe's the other day." She'd lowered her voice even more and shook her head. "They should be more careful." Then she'd tapped her nose twice and raised knowing eyebrows.

Camille had taken Connie's comments and gestures as a hint she should talk to Oscar. At the time, she just smiled, and moved on to Connie's slightly elevated liver enzymes. Somehow, Connie needed to understand some dietary changes were imperative.

Maybe she should have talked to Oscar about the affair. *Maybe* Faye-Anne would still be alive if she had.

Camille alternated her focus between Deirdre and Oscar. Both were important. She heard Thompson cough several times, but didn't look his way. She did wonder if they'd taken Faye-Anne away yet. She doubted the medic van turned on their sirens when a dead body was their cargo. *Poor Faye-Anne.* And killed right here in NewTown's clinic. "Good grief," she whispered to herself. No one else seemed to notice.

After a bit more "comfy" chat with Deirdre, Parker asked a couple benign questions like—*what did she do in the late afternoon; how many patients came and went; could she provide a list of their names?*—then he finally got her to the time period that counted.

"The last time I saw Faye-Anne," Deirdre said, while dabbing her nose with a tissue, "was when I went to the restroom." She looked up to a spot in the ceiling. "I hardly looked at her." She caught her breath, then brought her gaze back to Parker. Several tears escaped. "I should have been paying better attention."

She feels guilty, just like I do.

"Why?" Parker asked. "Was there something special about her behavior?"

"Well, yes."

"What was this special something?" His tone was patient.

"Faye-Anne said she was sick," tears started to stream, "and that she'd probably be heading to the restroom soon herself." Deirdre tried clearing her throat. "Faye-Anne is always claiming there's something wrong." She blotted at her eyes furiously as if she could actually stop the flood. "I thought she was just making it up so she could leave me with the closing." Her next words were barely discernable. "Said she was nauseous and her throat hurt. Oh God," she gasped. "I should have paid attention, I should have paid attention."

Parker reached out and touched her arm. "Ms. Lorrie, you can't blame yourself."

Left unsaid, Camille mused, was *unless you murdered Faye-Anne.* She remembered the white spittle in the corner of Faye-Anne's mouth and interrupted firmly and without pre-thought. "Pull yourself together, Deirdre." The young woman was a trained nurse, a witness—and needed to act like one. "Had Faye-Anne been drinking or eating anything right before she got sick?" Camille stood up, walked over next to Thompson, and stared intently at Deirdre— willing her to remember. "It's important. The ME might need to request an expanded toxicology panel." She felt Parker staring at her, but didn't take her gaze off her nurse.

Deirdre stopped sobbing, and looked up at Camille. "Well," she said, as her eyes widened and her cheeks reddened. "Patricia insists we have an afternoon energy drink. I drank mine right after lunch."

"And Faye-Anne? When did she drink hers?"

"Gosh, Doc Madison, I don't know." She bit her lip and squinted her eyes. "I just don't remember."

Camille heard Parker clear his throat and she finally looked his way. Camille wasn't sure about the look he was giving her, but before she could continue, he asked, "Who made your energy drink this afternoon?"

"Patricia, of course," Deirdre said without hesitation. "She always makes them."

Camille gasped softly—then quickly explained, "No one has called Patricia."

Parker tilted his head, then his eyes widened, and a chagrined look flashed across his face.

"You do remember, don't you?" Camille said. "Patricia and Faye-Anne are sisters. Someone has to break the news to her."

Parker nodded, and Thompson said from behind him, "Maybe she already knows."

His meaning was clear, and silence engulfed the room for a moment before Deirdre said, "And there's Nealy, too." Evidently having conquered her crying jag, she sniffed, then exhaled slowly.

"Who's Nealy?" Parker and Thompson asked almost in unison.

Deirdre looked up and said, "Faye-Anne's husband." She shook her head. "Her full name is Faye-Anne Miller Jones."

Camille hoped her jaw didn't drop and wondered how many more secrets would be revealed before this was over. *If I could just make all this go away.* Instead, she straightened her shoulders and steeled her emotions against revelations to come. *I need to be strong and have a clear mind.*

From his corner hidey-hole behind the door, Oscar stammered, "Faye-Anne was married?"

In Chicago, on the twenty-second floor of The Salk—having eventually gone to bed in her antique-furnished and old-world-appointed bedroom—Margot was vaguely aware she was tossing around fretfully in her Louis XV four-poster. Most probably her comforter was on the floor, her sheets pulled from their corners and rumpled, and her silken Asian-floral nightgown sorely tested.

Yet she didn't actually want to wake up. Somehow Margot knew—whether fully awake, sound asleep, or in the ethereal land in-between—it wouldn't make any difference. Her body knew there was danger brewing. Unfortunately, even in her groggy semi-slumber state, neither did enlightenment regarding the danger's source present itself— nor any idea of how she could possibly stop what awaited.

The scariest part was, she couldn't get rid of the unsettling and inexplicable feeling that whatever turmoil was swirling and building—she was at its center.

Chapter Two

Saturday

    Chief Parker Reed decided the pullout at Harvard Road was the spot where he wanted to start Saturday. It was his habit, more like addiction, to begin every day greeting the morning sitting in his police-jeep at a favored roadside haunt—a cup of coffee at the ready. It was a time to review the previous day and set his agenda for the new one. This morning, he'd passed on his uniform, but his mind and heart were definitely on duty.

    On the job ten years, he knew a lot of places to park, sit, and do what he called his "ruminating." Many favored spots had views to the east and along Route 66. This morning, however, he was drawn to Yermo Road at the Harvard I-15 interchange. There was a collapsing structure that used to be a fruit stand—now often vandalized, but occasionally used as an easy coordination spot for cops. This morning he'd pulled in on the backside of the building, his jeep invisible from the freeway unless you really tried to look. A perfect speed trap spot for CHP Officers and Mojave County Deputies. This morning, just a place for him to be alone and think.

    The weather had surprised him. Last night's wind storm had blown on through to Nevada and Arizona—not lingering as he'd expected. It amused him how distasteful Camille found the wind. *The Mojave is not for everyone.* He thought it might not be for her—and he wished it weren't so. *Yes,* he liked Camille. Did he love her? Well that was the question, now wasn't it?

    He sighed loudly and tried to forget about his personal life. His sky this morning was a gentle light blue, illuminated by a sun barely peeking over the horizon, and he had a cup of homemade brew in his double-walled insulated aluminum cup—very similar to the ones he noted last night Patricia used for her energy drinks.

He was hoping for a slow-developing and mellow colored sunrise. *No drama, just a quiet time to think.* He'd muted his cell phone, since he wasn't officially on duty—but didn't turn off his radio.

Parker wanted to focus his mind on Oscar Lewis and the evidence he hoped to gather today to see if there was a provable case against Camille's "Doctor Kildare." Someone killed Faye-Anne Miller, and Lewis was *numero uno* on his list. He certainly wasn't buying last night's act. Doctor or not, Lewis was a disingenuous weasel, and Camille was deluded in thinking he could walk on water. *And if Lewis is responsible*—Parker pushed consideration of how Camille might feel away. *Why anticipate trouble?*

His personal "little voice" of reason and fairness told him he was latching onto Lewis first-and-foremost because of jealousy. *He wanted to be the center of Camille's universe—not "Doctor Kildare."*

Still, husbands and lovers are always prime suspects, aren't they?

It certainly hadn't been fun phoning Patricia last night. He'd felt it his duty to give her a follow-up call even though Detective Al Hollist, who technically had jurisdiction, drove out to officially notify her. Heck of a thing, telling someone they'd lost a loved one. *And a sister, at that.* He thought Hollist a good officer, but not long in empathy or expressing condolences.

On the far-off chance Lewis *wasn't* a murderer, at a minimum, the doc had *something* he didn't want known. He needed to discover what that "something" was. Admittedly, Faye-Anne's murder had been a surprise, but he'd recovered now. *Time to get to work, for real.* He'd certainly come across many flavors of victims and villains, but there was something additional going on here. *Yep,* this morning he needed to think about what he was sensing.

"Ha!" he scoffed into his empty jeep. "Surprise me, but fool me too? Hardly." It was at moments like this—when he had no one to confab with except himself—that he wished he'd kept Dogue. But he'd known at the time he asked Camille to adopt the homeless German Shepherd that the stray needed a warm and stable home. A cop's life, even in a small town like NewTown, didn't allow for regular hours—or long doggie walks.

Forensics might just come up with enough evidence to charge Lewis, but he wasn't about to wait around for that. *I need to focus.* Nonetheless, as the sun rose and his morning sky lightened into a paler blue, Parker's thoughts settled in on Camille and his own personal dilemma.

Should he tell her the truth about his past—or not? He hadn't really lied, *yet*. However, in his mind there was some Sunday school admonition about lies of omission, wasn't there? Well, this lie of omission was definitely becoming a matter of convenience. Romantic convenience.

So much easier to become friends without old baggage getting in the way.

A *demilune* hutch commanded Margot's foyer. This Italian Baroque console was oversized with tapered legs and adorned with leaf and flower carvings. A huge matching mirror hung above the antique piece, and Margot thought both the spot and the furniture perfect for arriving and leaving her home. Of the several mirrors in the house, she considered this mirror her truth teller.

This morning while she waited for an airport limousine to arrive, George brought a pot of Earl Grey tea on a silver platter and sat it next to her clutch-purse and traveling gloves on the hutch's spotless green marble circular-top. So highly polished, it gleamed up at Margot, seeming alive with its own energy.

Barisa Callas Garcia de Arroyo Cooper—Cook Phillip's Argentina-born wife and Margot's housekeeper—was a cleaning marvel who abhorred dirt, dust, and clutter. Indeed, Margot was very thankful for Cook Phillip and Bari—and overpaid them accordingly. She ran her hand over the marble top. *Spotless.*

She didn't consider herself vain or possession-proud, but she did think her entry arrangement ideal for gathering her purse and keys, while simultaneously checking whether she was presentable enough to enter the world outside her domain. And when returning home, it was a quick and easy spot to assess what damage her latest foray had done. A place to take account. *What a stuffy old woman I've become,* she mused.

Margot had done her own packing, and at her side, a medium-sized Pierre Cardin roller bag and matching folding garment-bag sat waiting on her Chinese Khotan entry rug.

"The bellman called," George said. "He estimates your limousine will be here in five minutes." He smiled and poured her a cup. "You might not have another opportunity to enjoy black tea of this quality once you get out West."

They looked at each other in the mirror above the hutch.

She laughed lightly, and returned his reflected smile. "You make it sound like I'm heading off to the Sahara." The tea's aroma was lovely. She took a sip from the china cup. *Perfect.* She expected it would be—hot and heavy with sugar and lemon. George didn't leave her tea preparation to Cook Phillip. Like her evening hot chocolate, he made it himself.

No, George never failed her. And exaggerated accent withstanding, she loved hearing his voice. Baritone, sonorous, and oh, so proper. And the jacket, a blatant over-the-top affectation, was for her, the perfect touch. George explained early on he'd immigrated first to Britain, but now called the United States his home. But with the English gentry was where Margot guessed his heart was, and would remain. She'd never asked where he'd been born, there were many possibilities, and she had no inkling to spoil what she called the "George mystery"—or run him away. She did know he liked jazz, and that he'd taken a vacation a few months back in Barcelona—though she'd never seen any "vacation snaps." Indeed, on some fronts, she'd barely manage without him. Her brother Graham had suggested George was a product of the US Department of Justice Witness Protection program, but she thought the idea more than a bit fanciful.

After several sips and a pleasurable sigh, Margot said, "It's just California. They do have flowery orange pekoe tea out there."

George had explained about tea grades when he'd first arrived for an interview. She occasionally wondered if the employment agency had tipped him off about her fondness for tea and chocolate. Didn't matter really—she'd thought him perfect on all fronts.

He made a face and kept further thoughts on the topic to himself.

The intercom buzzed. Her limousine was waiting down below. Both turned from the ornate mirror with a sigh. Familial duty called.

It was a long drive to O'Hare Airport, and the whole operation of flying had become so unpleasant these days. But Graham had pleaded she come right away. And something in his voice caused her to fear the worst—a serious illness.

Cancer? She hoped not. In addition, she felt Camille was somehow involved. *But how could that be?* Well, she would at least visit her niece. Maybe stay with her a couple days.

She also felt her own participation was crucial. *But, again, how could that be?*

"George," she asked while putting on her 40s-styled eight-button length travel gloves. "Do you believe in psychic premonitions?"

"No, Madam," he said without hesitation. "I do not." He cleared his throat. "However, I do believe there's something to be said for 'second vision.'"

Startled, she turned to look at him straight on. He was smiling broadly.

Just like Harvey used to do—George so likes to tease me.

Camille's head hurt like hell, and the sunlight streaming through her window and assaulting her barely dilated pupils didn't help matters. She was beginning to believe the Mojave sun was relentless. Second only to the winds—which she'd whined about several times before finally leaving the clinic last night. *Parker must think I'm the biggest cry-baby.* Still, she took a moment to listen to the world outside her window before forcing her eyes fully open.

She considered herself a morning person, but this was a bit too much daylight so soon after last night. She closed her eyes again—tightly—and let her mind meander. *Relentless sun, winds, sand—all good reasons to consider moving on.* Indeed, maybe this had been a big mistake in the first place, taking a job because her boss had known her deceased uncle-in-law years ago.

And now, her father Graham was quick to remind her how lucky she was to have three offers for her next position. She figured he was behind the Palm Springs practice offer, but the LA and Loma Linda VA hospital letters, those were surprises. All three were higher salaries than her current one, and she wouldn't have to pay her own malpractice insurance.

But, six months wasn't a very long time to give NewTown a try. Not really fair. *Then there's Parker Reed.* She sighed, and Dogue, still half asleep across the foot of her bed, stirred slightly. If it weren't for Parker, she wouldn't have Dogue—and even though it had been only a few months—she couldn't imagine life without her German Shepherd.

The doublewide she rented from Oscar and Ann Lewis sat on a ten acre parcel, five-hundred or so feet to the side of the Lewis' larger home. Her mobile was fairly modern and faced a north-easterly direction. So did her large master bedroom window, and Camille loved her open and uninterrupted view out across an alfalfa field, followed by several miles of barren desert—then finally encompassing the rolling Cady Hills. She hadn't bothered with blinds or drapes; consequently, the impact of morning was never mitigated by window dressing. *Sometimes* a good thing, *sometimes,* not so much.

Should she try opening her eyes and facing the sun again? *Not yet.* Of course she knew the real reason she felt so awful. Faye-Anne Miller was dead. *Murdered.* Added to that pain, Parker most assuredly wanted to pin the poor girl's murder on her mentor. Maybe he was right. Then her mind brought back Oscar's face last night, his eyes in particular. Scared, pleading, and just skirting shock.

"God, this is horrible," she said out loud.

Even though her eyes were closed, Dogue clearly assumed she was talking to him, and barked. She liked his bark, deep and commanding as befitting a Shepherd. "Breakfast time, huh?" In their short time together, woman and canine had established a deep bond, and a mutually agreed upon routine—morning chow, *then* a walk, *then* she'd conveniently go to the clinic—and he'd snooze most of the day away.

"You'll have to wait," she informed him.

Camille could feel warmth from the sun's rays on her face. Soon, she'd have to open her eyes. "Ugh," she said, and wiggled her right leg a bit. Dogue barked again.

Oscar's agreeing to half day Saturdays at the clinic meant she was the one to pay the price this morning. She doubted *he* would be there. *Maybe Parker or the deputy had arrested him.* They were all still at the clinic when she was sent home last night.

Camille tried opening her eyes again—slowly. *Not so bad this time.* Thinking back, she realized no one had taken her statement. If the time of death was right, she'd had opportunity to kill Faye-Anne before rushing off to Velma's. She sat up in bed while Dogue turned his head quizzically.

"Even you know something's wrong, don't you?" *I seem to be talking to the mutt more and more.*

A surprisingly intense longing for her aunt Marg swept over her, and Camille had the oddest feeling that somehow Margot Madison-Cross was about to play a significant role in her life over the next few days. *How can that be?* The Dear was back in Chicago, enjoying her cityscape and pampered life in the Windy City. As far as she could remember, Auntie Marg and Chicago went hand-in-hand.

Camille also knew how much her aunt had done "behind the scenes," as her father had explained many years earlier. He'd been talking about greasing medical-wheels, and she still remembered one of her dad's rather uncharitable quips about Uncle Harvey. *"I doubt Harvey realizes how much Marg does behind the scenes for him. Ungrateful…"* He'd let it go—but she'd always wondered if some event her father would never tell her about hampered the two men's relationship.

He'd been correct about Auntie Marg's contribution to Uncle Harvey's practice. She could still see his office building—its marvelous stone edifice and side parking lot. A rarity in that area so near the Water Tower on Michigan Avenue—around Erie if she remembered correctly. Her memories were still amazingly vivid and she wondered if the building were still there. *What a different world— miles and years ago.* "I was just a child."

Based on his ear position and twitching, Dogue still seemed interested in her words, even though she had yet to use the magic word—biscuits.

What was all this thinking about her aunt, Chicago, and the past? Maybe she should call her—reconnect, find out if something was the matter? Better safe than sorry, as her Uncle Harvey was used to saying.

Thoughts of his old practice in Chicago brought Camille's mind back around to her own present day medical world. Patients would be arriving at the clinic around nine, and she had a lot to do before then. One item was to figure out what Parker was up to regarding Oscar. Maybe insert herself into the investigation even more.

Then from some other emotional direction, and only for a second, Camille felt a wave of excitement wash over her. *But that shouldn't be, should it?* What could possibly be exciting about finding a murderer?

Dogue barked again—entwined with a whine, but before she could pull herself out of bed, her home phone rang, and she reached over and grabbed the bedside receiver.

It was Deirdre, apologizing for calling so early, but she'd forgotten to give her a message last night. Her father had called. His message? Call her Aunt Marg.

Yet again, Dogue barked—this time rather insistently.

* * * * *

Even though flying first class and having access to a lounge, Margot found the rigmarole at O'Hare airport tiring. The actual flight was uneventful—the movie was one she'd seen—leaving her with more forced-captivity time than she wanted. Time she spent thinking and fretting.

She'd brought along a recent medical monograph—usually a treat. But not even part two of a brain tumor research project was able to grab her interest for long. She did open its mailing envelope and took a peek at the final findings and summary. Even now, with Harvey gone seven years and her connection to the medical world waning, she was still driven to keep up with the "latest."

By the time Margot landed at Ontario International in California—she was most definitely out of sorts. There weren't any non-stops from Chicago to Ontario—forcing her to spend several hours in San Francisco.

So she arrived in California, put out, put upon, and cranky. All emotions she felt capable of handling. Most worrisome, however, was an irrepressible and growing sense of fear.

Around mid-morning Saturday, Camille sensed Parker's presence in the medical center before he actually arrived at her office. *The electricity of romance novels?* She suspected human pheromones more likely, and didn't look up immediately when she heard footsteps in the hall, followed by a perfunctory knock on her partially opened door. When she did bring her eyes up from Gloria Daniel's file, she saw NewTown's Chief of Police didn't look happy.

He tossed a thin unmarked file folder on the corner of her cluttered desk. A minor splash of manila in a sea of folders requiring her attention.

"Got a sec?" he asked without preamble. "And where's Dogue?"

"Do I have a choice?" Camille heard irritation in her voice, *but really*. Sometimes Parker was infuriatingly rude and presumptuous. Admittedly, she was also mad he'd waited so long to let her know what happened last night. "And," she added. "My fierce guard-dog is probably asleep in the middle of my bed." She snuck a quick glance at her watch, and was surprised it was after eleven. "Are you about to tell me he needs a baby sitter?"

"No. But he does need company. Especially on the weekend."

She looked up from the latest test results and notes on Gloria, a mild diabetic who was doing remarkably well with diet, Metaformin, and exercise. She'd rather deal with Gloria's test results—110 mg/dl for the fasting plasma glucose test, 6.0% for the HbA1c, and 120 mg/dl for the random capillary blood glucose—than Parker. Gloria was one of those patients her Uncle Harvey called "the-easy-ones." His larger-than-life voice still rang vibrantly in her ears. *"The-easy-ones are the patients you tell what they need to do, and they do it."*

A long list of test numbers she could deal with; high blood sugar and low blood sugar were things she knew about. Indeed, patients she understood. Parker, not so much.

Nonetheless, Parker was here and now. Through a polite smile Camille used with recalcitrant patients, she tried to assess today's version of NewTown's finest. As usual, he looked sexy—even though dressed casually in well worn work boots, bleached Dockers, and an aged plaid work shirt.

Camille doubted she was emitting an in-kind appeal. It had been a long morning—ten patients already—*not surprising it was almost noon.* But that was good, patients coming in on Saturday. Also on the good side, Oscar's wife Ann had come through with her usual efficiency. She did a lot of the day-to-day office management activities and procurements; this morning, freshly laundered whites and scrubs had been waiting when she arrived. A murder had happened just last night—*but we'll all look professional this morning*—due to Ann's logistical abilities and willingness to dash in on short notice if something was needed.

41

On the bad side, Oscar had yet to appear, and she didn't know why.

Parker pulled a chair within a foot of her, turned it backwards, sat down straddling the seat, and crossed his arms over the chair's back-bar—each movement an identifiable and deliberate step. "You know you look real good in a stethoscope." His smile was broad, his tone flirtatious, and his eyes mischievous.

She picked up the folder he dropped on her desk. It was a transcript of the Medical Examiner's intake report. Camille knew the ME, his daughter had gone to medical school with her in La Jolla— and she considered Doctor Peter Matthews excellent at his job. "You brought this to me because?"

"Because you insist on believing your wonderful 'Doctor Kildare' is innocent."

Camille was surprised at his retro-reference. *Always something new with this man.* "Richard Chamberlain or Lew Ayres?" If she left NewTown and moved on, their relationship would most likely fizzle. A good or bad occurrence—she wasn't yet sure.

"Lew, of course. 1938 I believe."

She scanned the report quickly. Matthews had noted the blow to the parietal lobe, even speculated it had been made with a hard— *probably* a metal-surfaced object—and *probably* resulting in a fractured skull. Camille knew such a blow would cause massive brain injury, and almost immediate death. *Painless?* She doubted any death was painless, including the supposedly peaceful ones. Although, she had actually talked to several joyous people who'd experienced clinically defined death, and returned from the "white light" to talk about it.

Matthews also noted "Doctor Camille Metoyer-Madison has recommended normal and advanced tox screens." His tracheal examination indicated the possibility of poison. Agent unknown. Cause of death was noted as "not immediately determinable." A full autopsy was scheduled for today.

With the thought of Matthew's impending autopsy—the lifeless face of Gabriel, the last twelve-year old boy she had assisted with in Cook County Emergency in Chicago—was suddenly looking up at her. More like she was staring down at him--*dead little boys don't look back at you*--even when they're named after an angel. She closed her eyes for a second, banishing Gabriel back to the recesses of her memory.

Oscar had been right about leaving Chicago, the city Auntie Marg loved so much. *Doctor* Oscar Lewis had told her what to do, and she had done it. Just like Gloria Daniels had done with her.

This time, however, if she did make a change, she would figure things out for herself. *Maybe* Palm Springs near her father, *maybe* the LA hospital with big-bucks potential, *maybe* the VA in Loma Linda helping veterans—*or even stay here*. Whatever she decided, it would be *her* decision.

Opening her eyes, Camille met Parker's inquiring gaze and said, "Why would Oscar bludgeon the woman?" She laid the folder down on her desk. "So many ways he could kill her with drugs, and Peter would never find a trace. Some are unidentifiable even with all the tox screens in the world."

"He did it in a moment of passion."

"You're talking about the fractured skull part?" She shook her head. Didn't seem logical. "Are you suggesting two killers? And do you mean 'passion' as in losing control and doing something stupid like bashing your lover on the head in your own office?"

He looked at her for a long moment before saying, "Passion as in—they had a 'thing' going, and she threatened to tell his wife." He crooked his mouth, and smiled in only one corner. "People in love, or 'in hate' for that matter, do some damn stupid things."

She couldn't argue with that.

"Would you like to go with me to see Ann Lewis?" he asked, standing. Then he turned his chair back around, and replaced it against the wall.

Such a chameleon he is. "When?" she asked, trying to keep the excitement out of her voice. "And is that why you aren't in uniform?"

"As soon as you're finished. You're only here half-day, right?" He smiled charmingly again. "And yes, I'm guessing Ann will open up more if she sees me as a friend, not a cop."

Camille doubted Ann was so pliable, but Parker might know her better than she did. "Do you think Oscar will be there?" She would like to see if he was doing okay. "You didn't arrest him, did you?"

"Not enough evidence."

"Good." Camille blew out a breath. "I'll be able to see how he's doing. Deirdre said he didn't call in this morning. And I've just been too busy."

"So," he asked, "you haven't seen him since we were all in this office last night?"

"No…"

"No one seems to know where Oscar is. Seems your 'Doctor Kildare' is making himself scarce."

Camille pushed her chair back and stood. "Oh, God, what have I done?"

"You?" Parker extended his hand to help her. "What are you talking about?"

"Acute Stress Reaction. We need to find him. Now." She felt like crying. "He could be dead. Lying in a ditch somewhere, not knowing where he is."

"Mojave County and Barstow Police have already put out an APB. I've got a friend out looking—"

And you didn't tell me. "No accidents reported on I-15 or Route 66?" Her mind raced. "And Ann says?" *Parker already knew Oscar was missing.*

"Still hasn't seen him since he left home yesterday evening. She expected him to come home after we left the clinic. He didn't, so she figured we'd arrested him." He looked away for a few seconds.

"Ann was probably pretty upset." *I should have sent him to the hospital last night.* "You should have told me what was going on when you first walked into my office." Her voice was accusatory, and her words, she hoped, a stinging rebuke of his highhanded tactics at her expense. "If I'm one of your suspects, you need to tell me right now." Her finger easily found the programmed button for Community Hospital on her desk phone. She had a gut feeling.

44

Parker didn't offer a rejoinder. Rather, he chose the course of looking justifiably chastised and chagrined.

She wasn't buying his contrite looks. "Oscar better be okay," she said very slowly—each word laced in emotion and anger directed at Parker—*and herself.*

Even though Parker was driving with sirens blaring and lights flashing, Camille felt like it was taking forever to drive the thirty miles into Barstow. She had to exercise a lot of self control not to squirm like a child in the passenger seat.

On one level, it was exciting, sitting next to Parker, cars pulling over on the shoulder as they passed. Her conscience, however, insisted on reliving and scrutinizing her actions regarding Oscar's medical care. In the pit of her stomach, she felt awful. *Guilt.* She tried being the best doctor she could, just like Uncle Harvey, but when her mentor Oscar needed her, *I failed.*

Thank God, she silently prayed as they passed the Barstow Daggett Airport exit. *We're getting close.*

Sure, last night the arterial palpation of his heartbeat was in range, his skin color was normal, and when she'd applied pressure to his ear lobe, color had come right back. She'd asked him if he felt weak, or giddy, or nauseous—and he'd assured her he was fine. Camille still doubted he was in physiological shock last night.

But psychological shock? Now that was a different matter. She'd specifically asked him if he felt disoriented, in a daze, confused—she couldn't now remember what else she'd pressed him on. But again, he'd said no, he was just fine. However, something in his eyes had said he wasn't—and she'd believed his words, not her instincts.

Camille cursed under her breath.

"Are you okay?" Parker asked, not taking his eyes off the road.

"No." Miserable actually, but she still hoped for the best. "Nurse Tamarack at the hospital said Oscar was sitting in Doctor Kubiak's office." Camille looked at Parker's profile. "Must mean he's okay."

"If you say so." He still didn't take his eyes off the road. "You're the doctor."

Something in his voice told Camille that Parker wasn't the least concerned about Oscar's medical condition.

Despite her fear about her brother's condition, and a lingering undefined foreboding, Margot was looking forward to eventually seeing Camille again. What had it been? *Three years almost.* It was late, and finally relaxing with Graham on his spacious hacienda patio with a glass of wine on the table beside her, Margot prayed she wouldn't be bringing bad news to her niece when they finally did meet.

Your father is very ill, she mentally practiced the words; though Graham had yet to tell her. She knew, however, his news *was bad,* and whatever it was, he was relying on her to tell Camille.

She recalled his words from Friday night, "Had an accident last week, almost died. Time for some truth telling." Then his cryptic proclamation, "We're all living a lie."

On second thought, now that she was actually in Palm Springs, his statements didn't really indicate an illness, rather some kind of intrigue. *He couldn't possibly have guessed the biggest lie of them all? Could he?* Those involved were sworn to secrecy. *No,* her brother was just being melodramatic. Gray never changed. Evidently, neither had she. He'd thrown out his bait, and she'd swallowed it whole.

Sitting in a lounge chair next to him, waiting for his "bombshell," she didn't know whether to grimace or smile. Despite his faults, and once again taking in his deep-set eyes, the *pièce de résistance* of his eager and boyish oval face—she felt love and joy side-by-side with dread. Indeed, life without Gray's steadying anchor would be quite unbearable.

"Don't take this the wrong way, Marg," Graham's voice was playful. "But I suggest you stop at Lenwood Mall on I-15 near Barstow before you get to NewTown."

"Because?" Margot was also overly tired—worn out actually, and with an unwanted flash of irritation, wondered why he was so concerned about her wardrobe. She reminded herself how this trip was worth it just to see Gray and hear his voice again, even if he insisted on teasing her.

"It's an outlet store place," he explained. "You need to dress-down a bit."

She was also upset because of the bandage on his forehead. She didn't like the looks of it, even though today he said the accident and his injury were minor. Friday, his words were *almost died*. Later, but soon, she would push him for more details about what happened. Admittedly, other than the bandage, he didn't look ill. That was a good sign, wasn't it? And he felt well enough to tease her, another good sign.

She ran her hands over her Dana Buchman lounge-pants clad thighs. The material was smooth and comfortable, but Gray's idea was actually a good one. The plan was for her to drive to Camille's in the morning, and he'd explained NewTown was in a different type of desert than Palm Springs—more rugged. *Yes*, jeans were probably what she needed.

Nonetheless—she guessed a remnant of childhood sibling jousting—Margot lied. "I'll be fine with what I have." The trick was to look him straight on, maintain a deadpan countenance, and *look into his eyes as if I can see right through to his soul*.

She couldn't quite picture NewTown, but a couple desert images from the TV space-western *Firefly*, and the rather old movie *Bagdad Café* came to mind. Harvey had enjoyed both dramas, and she'd watched with him. *Before he was snatched from me*.

Graham smiled, then asked, "How's George?" He cocked his head a bit and made a teasing face. "Still have a crush on you?"

"Don't be silly," she said. "George is an employee."

"Hmm."

Her day suddenly felt very long—and *despite* the pleasant Palm Springs temperature, *despite* his 180° desert view, *despite* the dry and mellow wine, and *despite* her brother's welcoming hospitality— Margot found herself completely out of patience and energy. They needed to get down to business.

She picked up her half-full glass of wine and said, "Well, Gray, don't you think it's about time you tell me what's going on?" The wine's bouquet was lovely. "And is this a California wine? I meant to ask earlier." He'd decanted and poured at the mini-bar behind them, and she hadn't seen the label.

He turned his eyes from her, and looked out toward the rolling terrain off his patio. "No," he answered her second question. "It's an Ethos Reserve Cabernet Sauvignon from Chateau Ste. Michelle Winery in Woodinville, Washington." He took a long sip from his own glass while continuing to stare out in the direction of the San Jacinto wilderness. "I've been to their winery, you know. Lovely grounds."

Margot sighed; for now her feet, clad in *French Sole* ballet-pumps and visibly swollen from her cross-country flight, ached. Ironically, the slippers were called *Camilla*. Fortunately, she could feel soothing warmth from the red *Saltillo* tiles covering the floor below her thin shoe soles. *Residual heat from the morning sun?*

Graham stood, turning his back to her, and walked forward to the edge of his patio. "It's hard finding the right words."

It must be cancer.

An overwhelming urge to cry grabbed her throat. A world without Gray was unimaginable. She looked down and saw her hands were clasped tightly in her lap, her ruby staring back at her. Margot braced for the worst, while a gentle and fragrant breeze found its way through the patio—mocking the moment. *A May afternoon, sipping wine with my brother, should be lovely.* Yet, she almost shivered remembering the windy fifty-something degrees at O'Hare when she'd stepped out of her limo at Terminal-2 this morning. The air had not only been cold and damp, but had also smelled of diesel fumes.

Fair weather or foul, however, her brother was finally about to explain how ill he really was, and though she thought she'd prepared herself for this moment last night—and then on the flight—she hadn't. *Not really.*

Finally Graham turned back to her, and what seemed to Margot as if he were moving in exaggerated slow motion—came back to his chair, sat down, placed his wine glass on the table between them, looked her straight on, and finally said, "I'm not Camille's father. Your deceased husband," he made a quickie sign of the cross, "Harvey is." Then with his hands, he gestured pleadingly. "And I need you to tell her."

Margot was shocked.

Not clinically—she knew the difference between medical terms and everyday vernacular. Her husband had been the doctor, but she'd read countless medical monographs over the years. She'd always been as well informed as Harvey—even better at times. He'd had to concentrate on his patients, while she'd had time to read.

But at this moment, she didn't need medical savvy to know her racing heart and flushed feeling were telltale signs of the depth of her surprise. Nonetheless, she needed to stay calm so she could think rationally.

"Why do you think Harvey is Camille's father?" She hoped her voice wasn't quivering. "You do know what you're saying, right?" Margot made herself take a moment, inhaling and expelling a deep slow breath before putting her next words into the world. "You're saying my husband of thirty years," she made her own sign of the cross over her chest, "and your wife of thirty-plus years, were having an affair?"

Graham averted her challenging eyes, and returned his gaze to his expansive desert view. "Yes, Marg. I know what I'm saying."

For a moment, she was speechless, and a heavy silence settled over them. This was definitely not what she'd expected. Her sister-in-law Meredith had clearly lied. *A lie of convenience?* So much like Meredith. If a lie worked best, made her life better, then a lie it would be—no matter who else got hurt. *Oh, Meredith!* If she had to say something, why not the whole truth—instead of this silly half-lie?

Finally Margot said, "I don't believe it."

"It's the truth." Graham's tone was soft and sad. "I've accepted it." He turned back toward her, looking at his empty glass on the table instead of meeting her eyes. "Camille should know her medical heritage," he said. "You must agree with that?"

She wanted to laugh from irony, or was it frustration? "You think there's something in Harvey's medical history Camille should know about?" She heard the edge of anger in her voice, but couldn't help it. "Harvey died in an airplane accident. Not from an inheritable disease—last I heard."

"Now, Marg." He looked at her, and she could see exasperation written across his face. "No need to get testy," he said. "You must believe the truth is better than living a lie?"

No, Gray, I do not.

Suddenly, Graham jumped up and rushed to the front of the patio again—waving his arm and pointing his finger. "Look!" he shouted. "It's that damn trespasser again."

Camille had yet to meet Doctor Carol Kubiak even though she'd talked with her on the phone many times about her patients who unfortunately found themselves in Carol's Emergency Ward. The image she'd built in her mind from Carol's voice was of a tall, hefty, and stern woman. Reality was, Carol couldn't weigh more than a hundred pounds, or stand an inch over 5'4," and she greeted Camille and Parker with energetic handshakes and a broad-faced smile.

Carol had come out to the emergency intake waiting area to meet them, then without much ado ushered them to her office— where a disheveled-looking Oscar was sitting on a battered leather couch against the back wall, nervously thumbing a magazine. With a quick apology, Carol rushed off, closing her office door behind her. There had been a big accident in Victorville involving several motorcycles, she succinctly explained, and the overflow of injured was headed her way. They could use her office as long as they needed.

Oscar, looking rumpled but seemingly in control, stood before Camille could speak, and said, "I should have called you, I know that." He squared his shoulders a bit, and looked directly at her. "I'm really sorry."

She searched his eyes, looking for signs of stress, anxiety, or depression. *Nothing.* "Did Carol examine you?"

Oscar nodded unconvincingly, took a quick deep breath, then turned to Parker, and offered his hand. "I guess I owe you an apology too."

Parker reciprocated the handshake, smiled through tight lips, and didn't comment.

"You probably want to know where I went last night," Oscar said.

Parker held his forced smile, stepped backward, and flipped open his cell phone.

Watching both men, Camille saw a wave of something—*fear maybe*—flash across Oscar's face in reaction to Parker's actions.

"Cancel the APB on Lewis," Parker told someone on the other end of his call. "I'm with him now. Not a hostile situation."

"Not a hostile situation," Oscar repeated, then flopped back down on the couch and said, "Jesus." He rubbed his hand across his mouth before sighing heavily. "I just needed time to think."

This was a different Oscar than the one Camille knew. *Or thought I knew.* In an instant, she realized how hard it was to see an unpleasant side of someone you cared about. Like watching your favorite actor on a late night talk show—and realizing they're an idiot. She didn't want to see anything distasteful in her mentor.

Parker went over to Carol's desk, sat down in her swivel chair and leaned back comfortably as if it were his own. Camille thought

51

his actions presumptuous, and his demeanor unfriendly. *A tactic?* She wondered.

He paused a few more seconds, then said, "You do know a Barstow detective is heading here right now to interview you?" He looked at Oscar intently. "I would have interviewed you myself." He shot her a quick glance before returning his stare to Oscar. "But I was *told* I was too close to all the suspects. Conflict of interest, you know."

Camille didn't remember that, and again thought Parker's demeanor and words were tactics. Of course she hadn't been with him *all* Friday night, but she thought he was lying to get Oscar to open up.

"But if you want to try out what you're going to tell the detective on me..."

"There's no 'try-out' about it." Oscar's voice wavered for a second. "I didn't kill Faye-Anne. We've known each other for years."

"You want to tell me what you did last night?"

"When?"

Camille wondered what Parker expected him to say? At the same time, she couldn't understand why Oscar was being so cagey.

Parker sighed. "Come on, *Oscar."*

She'd remained close to the door, and consequently had a side view of Parker's face. His profile, combined with the thought he might be lying to draw Oscar out was disconcertingly titillating. *How could that be?* True, he was a handsome man, but that wasn't anything new. Indeed, her libido's timing stunk—and she wished her Auntie Marg was around to talk about this Parker "thing."

"I didn't kill Faye-Anne," Oscar repeated.

Camille figured she shouldn't be butting in, but did anyway. "What did you do last night?"

"Nothing different, I tell you. Nothing different."

She went over to Oscar and sat down on the couch next to him. She was his friend, and he needed help; maybe her friendly voice would get him to open up. She was no longer worried about him being in shock, but she did think he looked tense—like an overly wound spring. Both his hands were clasped tightly around his right knee, and she placed both her hands on top of his. "You asked me to help you. Do you remember that?" She gave his hands a little squeeze.

He nodded.

"Well, I think Parker just wants to know what you did after you left the clinic. You know, establish a timeline." She waited, but no response—though she thought she felt his hand twitch under hers. *Something is going on.* "I remember we both left around four. You said you were heading home for dinner, if I remember correctly." If she could just prod him a little, break the grip of whatever was holding him captive.

He shook his head, then stood up abruptly, jerking his hands from underneath hers in the process. "I can't remember."

Parker said, "You can't remember what you did after you left the clinic?"

There was a peremptory knock on the door before it opened, then a smallish but muscular man in jeans, T-shirt, and cotton sport jacket came in and announced, "I'm Detective Hollist. I've been assigned the case as an assist to the Sheriff's department." He took several seconds to visually sweep the room, then said, "I'm here to interview Oscar Lewis."

Parker had explained the "pecking order." Besides the CHP, there were County Sheriffs, City Police Departments, then unincorporated area police like him—"*I'm bottom of the pile,*" were his words. Consequently, she instantly disliked this man Hollist who had taken over Parker's case.

She stood, stretching tall as she could, and gave him a challenging look. She'd stolen the mannerisms from her aunt, though Camille knew she didn't have the same weighty gravitas. "He is *Doctor* Oscar Lewis," she said. "And do you have identification?"

Hollist tsked, rolled his eyes, flashed a wallet mounted badge—then snapped it closed within seconds. She wasn't even sure what "city" he was supposed to be from.

"May I see that a little longer?" Camille asked. Out the corner of her eye, she caught Parker hiding a grin, but she didn't care.

"No, you may not," Hollist said, then looked pointedly at Oscar standing next to her. "*Doctor* Lewis, I need some of your time. We can talk here, or you can come into town." He gave Camille a challenging look before returning his gaze to Oscar. "Your call." Then he smirked and added, "Doctor."

Oscar lowered his head, brought his hand up to cover his eyes, turned slightly toward Camille, and winked at her. Then he returned his hand to his side and said to Hollist, "Let's go into town."

It was mid-afternoon in Barstow. A funny time, Camille had noted on several occasions in the past—and again now. Stores were seldom crowded, traffic was light, and the whole town seemed eerily quiet—like it was asleep until people started getting off work. Town *siesta* time.

Today was no different; even Community Hospital's emergency parking lot was almost empty, despite Carol Kubiak's forecast of patient overflow.

"Do you know that Hollist character?" Camille asked Parker, glancing back toward the hospital emergency entrance.

Parker answered with his own question, "And do you know how your face looks?"

"I look PO'd, right?" Camille thought she had a good poker face when it came to patients, but clearly in her personal life, not so much. They were almost to his Jeep, but Hollist's actions still rankled. "He seemed awfully arrogant to me."

She was also irritated with Oscar. Evidently, he'd been faking last night and today. Biding his time. *But why?* Trying to get an alibi in place was the obvious answer. "You think Oscar killed Faye-Anne?"

Parker silently opened the door for her, walked around to his side, and didn't attempt to answer until they were both buckled in.

"What I think," he said starting the Jeep, "is something is going on with your 'Doctor Kildare.' And until I find out what that is, being a murderer is as good an explanation as anything else."

"But you've known him longer than I have," she insisted. "You actually think he could kill someone? He's a healer for goodness' sake."

He ignored her question, and said, "When we get to NewTown, I'm going out to talk to Patricia personally." He gave her a quick look before pulling out onto Main Street. "Want to come with?"

"For real?" *I sound like a kid.* Since Oscar was "found," evidently he didn't feel the need to still talk to Ann.

He laughed. "Yeah, for real."

Camille looked out her window. Main was almost deserted. "Someone did tell Patricia her sister was dead last night, right?"

"Officially, Hollist."

"Oh God. The man's not exactly 'Mr. Comforting.'"

"I called her afterwards, and evidently he wasn't that bad."

"If you say so." She didn't know why she was being so mean spirited. Her encounters with police professionals hadn't been frequent, and she'd had amicable dealings with them her whole life. *Truth be told,* the fact Faye-Anne was dead was beginning to affect her emotionally—grief gnawing at her psyche. Whatever Faye-Anne had done, the poor girl was far too young to die. And she was taking it out on the easiest target.

And poor Oscar. He must be going through hell. But why disappear, and why wink at her?

Once again she wished for her Auntie Marg. She should call her—though over the phone wasn't the same. She certainly needed someone to talk to who understood her. Even before her mother died, she always went to her aunt.

Then she remembered Deirdre's message to call her aunt. "Darn," Camille said, and hit herself on the forehead in a comical manner. She'd also meant to call her father. "I forgot to call my relatives."

Parker didn't say anything.

Poor Ann, probably worrying about Oscar. Maybe even wondering if he murdered Faye-Anne—*a philandering murderer no less.* Though last night, when Camille walked over to the main house right before bedtime, Ann hadn't given any indication she knew Oscar was having an affair. Just expressed sorrow Faye-Anne was dead. *How does a wife know about those things anyway?* She almost sighed, but caught herself. For some strange reason, she didn't want Parker to know what she was thinking or speculating.

Camille planned on walking over and talking to Ann again when she arrived back home—even though Parker wasn't intending to conduct an official interview. Check out how she was holding up. Maybe Oscar would be home from *his* interview by then—*or arrested.* Indeed, sitting next to Parker—who she figured must be experienced in recognizing evil—Camille entertained for the first time the possibility Oscar might have killed Faye-Anne. It was a horrible thought.

Parker had one hand resting on the gear-shift knob, and she wanted to reach over and hold it. Tightly—or was it tenderly? *Good grief.*

Instead she asked, "They're running the expanded tox-screen like I suggested, right?"

"Yep."

When Oscar first offered to rent her their mobile, he specifically stressed, "Be careful handling any part of the oleanders. They're very poisonous. Only takes a small amount."

Of course her medical curiosity had been teased, and she immediately researched the *Nerium* oleander and found out that similar to digitalis, it contained cardiac glycosides. In fact, she'd found a whole list of pharmacological compounds that were in the plant. Most upsetting was the reporting that it only took 15 to 20g of leaves to be fatal for a horse. Even using fresh twigs as grill skewers was not advised.

To her, the oleander flowers, especially the white ones, were beautiful. But she'd never forgotten Oscar's admonishment, or her research.

*   *   *   *   *

Camille hadn't been to this part of NewTown before, and based on her current experience, hoped she wouldn't have to ever come this way again. One mile of bumping, bruising, potholed dirt road was bad—but four miles were excruciating.

"Are we there yet?" she asked Parker.

"Still another mile." He seemed unaffected by the potholes or dirt cloud swirling around his Jeep. "You sound like my brother when we were little. Could never wait to get wherever we were going."

Camille almost asked if he'd also vied for the window seat. Fortunately, before speaking she remembered his older brother Patrick, a career marine, had been killed in action. "No wonder your cars are always dusty." Their windows were closed, nonetheless, Camille could taste sand, and she wondered about silicosis, or some other dreaded fibronodular lung disease. There was also coccidioidomycosis, "Valley Fever," caused by arthroconidia—air borne mold spore filaments. She'd been presented with a case of it in an older alfalfa field worker suffering from allergies that masked some of the symptoms. Remembering, she felt ashamed—she'd almost missed the diagnosis. Faye-Anne was the one who'd mentioned the disease to her, and Camille almost teared-up remembering.

Fortunately, her attention was drawn to the sight of an odd looking building in the near distance. "What's that over there?" she asked. "To my right. Set back. That big thing with the curved roof?"

"Our former Chief of Police lives on that property."

"But what is *that* building?" Sometimes Parker was annoyingly obtuse. On purpose she was sure, and very irritating. A trait that would probably not weather well in a long-term relationship. "I'm asking about the building set back and to the left of the house where I'm assuming your old Chief *actually* lives." And to make sure she'd get a direct answer, Camille added pointedly, "The huge rounded-arch shaped thingey."

"Quonset hut." He laughed. "With all your education, would have thought you'd know that."

Now that he'd named the type of building, she recognized the word, and remembered seeing pictures of similar structures—popular in World War II. But his remark about her "education" was an odd thing to say out of nowhere—and snide.

"Meaning, because I'm a doctor, I should know everything?" She turned to better see his expression. "Do I act like that? Like I'm a know-it-all?"

Parker didn't answer right off, but rotated his head back and forth, side to side, for a few moments, like he needed to stretch his neck and shoulders. Next, he looked out his side window for a second. Finally, after a long breath, but still not looking at her, he said, "You've got it all wrong."

A long silence followed, and Camille thought it a good idea to change the subject. "So, what does your predecessor use it for?" She looked backward out her side window, but the only thing visible to their rear was a cloud of dust.

"Chief Martinez used to have a yearly shindig there. Inside and out. Every Fall," he said, his tone one of remembered appreciation. "Troughs of iced beers and sodas, several barbecues going, a band. Everybody used to come. Even your 'Doctor Kildare' and Ann. The Chief stopped doing them a few years back."

"And now?"

He shrugged. "Just storage I think. Things change. People move on, others die." He sighed. "Probably sticks in my craw how much education you have. Lotta years to become a doctor."

It took Camille a couple seconds to disconnect his comments, and before she could respond, they hit a deep ditch, or a high bump—she wasn't sure which—and despite her seatbelt, her head almost hit the ceiling.

"Good grief!" she yelped and put her hand on the top of her head as if a meager hand could protect a skull. "I think I've just jarred my brain." She had treated several soccer players in the past.

"I wanted to go on to graduate school," Parker said. "We're almost there."

He slowed down and turned to her, an expression on his face that was new to Camille. Openness, a desire for acceptance? She wasn't sure.

"But I didn't."

Camille didn't know what to say, and turned to look and see where "there" was—and was flabbergasted at what she saw.

"I...I...," she stammered. *Wish Auntie Marg could see this.*

Parker smiled smugly. "The Chief's place is only about half a mile back. And this is the last spot on this road. If you want to go further up into the Cady Mountains, you need an ATV. Or you walk."

Camille said, "This is an amazing spot." She was genuinely impressed with the Miller sisters' place. She was also thinking about a hook to draw Patricia out. Help her with talking about Faye-Anne's death—and maybe help Oscar in the process.

They were sitting in a large room of an old but well maintained sprawling ranch-style log house situated at the base of the rolling Cady hills. Outside was a small clear blue lake surrounded by stately Date Palms—quite strikingly visible from the road—and now a centerpiece attraction through the living room picture window. All sides of the property she could see were bordered with mature oleanders.

The overall effect was of a sparkling jewel in the desert. *Who would have thought?*

Patricia was dressed in shorts, t-shirt, and synthetic Wal-Mart-issue mules—striking in that her entire ensemble, including her shoes, was turquoise. Camille was wearing walking shoes, but the mules caught her eye because she had identical ones at home—except hers were red. *Funny what catches your attention in situations like this.*

"It's like—," Camille was stuck for an appropriate simile. "An oasis," she finished. *Or was it a metaphor?* She could never keep them straight, despite all the education Parker claimed he found intimidating. Actually, she wasn't sure she completely believed his "education regret" spiel. *He's a Police Chief, for goodness' sakes.* Couldn't have more power than carrying a gun and having the authority to arrest, or even shoot someone. What the heck did he want more degrees for?

She brought her thoughts back to Patricia and said, "I can't believe you and Faye-Anne drive all the way out here on that road every day." The realization hit her hard that Faye-Anne would never drive their road again.

"Potholes keep the bad guys away," Patricia said, her voice listless.

Camille didn't want to push, so she leaned back for a moment and more thoroughly took in her surroundings. She and Parker occupied opposite ends of a comfy loveseat, and Patricia was slumped in a plump turquoise armchair facing them. The decorating motif was completely unified by a predominate Southwestern theme. Indeed, what caught her eye right off were the Native American design rugs on the floor, a cowboy blanket draped across an entry table, and a R.C. Gorman print on the wall. *Or maybe an original?*

Camille didn't often interact with Patricia at the clinic, usually Deirdre assisted her with patients. However, she'd thought Patricia competent. She was a nice looking brunette, whose best asset—and similar to Faye-Anne—were her expressive large brown eyes.

But this afternoon, Patricia's eyes were lackluster—in fact, she looked and held herself like a dead-woman-walking. Nonetheless, when they arrived, Patricia insisted on brewing and serving fresh coffee in large mugs, accompanied with chocolate chip cookies. The refreshments now sat untouched and lonely-looking on a low hand hewn burl coffee table.

An aged and brown-blotched Saint Bernard lumbered in with Patricia when she'd returned from the kitchen with coffee, then sprawled herself on the tile floor between them and the entry door.

At the time, Patricia introduced her as Oozie. "Believe it or not," she'd said, "Oozie's a great watch dog. Knows things, hears things, way before we do. Faye-Anne thought she was psychic—" She'd choked up, then quickly placed the coffee service on the table and sat down.

Camille wasn't confident she could help Patricia, but hoped she could assist Parker. She leaned forward and asked softly, "Are you feeling depressed?" Of course she was, but *how* depressed was her medical concern. "Would you like to talk to a grief counselor?"

"Huh!" Patricia half laughed, half grunted, and her eyes widened for a second. "So they can tell me how much I miss my crazy sister?" She sniffed. "And it'll take time…"

Camille scooted to the edge of her cushion and leaned forward even more. "How much did Detective Hollist tell you last night about how your sister died?" Parker had yet to ask any questions, so *what the heck,* she'd take the lead until he stopped her.

"Last night?" Patricia looked vaguely to the ceiling then back directly at Camille. "Hollist? Oh, you mean the jerk who came around and told me my sister was dead." Her face tightened, and emotion swept over her features. "Like she'd been road-kill or something."

Yet, she'd told Parker Hollist was okay. Or maybe, Parker was protecting a brother-in-arms? *Jeez. People and the games they play.*

Like with her, Hollist's coldness made him an easy target for anger over Faye-Anne's death. Camille noticed a slight twang in Patricia's voice she hadn't heard before. "Trust me," she said, in as compassionate a tone as she could. "I know what you're going through." Many faces flashed at camera shutter speed across her memory. Shocked faces of family members standing in Cook County Hospital emergency, trying to grapple with the loss of loved ones. Often, their own children.

Camille forced herself to continue. "It's a horrible thing that's happened." She leaned in even closer to Patricia. "And your pain isn't going away soon." She glanced quickly at Parker to see if he was going to say something, but he was watching Patricia intently. *What a way to know people,* she thought. Always anticipating a lie, and looking for a clue to their deceit.

"I'm usually at the front desk, you know," Patricia said. Curiosity flashed in her eyes for a second. "How's Deirdre?"

Before Camille could respond, Parker asked, "Was Deirdre fond of your sister?"

"Not really." She turned to him. "I know for sure my sister and Deirdre both cared about Doctor Lewis more than they should."

Camille held her tongue as Parker leaned forward. "Do you know if either your sister or Deirdre were having an affair with Doctor Lewis?"

A long, but not uncomfortable silence hung in the air for a few moments. Finally Patricia said, "Faye-Anne was. I don't know about Deirdre. We had a big fight about it—Deirdre and me." She paused. "Sis was a flirt, and in some ways manipulative. But I didn't want to see her unhappy. So," she blew out a resigned whiff of air, "I told Deirdre to leave Doctor. Lewis alone."

My goodness. The sister of Oscar's mistress telling her sister's possible competition to lay off. Then she remembered the spittle in the corner of Faye-Anne's mouth. "Deirdre said you made energy drinks for everyone. Is that true?"

"Most definitely." For the first time since they'd arrived Patricia's voice sounded more like her old self. "Nursing takes a lot out of you." A touch of a smile appeared for a second. "Well, you know that, being a doctor and all." She shrugged and dipped her head like a child. "We actually walk several miles in one day at that office."

Camille hadn't thought of that. She knew she walked a lot in and out of exam rooms. But not like the nurses.

"I've done a lot of research on supplements, you know," Patricia continued proudly. "Particularly natural ingredients like antioxidants and energy enhancers."

"You mean like fruits and vegetables?"

"And berries and grapes. I prefer to make my own drinks." She inclined her head toward the hallway leading to the kitchen. "I even grow my own raspberries, strawberries, grapes, and jujube on the property here." She sniffed. "We have a high quality blender, and juicer."

Camille smiled and nodded. She'd never heard of jujube, but now wasn't the time.

"I make the drinks every morning and bring them in."

"Of course." Feeling like a dunce, Camille said, "The metal containers in the refrigerator." *How could I forget about them?* Containers personalized with Patricia, Faye-Anne, and Deirdre's names. There could be important evidence sitting right there in the refrigerator. *Unless the murderer has retrieved them already.* She looked at Parker who was still intently watching Patricia. "Chief Parker," Camille said. "We need to stop by the clinic."

Patricia took in a sharp breath. "You think there was something in the drinks I made?" She shook her head vehemently. "I make them myself! Fresh every morning." Her voice faded almost to a murmur. "One of my mixes is sort of bitter." After a moment, she continued, her tone now shaky and shrill, "That detective last night said I can't even have her body."

Camille thought Patricia needed counseling, and fast. "If I give you the name of a doctor I know in Upland will you promise to go?" Once again, she remembered Uncle Harvey's lament of how his patients never listened. "You're a nurse, like your sister. You must know how important it is to have grief counseling?"

Tears flooded Patricia's eyes. Camille got up, went over to her, squatted at her feet, and took Patricia's hands in hers. They were cold and quivering. She thought she heard Oozie voice a complaint—but even as big as the dog was, she would just have to ignore the Saint Bernard. Besides, if Oozie was as smart as Patricia claimed, she would know she meant her mistress no harm.

She had to get through to Patricia. "Promise me. Please."

Finally Patricia nodded consent as tears flowed down her face.

Clearly her tears were real, but for a tiny moment, Camille wondered. *Parker's cynicism rubbing off?*

Margot sat straight up in bed—not quite gasping for breath—but definitely in distress. Her breathing was rushed, her heartbeat rapid, and much of her body was covered in perspiration. She patted her chest—her silk Asian motif pajamas were soaked.

She blew out a breath and said, "What is this all about?"

Nightmares were not an unfamiliar occurrence for her, especially after Meredith's death—and again for a long time after losing Harvey. But they'd always been composed of ramblings and wanderings through snapshots of existing traumas intermixed with age-old anxieties tucked away in the limbic system parts of her brain. Admittedly, her pictures and emotions were often bizarrely concatenated, but always with some frame of reference if she thought long and hard enough. Usually a rehashing of the past, even if reframed in anticipation or anxiousness over a future event.

This was different.

"Oh my," she said with a sigh that seemed to help slow her heart rate.

Though Margot was alone in the bedroom of Graham's guest casita, speaking out loud seemed to have a calming effect. She'd begged off with her brother for an early evening, deciding to rest her eyes before calling George, then reading herself to sleep. Her drive to NewTown was planned for the morning.

It would be late when she called Chicago, but she knew her butler was a night owl. However, instead of resting her eyes for a few minutes, she'd immediately drifted off to a nightmarish place she'd never been before.

Now physically calmer, Margot closed her eyes and tried to bring back the images that had so frightened her. *Yes*, she was trapped in the dark, scared, alone—and someone she loved needed her help. She didn't like the emotional feelings emanating from her attempt to recreate where her mind had gone, and inexplicably she could feel her physiological reactions returning. Immediately she re-opened her eyes.

"The oddest feeling..." *Dare I say it?* "A precognition?" *Yes; denial would be a lie.*

Also—and this was the worst part—Camille's beautiful face had been staring back at her. Horribly composed in a lifeless image.

Margot started to shake, but immediately willed herself to stop. *This is silliness. I can't possibly know what's in the future.*

She was able to control her trembling, but she couldn't stop the coldness that seemed to sweep through the bedroom.

"You aren't mad?" Camille asked. "I didn't really mean to take over—"

"You did what I'd hoped you'd do." He shifted his weight in the Jeep's driver's seat. "I watched, while you talked."

They were bumping back down what Camille now knew was Tappy Road, heading toward blacktop. She could hardly wait to return to pavement. Her backside and lower back ached, and she guessed Parker, despite his stoic body language, wasn't fairing any better.

"You don't like interrogating women, do you?"

"Not ones that need coddling to get information." He glanced at Camille. "She needed handholding, literal and physical—and you did both." His tone was complimentary.

It felt good, him liking how she'd handled herself, and she took a few seconds to bask in his praise before returning her thoughts to Faye-Anne. She'd left her car in the clinic parking lot. "Instead of just dropping me off at my car," she said. "Would you go inside with me to check something out?"

"Does this have to do with Patricia's health drinks?"

"Not as clever as I think I am, huh?"

He refrained from comment.

"When do you think you'll get a prelim on that tox panel?" she asked.

"Monday, hopefully."

They finally hit the two-lane paved road that ran north to south through NewTown, and she noticed Parker's shoulders relax—and for a few moments it felt like they were floating on a cloud.

"That road sucks," she said, hoping never to have to go down it again. An unexpected tingle shot across her shoulders, but she shook it off. "Probably caused me a pinched nerve."

He laughed, and asked, "What do you think you can actually find or do at the clinic?" He looked at her again, this time a little longer before returning his attention to the road. "You do know some parts of the clinic are still a taped crime scene?"

Sometimes she really liked the sound of Parker's laugh, and this was one of those times. "I know." *I need to keep my mind on solving a murder.* "I'm guessing that young deputy is still stationed at the back door?"

"Yeah, him or Thompson."

"I just want to look in the refrigerator."

Her cell phone rang. *Auntie Marg!* What a wonderful surprise.

Margot liked Graham's antique-white rotary phone. It was so much more comfortable speaking into a regular receiver. She was not fond of cell phones. Having gotten past her nightmare, she was now ensconced in a comfy rust-colored lounge chair in the *casita's* sitting area talking to George. She'd changed into fresh lounging pajamas, and was almost ready to call it a day.

Chair side was a pedestal-table large enough to hold the stylish retro-phone, a snack, even a couple books.

"George," she said. "Did I wake you?"

"No, Madame."

She smiled at their salutation silliness, but moved on quickly to say, "I'm visiting with Graham now, and I just talked to Camille. She knows I'm coming. I'll see her tomorrow."

"Excellent Madame. Do you have directions?"

"Yes." Her drive would be into unfamiliar territory, but she didn't want him to worry. "Camille was very clear. And it doesn't sound complicated."

A comfortable silence fell between them for several moments before she continued, "Meredith lied to Graham, and now he wants me to pass that lie on to Camille." George didn't need to know specifics.

She thought he coughed, but wasn't sure. "Is it a matter that will be upsetting to your niece?" His tone was interested, but not pushy, and she thought George raised an interesting question. Would Camille be hurt by Meredith's lie?

"It could be devastating."

"Why would she tell such a lie?"

"For convenience sake, I'm guessing." In the past, she'd shared many items with George, but here she would have to deceive even him. So many little lies, she speculated, *were* lies of convenience.

She changed the subject. "It's very beautiful here."

Margot had stayed in her brother's guesthouse on two earlier trips, and found it comfortable. Not only was there a kitchenette area, but also a private patio and Jacuzzi—designed so you felt like you were sitting on the edge of a cliff. Graham had a good eye for architecture, color, and design, and he'd taken layout and decoration of his *casita* seriously.

She thought the view from the sitting room, though not comparable to Lake Michigan's waterfront, quite dramatic in its own way. Especially at sunset. Paint-brush-like splashes of red, orange, and blue were beginning to spread across the horizon above the Mesquite and Palo Verde tree laden hillside. It was not her Grant Park twinkling lights—but still.

"It's not the lake," George said, his tone doubtful. "Though I never met your sister-in-law, from everything you've told me, she must have been a complicated person."

Margot could almost see him in Chicago, his handsome, but rather bland looking face scrunched up, contemplating—and she smiled before quite frankly saying, "I think a lot of Meredith's actions sprang from the affects of alcohol." She wondered if George were talking to her from his quarters, or from the kitchen. "Nonetheless," she said after a few seconds pause, "she was always concerned about Camille."

Yes, Meredith had the mothering instinct. *Not like me.* How any woman, actually, managed a screaming baby was still beyond her understanding.

She reached over with her free hand and picked up the still-frosted glass holding the rest of a tequila drink Graham had brought. Margot couldn't remember what the strawberry concoction was called, but her first taste before calling George had been lovely. Sweet, fruity, and refreshing. She took another sip now, then changed the subject. "I've rented an auto to drive to NewTown tomorrow. I'm leaving early in the morning."

"What type of car, Madame?"

He'll like my choice. "Mercedes-Benz GL450."

"Excellent."

"Graham rented it for me in Palm Springs." Her brother seemed to have "connections" everywhere, and for everything.

"Does your niece know you'll be in the area?"

"Yes, just talked to her." *Weren't you listening?* Was he doing something else while talking to her?

"And the weather out there?" He sounded doubtful a positive response was possible.

She thought for a moment. "It's lovely. Around seventy-eight right now, and cooling down."

Regardless, George's tone was cautionary. "Be careful Madame. You *are* on the West Coast."

"I will." It was hard not to laugh. "I'll call you tomorrow evening. And by the way, you didn't say what the temperature *there* is tonight?"

He cleared his throat before answering. "Fifty degrees, Madame."

After she replaced the receiver in its cradle—and while thinking how nice it was to actually "hang up" rather than press a *tiny* little button on a *tiny* little phone—Margot finished her drink in one not-so-ladylike swallow. Then she sighed and surrendered her body into the accepting cushions of her armchair—letting even her head fallback onto the chair's plush headrest.

Tomorrow would be a hard day. For a moment, fatigue followed by irritation took over, and she told her empty glass, "Gray believes it was *his* wife fooling around with *my* husband." *Yet he wants me to tell Camille, instead of him telling her.* "Coward," she whispered.

Today had been filled with emotional and verbal minefields. She doubted tomorrow would be better. As George had advised, she would be careful. Egocentric or not, and even though she didn't know why—all her senses were on alert. She was moving into the center of something. *Something* very unpleasant.

It had been so lovely hearing her niece's voice on the phone. Maybe she'd figure out what was going on when she actually saw Camille in the morning. Tomorrow would be a better day.

After all, it would be Sunday. *What could go wrong on a Sunday?* Indeed, she could almost hear the chimes ringing before the eleven o'clock Sunday service at St. James Cathedral on Huron Street back in Chicago.

Chapter Three

Sunday

Unlike yesterday, Parker decided to wear his uniform. Today, he would not only be psychologically ready for work, but also "formally" attired. As if "how" he dressed could speed up progress on the case. His was a seven day a week job—a fact that didn't bother him at all. He liked what he did, but on weekends, the uniform was an item of impulse depending upon his mood.

He also didn't care who technically claimed jurisdiction—this was his town, his friends, his case.

This morning, he parked on the shoulder at the end of a side spur off Route 66 about ten miles past the second NewTown I-40 east exit. A spot he was particularly fond of.

Part of his Police-Chief-enjoyment came from knowing where he physically was on planet earth in relation to incident calls—or anything else for that matter. Long before all the latest gadgets, he was his own personal GPS system. Even as a kid, he always kept track of North, South, East, and West. He was the family human-compass, and was usually right. Parker thought it had to do with some kind of internal magnetic system. At this morning's chosen spot, directional points were easily discernible. Surrounded by what he considered unique pieces of scrub-desert, it was an area with no pretensions to be other than what is was, Mojave High Desert. Not too far away was a dry lake bed, and not much farther, before Ludlow, and near Amboy were volcanic remnants.

Also unlike yesterday morning on Yermo Road, weather-wise this morning, a thin stretch of clouds spread themselves across the eastern horizon. Not unusual for a spring morning—but more clouds than he'd expected, and the blue sky backdrop, like the foreground terrain was extremely pale. Combined with the sunrise itself, he especially liked how all the subtle shades of sand and tan blended together in early morning light, letting the lines of new-day sunrise yellow, orange, and red be the headliners of the show—with a soft desert-pallet as their backdrop.

Clouds, sun, brightness, spots of overcast—this day had yet to decide what it wanted to be.

Parker once again wanted his morning thoughts focused on Faye-Anne's death, and Oscar's part in her death. *That hospital act was incredible.* He thought Oscar was playing a dangerous game. *But why?* Didn't he know, if guilty, *he would* eventually catch him? He laughed at his own arrogant thought, then said aloud, "Yep, super-cop will get you alright."

He didn't even have a definitive answer on the cause of Faye-Anne's death yet—even with the obvious signs of bludgeoning. He figured results were slow because of the extended tox-screen Camille had so astutely asked for—but the thought had surfaced that Deputy Thompson might be holding back. He doubted it, though. *No,* he wasn't worried about Thompson. Indeed, the deputy had sent the drink holders from the refrigerator to Riverside forensics immediately. And he didn't think Hollist was getting in the way.

Still, he exhaled a long slow breath, releasing a building uneasiness. Growing within was a sense Faye-Anne's death wasn't just a case of criminal villainy. It felt more like past dramas inconveniently unraveling in the present. Sins and lies no longer tolerable. *But whose sins, and whose lies?*

His money was definitely on Oscar.

"Ten-twenty-eight," said a scratchy radio voice he recognized. Besides his internal compass, Parker had two scanners, a hands free cell phone, a CB, a GPS unit, and a top-of-the-line UHF two-way mounted in his Jeep. He also had a handheld lying on the seat next to him. The lights on his oldest and biggest scanner were flashing activity.

71

He smiled. This particular scanner was set on a frequency an old Air Force buddy of his used who was now on the Kingman, Arizona Police force. Sometimes he'd get a VHF repeater-ping like this from across the miles, and he would think of Jerome and the times they'd shared. To use all his equipment, he had two honking-big whip-like antennas on his back fender. His smiled broadened, thinking about all the equipment peppering his jeep.

He said aloud, "A lot of hardware for a podunk cop like me." He never tried to respond to Jerome. Even if he wanted to, Kingman was too far away. Often the way with catching the criminals—*too far away*.

Parker shifted his weight in his seat, patted the butt of his Glock 9mm in the tray between the front seats, and blew out another long breath of air—forcing his thoughts from Jerome and the past.

Okay, part of his anxiousness wasn't murder-related, rather a response to the knowledge Camille's Aunt Marg was coming to town. Camille was very excited; he wasn't so sure.

As far as he knew, she'd never been to New Town. *So why now?*

"Margot Madison-Cross," he said her full name out loud, and something primeval in his being—akin to his internal directional compass—told him his world was about to change. And this Margot woman would be in the center of whatever that upheaval entailed.

Graham cursed vehemently, then said, "Why aren't I ever in a position to go after that bugger?" He was standing on his second floor study balcony, and speaking to himself about the barefoot trespasser he just saw zigzagging from east to west across his property.

It was still early—the sun barely above the horizon—usually Graham's favorite time of day. Especially on Sundays. Today however, he'd not only woken up under a cloud of irritation bordering on anger, but his mood had continued in a downhill slide culminating in catching sight of the trespasser once again.

He rubbed his forehead with both hands. Another one of his headaches was taking shape. They were awful, and he was sorry he'd mentioned them to Margot. Maybe he should have let them do some imaging after his accident. *No—*the MRI, or CT, or PET, or *whatever else* they'd tried to foist on him were entirely unnecessary. He was just fine.

Fortunately he and his sister hadn't lingered over morning coffee, and their goodbyes had been quick. He'd wanted to spend the rest of the morning trying to figure out what was going on between them—alone, on his own. Last night's conversation needed to "sit" before they talked again. Margot hadn't shared enough of her feelings—and that omission on her part made him angry.

So after seeing her off in his driveway, Graham climbed the stairs to the second floor and walked out onto his study balcony where he now watched her silver Mercedes-Benz slowly make its way down his twisting and turning road toward the main drag into Palm Springs. *The same road I almost lost my life on.* He said aloud, "I'm a very lucky man."

She must have seen the trespasser too, couldn't have missed him. *Soon,* Margot would be navigating through Palm Spring's "civilized" parts, then heading north to the Mojave High Desert. *Soon,* she'd be talking with Camille. He took a deep breath, tasting the morning air, and felt a little calmer.

He could blame it on Margot, but in his heart, Graham knew it was innocence about to be lost churning his stomach. Something he couldn't do anything about.

He wished he had the *cojones*—a word his gardener Michael was fond of—to tell Camille himself. Actually, he was capable of telling her, he'd practiced what he'd say enough times in the wee-hours of the morning. But Margot would do a better job of it. *Suppose* Camille started to cry, *suppose* she got mad at him. It was seeing his daughter's hurt that he wasn't sure he could handle. Her world shattered, her trust in him irrevocably wrecked.

Margot must surely understand how important this was—yet last night she hadn't committed to tell Camille. And this morning, all she'd said was "I'll see how things are with Camille." *What the heck did that mean?*

Thinking back over the years, he remembered how close he, Margot, and her deceased husband Harvey had been. Still, it was a good thing he hadn't found out about Harvey fathering his daughter until after he'd died. To this day, he didn't know what he would have said to Harvey. *Done to Harvey.* He was able to forgive Meredith—but Harvey, he wasn't so sure about.

Even though he felt Camille needed to know her bloodline, he and Meredith—he made his habitual small sign-of-the-cross, and mouthed the words *God rest her soul*—were Camille's parents in every way that counted. *And look at her now, a doctor for goodness' sake.* He was so proud—and so had Harvey been when alive. Even helped her become a physician.

No, I can't take that away from him.

He took in another deep breath and watched Margot's left turn blinker come on as she reached the bottom of the hill. She was on the verge of leaving his protected world. That was how he saw himself and his place. Once back on county pavement, it would be *their* world. Up here, he could just hunker-down, close his eyes, and believe what he wanted.

"King of the hill," he said. "Modest as it may be."

However, being king of your own hill only went so far when it came to doing what was right. That realization had been crystal clear in those seconds when he thought he was going to die. Not telling Camille about her biological father wasn't right no matter how much he wished it otherwise.

Graham looked up—the sky was magnificent, the lightest of blues, unclouded. Hiding nothing. As his eyes returned to the horizon, he saw the intruder again—*bold faced trespasser*. This time however, Graham had plenty of light, and a good side view. Maybe he'd be able to describe the jerk to the police. And what the heck was the fool doing, zigzagging around from bush to bush and popping up unexpectedly. *Now, really.* The chutzpa.

But as annoying as the unknown trespasser was, his thoughts returned to Margot and Camille.

What a coward I am. And a hypocrite, for that matter. Asking my sister to do the dirty work. Still, he rationalized aloud, "It was *her* husband fooling around with my wife." And consequently her responsibility.

Graham looked down at his watch, a 1980's era Audemars Piguet "Royal Oak." A gift from Harvey twenty-plus years ago. Even at the time, the watch was an extravagant present, and Graham had accepted the timepiece as a mark of genuine friendship. An acknowledgement between two men who felt they'd not only finally "made it," but also had an appreciation for the finer things.

Now, standing on his balcony, contemplating where and how their lives progressed, he wondered at Harvey's motivation.

Three hours, and Margot should arrive in NewTown. *Okay,* he didn't really blame his sister per se, but still, after a little thought, he realized she was a significant part of his morning unhappiness. He had expected her to be more broken up by the news her husband had fathered Camille. He'd anticipated disbelief, or across-the-grave recriminations. Maybe even tears—though that wasn't Margot's style.

Like it or not, what rankled most was his own secret. He'd known for years he had low sperm count, "Oligozoospermia." He liked saying the awkward word because it was so hard to pronounce. Not something a man went around bragging about; but to lie to Meredith was something more than ego. Not actually a lie of commission, more a lie of omission.

Whatever you called it, he knew never telling her was the same as telling her an untruth. At first, he'd considered withholding the information just a matter of conflict avoidance. He now recognized his omission as the vain and misdirected machismo deception it was—and not one of his prouder moments.

Several noisy and mottled brown sparrows landed on his balcony's broad stucco railing. "Did you see that man running across *my* land?" he asked softly. "Come to think of it," he told the chattering little birds as if they were following his bouncing chain-of-thought. "Can't remember ever seeing her cry as a kid."

Then he remembered a late afternoon in Chicago—*how could I ever forget*—the sky had been Midwest winter cloudy, and a ferocious wind had kicked up from the lake. They'd waited for a bus on Michigan Avenue for what seemed like ages, and he thought he was going to freeze, and had started crying.

He was only ten at the time, Margot was twelve—going-on-forty. In a juvenile way, he'd realized even then, her lack of tears wasn't because she didn't feel. She'd tried to explain, "I hate crying. It's a loss of control that makes me feel miserable."

Remembering the episode, and while scouring his landscape for another glimpse of the intruder, Graham laughed outright. He couldn't remember a time when Margot hadn't talked like a grownup.

With his laughter, the nervous little birds flew away into the branches of a fruitless Mulberry that had reached second story height. *All my landscaping is finally maturing.* An enjoyable line of thought, but even his quite successful efforts at desert landscaping weren't strong enough to divert his attention from his sister and daughter.

Margot's distaste for crying aside, he still had expected a stronger reaction from her. Thinking back on yesterday, she had seemed more surprised Meredith had told *him*, rather than at the deed itself. He shook his head—*no*, that wasn't exactly right. More like—he couldn't quite put his finger on what her reaction told him. Graham did know, he had certainly expected more.

"Ah!" A logical explanation came to him. Harvey must have told Margot before he died. *She was just surprised Meredith told me.*

He looked down his winding road a final time before going inside. Not a barefoot trespasser or car in sight. Margot had successfully headed out—on her way, hopefully, to break the news to Camille. It was an easy drive, even though his sister was a hesitant driver. *And terrible at directions.*

Their Route 66 adventure as young adults flashed across his mind's eye one more time. He'd loved the Wigwam Villages, and the Rabbit Ranch, and Seligman—pictures, thoughts, remembrances came in a flood—and he almost cried out from the wave of emotion that swept over him. *You can't go back.* Graham fought back unexpected tears, and the memories causing them. Unfortunately, his budding headache was now a reality.

Turning and heading inside in search of aspirin, *Oh well,* he thought. *Margot has her cell phone.* He'd also noticed a GPS in the car, and she had said something—not jokingly—about always carrying pepper spray. *What could go wrong?*

The man drove past slowly, then stopped his pickup truck about twenty feet in front of her Mercedes-Benz. He also got out slowly before walking back to where Margot was standing by her car.

Wind and dust where swirling all around, pounding her with cold, then hot air—without any rhyme or reason she could identify. On top of the weather driven misery, out of nowhere, her eyes started to run, her sinus passages dried up, her throat turned to sandpaper, and she had the most intense urge to sneeze. Nonetheless, she didn't move—just watched as he approached her.

He was maybe six-three or so, dressed in jeans, western jacket, cowboy boots, and wearing a huge cowboy hat—*the kind Harvey's cologne was meant to conjure up*—and seemingly unaffected by the battering winds. His walk was stiff, almost limping. So much sand was clouding the air, Margot couldn't make out his face until he was a few feet away. Even then she couldn't get a good read on his eyes.

"Got a flat, I see," the stranger said.

"Just happened." The wind seemed to grab the words out of her mouth. She was sure her GPS had said Camille's house was on this road.

"Odd car to be driving out here," he said. "Truck or SUV is what you need." His tone was flat. "Can't count on them foreign made fancy cars on these roads." He gave her rental an accusing look. "Fancy hubs, but flimsy looking tires. Probably foreign too."

Margot was sure her Mercedes had quite substantial tires, still, she looked at her flattened one, and stammered, "I don't know."

"Got someone waiting for you?"

"Yes," she said quickly. "But I'm lost." Margot felt grit enter her mouth. "And my cell phone can't seem to get a signal." The storm was getting worse, turning afternoon into a sheet of sand, and her pantsuit was being whipped against her body from all directions.

"Those phone contraptions don't work behind these hills. Don't believe in them myself." He rubbed a roughened, possibly dirty hand across a bushy and unkempt mustache, then across his chin. "Need an old fashioned CB." He looked her up and down. "You're not from around here."

"No."

"Didn't think so," he said. "Not dressed like that. This ain't the city."

Her unconscious habit surfaced, and Margot slid her hands over her thighs and linen pants. She'd just bought the outfit at Liz Claiborne in the Lenwood Mall place Graham had suggested, then changed in the store, and thought she'd prepared herself quite nicely for the Mojave. Sadly, her pants felt sand permeated. "I got lost," she repeated. "I'm looking for the Lewis place." Maybe mentioning a local name would make a difference. At least she thought Camille had said "Lewis." *Oh dear.*

"A woman shouldn't be driving alone out here."

Suddenly, Margot felt a bit afraid.

He added, "Lewis place isn't anywhere near here." He stepped forward to within a couple feet of Margot and stared into her eyes. "No tow-truck is coming down this road anyway, even if your phone did work."

She hadn't thought the road that bad, smooth actually for dirt. She now saw his eyes were dark brown, tough looking, but revealing little else. She had her pepper spray in her hand behind her back—her finger on the trigger. But she sorely wished for her derringer, Paladin. *Darn airline regulations.* She swallowed hard, and said, "I need to get to a phone. Let them know where I am."

"This desert is a big place. Been here all my life." He turned and started to walk toward his truck. "I'll turn around and come back. Not my way, leaving a woman out here alone," he said over his shoulder. She barely caught his words before the wind took them away.

Margot's instincts told her this man was probably okay, yet she was apprehensive. The storm was getting worse, and he disappeared into swirling dust. However, she could hear his truck start, then the rumble of his motor as he came back. Within moments he pulled up next to her.

"Get in," he said. "I'll take you to the Lewis place. Lock your car."

Margot grabbed her purse out of the car, stuck her pepper-spray in her pocket, and locked the rental as he'd instructed. Then she climbed up into the cab of his pickup truck, and realized she didn't even know his name. She almost jumped down, but it was too late to turn back. And again, she had to stifle a sneezing fit. *Allergies?* The Mojave Desert was not turning out to be her friend.

After the truck started moving, she looked down and saw a large handgun lying on the hump between their seats. Then she heard her passenger door lock automatically.

"My name is Gus," the stranger said. "You shouldn't have come this way."

The last stretch of road to his house had been *awful*—pothole, then a bump, then a pothole—*awful*. The worst, Margot thought, she'd ever been on—even when she'd visited Alaska.

"Whattaya' think?" Gus asked proudly.

Once out of the truck, he'd positioned himself to the side of his front fender, facing what his gate sign announced as "Oleander Ranch." His stance was wide-legged, and he hooked his fingers in his pants pockets.

"Give me a moment," Margot stammered. She needed time to take it all in, and to choose her words. Especially since to the far left, a Quonset hut in the distance had a peculiar, almost ominous feel to it. *Was it his?* And how could she possibly "feel" a Quonset hut she'd never seen before?

He left the gun in the car, but she was still wary of this stranger, her rescuer. *On alert.* But she was stuck—no car, no cell phone coverage. Or could she get a signal now? She'd give it a try as soon as the right moment came.

The high winds had stopped as quickly as they started earlier, now producing an almost eerie calm. A few dust-devils danced around her feet, but nothing like earlier, and after the storm she'd just been through—the baby swirls were barely noticeable. Above her, the sky was clear pastel-blue, with the sun bright, hot, and almost directly above.

Are those dogs I hear? She'd never seen anything like what spread before her—land, buildings, and so much more.

"How much is yours?" Margot asked. She guessed five or so acres were fenced with chain-link, but miles of open scrub-desert stretched before them until her eyes took in low rolling hills on the far vista. Maybe one more house at the base of the hills? She even thought she saw the flicker of sun on water. But that couldn't be.

"A section."

Pride was in Gus's tone, and she would have to choose her words carefully. This was her first opportunity to really take in the Mojave while not driving, and she found herself at a loss for words— *complimentary words* at least. She could feel his eyes on her, watching for her reaction.

To Margot's right a couple hundred feet away was a large two-story house, partly brick, and partly wood siding. An expansive covered porch surrounded the building on three sides, maybe even around back. She couldn't see well enough to tell, and she didn't want to move closer. Besides the home, there were several sheds, lean-tos, and carport looking structures. To her left outside the fenced area was what looked like a well-maintained orchard with neat rows of shortish trees she couldn't identify.

"Pistachios," Gus said, reading her mind.

The barking was getting louder, more insistent.

What grabbed her attention again, visual and emotional, was a huge building in the far corner of Gus's property. Metal, clearly rusting in many spots, and gigantic.

"What kind of building is that?" She pointed and inclined her head. Of course, she already knew the answer. "It's huge."

When Gus didn't respond immediately, Margot turned to see she was still under scrutiny, and he was smiling. "Quonset hut." He winked. "And you know that already, now don't you? Got some special items in there. Want to see? Some pretty fine antiques if I do say so myself." Brazenly, he looked her over again—top to bottom. "Might get dusty, though." Then he laughed outright. "But you've already crossed that stream, now haven't you?"

Margot managed not to look at her clothes herself, or rub her hands over her thighs again. True enough, she must look a fright, but this disconcertingly loony man was not going to know she cared. "You're rather arrogant about your 'desert credentials.' Reverse snobbery I'd call it."

He laughed even louder and shook his head appreciatively. "Bunch of spiders in there." When she didn't react, he continued, "Afraid of them?"

"Hardly."

Margot picked up the sound of goats bleating, or was it sheep baaing? She wasn't sure, but the sound of horses whinnying and snorting was unmistakable. She even thought she heard cats meowing somewhere—inside or outside—she couldn't tell. *My goodness.* Her moments of post-storm quiet had suddenly transformed into a barnyard cacophony of animal greetings.

Gus turned from Margot and started walking toward his house. "Ann Lewis and our Chief of Police even got stuff stored in there."

"Mr. Gus," she called out, knowing her nomenclature sounded silly, but he'd yet to reveal his full name. "I really need to get to my niece's place." She turned to get back into his truck. "Are you, or are you not going to take me there?" She put her hand on the door handle, and hoped her voice sounded firm. "As you promised."

He ignored her and kept walking.

So she stood for a moment, her hand on the door handle, feeling stupid and vulnerable, while trying to figure out what to do next.

Gus called out over his shoulder, "Dogs want to meet you. Better to do it now. Then they'll know you when you come back."

Come back? The man must be crazy. If she ever got to Camille's place, she'd never be coming back here.

Gus stopped before reaching the porch, turned and said through a crooked half-smile, "Might want to try calling the Lewis place again. Get clear reception here."

She thought his smile rude and mocking. *Good thing I don't have Paladin. Just might shoot this irritating man on the spot.* Before Margot could contemplate further acts of mayhem, Gus opened his front door and five assorted-sized, assorted-breed, assorted-color dogs rushed out to greet her. The largest one looked to be part Shepherd, and she smiled, remembering her dear Faustus. All their tails were wagging and butts wiggling as they rushed toward her. Her pant-suit was already ruined, her shoes scuffed and dirty, and her hair and makeup probably in ruins. "What the heck?" she said smiling.

Margot squatted and opened her arms to greet them.

"Do you know how you looked when Gus dropped you off?" Camille's tone was teasing.

Margot laughed. *Indeed, what a sight I must have been.* "Goodness, I do feel better," she said. "And rather foolish." She'd showered, changed into a cotton tunic set, and slid her feet into lounging slippers. Camille had made iced-tea and it tasted grand. "There's one thing I can say for certain about your place here. The shower is marvelous."

She had a hard time taking her eyes off her niece. Every time she saw her over the years, Camille seemed dramatically changed. Her features of course, were the same, but somehow more mature—more woman-like, less of the child she'd doted on. This time, she could now see Harvey's DNA in her face, and she even thought she also saw some Madison genes in the set of her eyes. She so wanted to fold Camille into an all encompassing hug, then squeeze her tight like she was a little girl in need of a hug. She felt like a foolish old mother hen.

They were sitting in the kitchen, across from each other at Camille's small early-American kitchen table. Also unavoidable in catching Margot's notice and tugging at her heartstrings, was a wary eyed German Shepherd. "A present of sorts from the local Chief of Police, Parker Reed," Camille had informed her earlier.

The canine's name was Dogue, and he was sitting only a few feet away from the table, staring at her, ears straight up, and eyes intent—daring her to move. She remembered Camille taking in an aged cat when in college, but thought Dogue was her niece's first canine.

While smiling encouragingly at Dogue, Margot said, "I can't remember how many dogs that strange man Gus has." She raised her eyes in an expression of exaggerated disbelief. "Five or six at least."

"You know what his real name is?" Camille asked.

"Gus, you mean?"

Camille nodded.

"Gustav, maybe?" Margot guessed.

"You're close. Gusztáve Martinez." She smiled and added, "I'll spell it for you, G-u-s-z-t-a-v-*e*."

"A Russian first name?" Margot knew many families with Eastern European roots. Some whose immigration to Chicago dated back to Displaced Persons after World War II.

"Hungarian," Camille said. "His father was Mexican, mother Hungarian. Parker said both are dead now."

This Parker guy had come up several times since she'd arrived, and Margot was beginning to wonder. "And is Gusztáve," she accentuated her pronunciation, "okay?" Margot swallowed hard, remembering being lost in the sand storm just an hour or so earlier. "I have to admit, sweetheart, I was a tad afraid this morning."

Her urge to wrap Camille in a bear hug became even stronger, but she'd already made an emotional slobbering fool of herself when they'd first embraced. Unfortunately, with Gusztáve as witness.

"Well," Camille leaned across the table and lowered her voice, "he used to be the Chief of Police. Parker took the job when Gus retired." Her lingering smile was mischievous.

"Really?" She would have never guessed. "And he lives...." She caught herself. "In such an out of the way place."

"Maybe tomorrow I'll drive you around so you can see NewTown." Her smile continued. "People actually *choose* to live here."

Margot took a moment to again appreciate her niece, the newly desert-wise Midwest city-bred Camille. *Always a sensible and adaptable girl.* Hard not to be with Graham raising her, and Harvey butting in all the time. Then there was her genetic makeup—though Margot still flipped back and forth on the nature versus nurture controversy.

Dogue finally laid down, and she took a long sip of tea while a companionable silence filled the moments. Still, Margot couldn't take her eyes off her niece, and watched as Camille's face turned solemn.

After another moment or so, Camille said, "I'll find out how Father is doing from you later, if you don't mind. I just saw him last month." She took a deep breath and leaned forward. "Auntie Marg, right now I'm in the middle of a murder investigation."

Margot thought her eyes must have widened like a cartoon character. Indeed, she was momentarily speechless.

"One of our nurses was killed Friday night and Oscar is the prime suspect." She straightened and dropped back against the wooden slats of her chair. "There," she said blowing out a stream of air. "I've told you."

Margot could see Camille was glad to share what was happening—and her heart swelled even more from her niece's reflected fondness. She could also hear curiosity, excitement, and unfortunately, fear in her voice.

Had she psychically "sensed" two days ago what had happened? *Certainly not.* She couldn't deny she'd intuited *something* was going on. But no, she hadn't guessed Camille was involved in a murder investigation. *Of all things.*

A hard knock on Camille's kitchen back door surprised her, and she jumped slightly.

"Oh, by the way," Camille said standing up. "I asked Parker to come over and meet you." As she passed Margot, she put her arm around her aunt's shoulders, then leaned down and kissed her on the cheek. "I don't think he's ever met anyone like you."

Dogue got up and followed Camille, tail wagging. Margot hoped that was a harbinger of something good.

"The sauce is heated," Parker said, glancing at the oven. "And the bread should be warm." He turned from Camille's stovetop and said, "I forgot the wine. You have a bottle somewhere?" He gave her kitchen a more extensive, but quick visual sweep, settling on the refrigerator door. "Hopefully a chilled dry red?"

Margot thought he was careful not to let his gaze linger on either her, or her niece.

Camille rushed to explain, "This is the Chief's first time at my house."

Margot was sure a picture of romance in the making was presenting itself—and for a moment, a curious emotion swept over her. She'd think about it later, but guessed at the moment it was the thought—or picture—of her little niece kissing a man. An image she'd purposefully avoided since Camille left for college years earlier.

Nonetheless, it only took Margot five minutes from the time Chief Parker Reed stepped into her niece's kitchen for her to like him. He certainly was good looking, with a wry but captivating smile—reminded her of George in some ways—but that alone hadn't won her over.

Mostly, it was the way he carried himself, an aura of honesty—a "standup guy" Harvey would have called him. Of course, the way he looked at her niece gave Parker high marks. She doubted he knew he was so transparent, but she saw it in his eyes, the way he purposely didn't touch Camille, and a sappiness in the smile he bestowed her niece's way.

Within a couple moments after they'd exchanged greetings and he'd given his explanation for dropping by—"I made too much spaghetti and thought I'd bring over a late lunch"—Margot also decided there were hidden, deeper layers to this man than what his public persona put out. How she knew these things? Unexplainable, and not how she was accustomed to emotionally navigate through life. Nonetheless, she instinctively knew there were "things" Parker Reed didn't want anyone to know about. She *felt* their existence. *But how could I?*

Margot focused on trying not to give away her thoughts and speculations as Camille quickly set the table, and Parker brought over sauce and angel-hair spaghetti. He'd quickly plated the noodles in a large pasta platter he'd brought with him, topped them with sauce, and then meatballs.

"Auntie Marg has a cook," Camille blurted out in a nervous tone.

Parker gave Margot a curious look—similar to one Gus had bestowed upon her earlier. She laughed lightly, hoping to keep everyone comfortable. Then with a casual shrug and tilt of her head, she said, "Well, things are different in the city."

He sat down. "Back east in Chicago?" He smiled and added almost whimsically, "The beginning of The Mother Road."

"Yes." Margot nodded. "Though technically, Chicago is in the Midwest."

"Hmm." He stopped organizing food and place settings for a moment and said, "Former Chief Martinez is originally from Evanston, a place he said is near Chicago."

"North of the city," she said. *And all the time this morning, acting like he was the wise and wizened salt-of-the-earth desert-dweller—and me the idiot city know-nothing.* "I would have never guessed." Hadn't he actually said something about being out here all his life?

"I'll get the bread," Camille offered, then got up before anyone could object.

"After we eat, Chief Reed," Margot asked. "Would it be appropriate for you to fill me in on the murder my niece has told me about?" Murder was serious business, and she wanted to know what was going on. Camille could be in danger. Unconsciously, she smoothed her hands along the surface of her legs under the table.

He laughed and leaned back against his chair back. "Don't waste time, now do you?" Something in his eyes told Margot he was appraising her anew. "And please call me, Parker."

"Thank you, Parker," Margot said, and smiled slightly. "I'm concerned for my niece."

Camille returned, sat down, and placed butter and a basket of crusty French bread on the table. "Auntie Marg," she said. "I'm not in any danger."

She looks so young, so vulnerable. But Camille was a grown woman, a practicing physician. *And I'm turning her into a child.* In front of a potential gentleman-friend no less. *Time to change.*

"You're absolutely right. I'm coming off as a mother hen." She smiled apologetically at Camille. "You're quite capable of taking care of yourself." She could still feel Parker's gaze and turned back to meet his scrutiny. "I'm using concern for Camille to mask pure and unabashed nosiness."

Parker laughed. "I make a mean spaghetti sauce and even meaner meatballs," he said, looking back and forth from Margot to Camille. "How about we eat, drink a little wine, you tell me how good my cooking is—then I'll tell you both everything I know about

Faye-Anne's murder." To Camille directly, he said, "I have some new information about your 'Doctor Kildare.'"

"Doctor Kildare?" Margot asked.

"He's talking about Oscar Lewis," Camille explained. "The doctor who owns the clinic and I work for and rent from." She waited, and when Margot didn't immediately respond, she continued, "You remember him, right? He and Uncle Harvey went to Feinberg together way back when."

Margot nodded and reined in her surprise. She hadn't until this moment connected the names Doctor Lewis, Oscar, and Oscar Lewis, her husband's old friend, as the same person.

Of course she remembered Oscar. "What's his wife's name?" Margot asked while unconsciously holding her breath.

"Ann," Camille said. "She's my landlady.'"

Oh dear.

Camille and Parker continued talking as they ate, but their words seemed to fade into the background—and Margot couldn't quite make herself pay attention. Indeed, while they ate angel-hair spaghetti with meatballs, which Parker explained were made with ground chuck and hot Italian sausage, all smothered in a rich wine-based basil, oregano, and garlic laden tomato sauce—Margot's mind willfully wandered back to Harvey's early years at Northwestern University's Feinberg School of Medicine.

She still occasionally walked through Northwestern's Chicago city campus. It wasn't far from her penthouse—a straight walk up Michigan Avenue, then east on several choices of streets. Often she'd combine stops at St. James Cathedral and the Water Tower on her walkabouts. She couldn't quite see the city campus from her penthouse, but she could get a glimpse of Navy Pier—a place with an additional set of memories.

Back during those Fienberg days, Sunday meals were quite the event with their little clique. *She, Harvey, Ann, Oscar, Parnell, Glover, and Leila.* Out of the blue, her niece's involvement in a murder investigation was bringing back those years—those connections. For a second, Margot felt like she was losing her composure, an unusual and uncomfortable experience. Maybe it was just the memory of Leila's death from the brain tumor triggering her sense of light headedness. For sure, that had been the "worst of times."

Margot heard Camille say something like, *"Garlic is very good for you."*

Ironic. Just yesterday: she'd endured a traffic laden drive to O'Hare; gone through a tedious and lengthy security screening; endured a four and a half hour flight; taken in Graham's earth shattering revelation; barely survived a dust storm the likes of which she'd never experienced before—to now sit in her niece's doublewide kitchen eating spaghetti made by the Chief of Police. And probably having to reconnect with a woman she hadn't seen in years, and wife to the prime suspect—a man she also hadn't seen in years.

She still couldn't focus on the present, yet her senses vaguely registered, *"And fresh Roma tomatoes..."* Parker was evidently explaining his spaghetti recipe.

Indeed, Margot's moments of emotional amazement were so intense, she unconsciously looked away to be alone with herself. That's when she spied the large black spider high up in the ceiling corner behind Camille. Its web was quite elaborate—*a metaphor for the moment?*

The spider, mottled in color, mainly muted black with dark brown highlights, was neither hidden, nor making a spectacle of itself. She allowed her thoughts to wander farther afield. Meredith was never a good housekeeper. Now Camille too? She almost admonished herself aloud. Here she was—engulfed in some kind of mental fugue and looking askance at cobwebs—when she employed a housekeeper, cook, and personal assistant.

Margot forced her attention and gaze back to Camille and found Parker silently watching her. She looked down. Dogue was lying on the floor next to her, looking at Parker lovingly. Margot shook her head sharply, forcing her mental cobwebs to disappear, then looked up at Parker and said, "Excellent meal."

*　*　*　*　*

Camille telephoned Ann, just across the property, and asked her to walk over for a glass of wine with her visiting Aunt—also offering spaghetti if she was hungry. Ann agreed to come right over. Before she arrived, Parker succinctly brought Margot up to date on what happened Friday night and then Saturday.

When he got to their "refrigerator excursion" at the clinic last night, he said, "I expect a lab report in a couple days."

"You're thinking poison?" Margot asked Camille.

"Yes, I am." Camille pushed her empty plate aside and leaned across the table. "I saw a little spittle in the corner of Faye-Anne's mouth."

"Several things could cause that—" Margot murmured.

"Wait," Parker interrupted. "Don't tell me you're a doctor too?"

Camille quickly spoke for her aunt. "No, but my aunt knows as much as any doctor." She smiled proudly. "Auntie Marg did all of Uncle Harvey's research. Whenever I'd call Uncle Harvey for actual medical advice," she said wryly, "Auntie always knew the 'latest' in medical research." She turned her head sideways and squinted her eyes at Margot. "Now that I think about it, how much time *did* you spend reading medical journals?" Her tone was teasing.

Margot laughed, but didn't answer. After a moment, Parker poured everyone another glass of wine, then slouched into his chair, wiggling a little, as if he could make its wooden slats soften and conform to his form.

"And I thought," Camille continued, again contemplative. "The spittle was curious in itself, but then when Deirdre mentioned the energy drink…"

Margot nodded knowingly, and Parker murmured, "You two are going to be a handful." Before he could elaborate, there was a knock on the kitchen door. "Want me to get that so you and your aunt can solve this murder?"

Margot couldn't tell if he was pleased or not, but Camille smiled and winked, so she guessed he was teasing. She returned her nieces smile and steeled herself to meet Ann after all these years.

Evidently sensing her slight apprehension, Camille reached across the table, and gave her hand a quick little squeeze. "I thought you knew who Oscar was, and that he was married to Ann." She looked down for a few seconds. "Maybe since moving out here I haven't kept up with you the way I should have."

"We'll talk later. But not to worry, Sweetheart. Phone lines go both ways."

Ann entered Camille's kitchen, and reentered Margot's life with aplomb. "Margot, Dear, you haven't changed a bit," she declared.

Margot stood and turned to greet Ann, who insisted on an all encompassing hug. Nonetheless, even with the hug and complimentary words, Margot felt an underlying coolness emanating from Ann.

Almost immediately, more memories came in a rush—good and bad. What had Harvey—jokingly—but still uncharitably called Ann? *The ice-queen.* How could she possibly remember that? *Must have been important at the time.* Margot also remembered she and Ann had once been friends—well, more like acquaintances. Her true friend from that period had been Leila—until the end when she'd succumbed to a brain tumor. Margot immediately removed the picture of Leila from her mind before her eyes could water.

"I didn't know we'd be meeting. Reconnecting," Margot said. "What a pleasant surprise."

The picture of Ann residing in the recesses of Margot's mind was of a twenty-something collegiate she no longer was. Surprisingly, little had changed from that fixed-in-time image. Ann was still a striking woman, with skin that displayed few signs of age, heavy but naturally arching eyebrows, and full but classically shaped features. Her mouth in particular, was overly broad and full, but nicely shaped. Her hair was still dark brown and only slightly gray in the temples, worn in a stylish bob. However, she remembered Ann having short curly hair—*something about her hair isn't right*. And the tone of her skin seemed off. Otherwise, Margot thought she looked wonderful.

Camille found a matching chair and brought it over. "Ann," she said. "Squeeze in here between Auntie Marg and me." Margot thought her niece's tone deferential, and she guessed it was because Oscar was her boss, and together with his wife, they were her landlords.

"Here, take my seat," Parker said, and without waiting, got up, took the chair from Camille, and sat it and himself back away from the group of women.

To observe, Margot thought. Possibly he was considering Ann a suspect because of the alleged affair. *Poor Ann.* Knowing she could be a suspect, while being worried about Oscar—who it seemed was the prime suspect in Parker's mind.

Ann refused wine and food. Instead, she went directly to what was on all their minds. "Oscar is at home." She turned for a second and looked at Parker. "That detective Hollist seems to be in charge."

Parker nodded.

With a dismayed look, she turned back to Margot. "At least he had enough sense to let Oscar come home."

Margot murmured, "They must not have enough physical evidence." And was surprised she'd spoken out loud.

"Exactly," Ann agreed. "He's in bed sleeping."

Ann was lying—Margot knew it instantly. Oscar was not home, and Ann didn't know where he was. Margot said, "Tired. No doubt."

It was interesting how Ann seemingly wanted to talk directly to her, like they were still close friends. They hadn't actually seen each other for years, and when Margot looked to her niece's face for possible explanation, Camille's face reflected discomfort. *No*, more like worry. And she didn't think it had to do with Ann choosing to talk to her. Worry about Oscar, she guessed.

"And it's ridiculous to think he killed that nurse," Ann said.

Margot thought it indicative of something that Ann didn't use Faye-Anne's name. "Is it always Patricia that makes the health drinks?"

Ann's eyebrows raised, ever so slightly, and Margot wondered if Camille and Parker caught it. *Why?* Ann hadn't made the drinks.

"I can only gather you think there might have been a problem with her health drink," Ann said within a sigh. "I told Oscar he shouldn't allow those kinds of unproven pseudo-science remedies in the office." An expression of exasperation crossed her face. "But Deirdre took her side, and there you have it." She rubbed her hands dismissively, as if the discussion was dirty. "You remember, Camille?"

Camille nodded.

"Deirdre can tell you. I don't make the drinks. And the labels—" She tsked, then smiled graciously. "You'll figure it all out, Margot. You always were the clever one."

Me? Chief Reed was the investigator, not her. She'd just arrived in town, for heaven's sake. Margot continued to notice Ann had yet to say Faye-Anne's name, and wondered if Ann had guessed at an affair? She dared not ask now. Sometime when they were alone. For a second, her brother Graham's declaration about Meredith and her husband flashed across her mind—she pushed the thought away. *Not now.*

"But, wait," Ann said, and turned to look at Parker. "I'm sure Oscar said she'd been hit in the head."

"That she was," he said.

Ann turned back to Margot and asked, "Do you think we could get together for breakfast or lunch while you're here? Catch up."

"Of course."

It appeared Ann wanted to talk with her in private—and in an instant, a time years ago at St. Andrew Chapel in St. James Cathedral came back as if were yesterday. She and Ann were huddled in a back pew, and Ann had asked her, "Do you believe in right and wrong? So many things to me are relative." It had been the last private conversation they'd had. *So many years ago.* After Leila's funeral.

"Definitely," Margot remembered answering. And now, she almost cringed at her own remembered youthful arrogance, and so many similar all-knowing declarations about life.

"Then there's the past, present, and future," Ann had enigmatically continued.

Margot thought she heard Dogue growl, but when she looked down, his look was told her nothing, and her memory lost the rest of Ann's youthful pronouncements from way back then in Saint Andrew Chapel.

Heck with the past. "It's the present we should care about," she whispered to Dogue with much less certainty than she would have used thirty years earlier.

"Well," Camille asked after opening a second bottle of wine. "What did you think about all of that?"

Feeling a little warm and tipsy, Margot didn't answer her question immediately. Instead, she said, "Maybe I should have stayed with iced tea."

She looked over at Dogue stretched out underneath the arch between Camille's small kitchen-cum-dining area and the rest of the house. There was a breeze passing through the house created by the swamp cooler, and she guessed Dogue was attempting to stay cool. She wasn't sure how warm Spring was in the desert, but it certainly was more pleasant than Chicago.

Parker and Ann were gone, and they had moved to Camille's comfortable living room area, settling into cushy armchairs on the opposite ends of a matching loveseat. They were positioned to enjoy Camille's west-facing view. *Runs in the family,* Margot mused when she'd first seen her arrangement—*enjoying the view.*

There was also a well-used early American table, a fairly new upholstered couch, and two matching side tables filling out the room.

Off the side of the living room was a separate dining or lounge area that Camille had evidently not yet bothered defining or furnishing. One of three bedrooms was a dual purpose TV and computer room. Everything was "comfortable," but nondescript, and Margot thought her niece had yet to make this place her own.

Not planning on staying? She wondered.

Through the generously-sized front windows, she could see evening arriving behind a slow, pale sunset. Quite nice, possibly as nice as Gray's pricey Palm Springs view.

Margot brought her mind back to Camille's earlier question, and finally answered carefully. "I certainly didn't expect you to be embroiled in a murder case."

Camille laughed. "Crazy, huh? You happening to visit daddy at the same time Faye-Anne is killed."

"Did you notice Ann never used Faye-Anne's name?"

After a moment of thought, Camille said, "Not really. But…" She paused for a couple seconds. "I'm not sure about the significance of what I'm about to say. Because sometimes at the clinic I'm often rushing so I only get snatches of things."

"You want to give the patients as much time as possible."

"Yes, you understand." Camille leaned forward. "But I don't think there was much love lost between Ann and Faye-Anne."

"Was Faye-Anne a nice person?" Margot wasn't certain what she was asking, but hoped her niece understood.

"Vain. Sharp." Camille clicked through her teeth and shook her head. "My, that came out awfully fast." She emptied her wine glass, and chuckled. "Guess I must have noticed more than I thought."

"And what's with these energy drinks?"

Camille shook her head. "Not as complicated as Parker made it all out to be. Patricia makes the drinks at their house. Every day she brings the thermo-cups in, then takes them back home to refill. All three are labeled with their names." She eyed Margot curiously for a second. "Did you say you were at Gus's place?"

"Yes."

"Well Patricia and Faye-Anne live at the end of that same road."

Margot shivered and wiggled her shoulders. "Awful road."

They laughed together—comfortably.

"Is yours a small office?" Margot asked.

"Very small. Will you come and see it tomorrow?" Her voice was eager. "I'll give you directions."

She's forgotten my car is sitting on the side of some dirt road—somewhere. "As soon as I get my car situation straightened out."

"Do you need my help?"

"No, Sweetheart." She did, however, wish for George. He would take care of all this for her. Along with all the car stuff to deal with, she also needed to find the right time to tell Margot about Harvey—*if I do tell her.* Just because Graham thought the revelation was a good idea, didn't make it so. She caught herself sighing.

"Auntie Marg, is there something you want to tell me?"

Later. "Do you like being a Doctor?"

Camille smiled, got up, went over to her aunt and sat on her chair's arm. Then she leaned over and hugged Margot tightly, lovingly. When she let go, her eyes were moist, but her voice was strong. "I love being a Doctor." Then softer, "You and Uncle Harvey gave me that." Finally, and almost in a whisper, she added, "Thank you."

Margot felt an overwhelming and deeply repressed emotion start to swell—but a loud and demanding knock on the front door made both women jump and turn toward the entranceway.

Camille's front double French doors were eggshell colored, and twelve-paned. Margot thought they made for a lovely entry, and did a lot to make her niece's new home charming. Camille told her she'd had the doors put in herself, mainly because she liked seeing who was there.

This evening Gus awaited them. He was backlit by a low sun, and Margot was surprised he didn't look as desert-ratty as before. "It's Gusztáve," she said, quite unnecessarily.

Cleaned himself up a bit—hopefully not for my benefit.

"Thought you'd be pleased," Gus said, devilment dancing in his eyes. "Your daughter here being a busy doctor with a murder on her hands, and Doc Lewis and Nurse Ann up to their noses in it, and you not knowing anything about the desert." He shrugged and looked put-upon.

I'd forgotten Ann went to nursing school. Loyola's Marcella Niehoff, or was it also Northwestern? She couldn't remember which.

"My, that's a long sentence," Margot said. Cleaned-up, Gusztáve was turning out a bit more charming than she'd anticipated—and better looking. Especially with his larger-than-life mustache now trimmed and combed into submission. He was again in jeans, western jacket and boots—but not as dusty and scruffy looking as before. And his eyes, still menacingly dark, didn't seem as foreboding as during the storm, either. "I believe this is the third time we've met in one day. To what do I owe this honor?"

"Do you always talk like that, proper and snooty like?" He enjoyed a walloping swallow of beer, nearly smacking his lips afterward. "Ahh," he said. "Thanks, Doc. You're a good hostess." Then he winked at Margot. "I believe it's only twice, and if you remember, you were the one stuck out on Fort Cady Road, miles from where you should be."

They had moved to Camille's front deck, where all three sat in wooden deckchairs facing the nearly-set sun. Camille had brought Gus a beer and a frosty mug, and for herself and Margot—wine refills.

Margot returned to his earlier comment and said, "Doctor Madison-Cross is my niece, not my daughter." She noticed Gusztáve had stretched his right leg out straight in front of him, not bending at the knee—then she remembered he'd walked stiffly earlier, almost limping. She guessed at a knee injury.

"Whatever." He waved his hand cavalierly. "Doc Madison here is a good kid. Fits in well." He raised his beer glass to Camille. "And not to worry, Parker will figure out who killed that Faye-Anne gal. I'm positive Doc Lewis had nothing to do with it."

Margot leaned forward and asked, "Do you know Faye-Anne and her sister Patricia well?"

"You know the girls?"

"Oh, no. Never met them. Only know what my niece has told me." She cleared her throat and wondered why she was intruding in Camille's murder investigation. "That's why I'm asking you, Mr. Martinez."

He laughed. "So it's 'Mr.' now?"

She felt herself warm. "Gusztáve."

He smiled in return. "Nice girls. Faye-Anne was a little flirty. More ambitious than Patricia." He shook his head and fell silent for a few moments. "Don't really know them. Should have gotten better acquainted—don't you know?" He stared straight ahead. "Closest neighbor. Great dog."

Margot heard regret in his tone. She needed to keep an open mind about this man.

"Oozie," Camille said fondly. "She's pretty spectacular. Patricia says she's sort of psychic."

Margot cleared her throat dramatically and said, "You know, Gusztáve, I think I've been very ungracious." She waited until he turned and looked at her. "Let me formally thank you for taking care of the rental agency picking up my car. I was extremely negligent in not taking care of that myself immediately." She sighed lightly. "Though it has been an extremely hectic and fast moving day."

He laughed heartily. "There you go again, talking proper-like." He pulled an automatic automobile door opener out of his pocket and pressed the unlock button.

Margot looked through Camille's picture window, out into a darkness that seemed to have snuck up on them. The interior lights of a dark-colored new-looking SUV type car had come on. *An Escalade?* She wasn't sure, but its barely visible shape reminded her of a recent

Cadillac commercial. She couldn't determine its exact color, but it certainly looked substantial—at least from inside the house and at a distance. The lit interior also looked well appointed, though it was hard to identify specifics.

Something tickled something in her mind about looking at something from a distance and thinking "up close and personal" was what mattered—crucial actually. She almost tsked out loud in dismay at her mental loss of order and clear thinking. Not dementia, she was rather confident. But something was going on. Paranormal? Even more doubtful.

In a proud tone, Gus informed her, "Brand new. Only a thousand miles on the dash, six-point-two litre vee-eight with all-wheel-drive. Got it as a replacement, same price as that foreign car, and unlimited miles." Instead of handing her the opener, he dropped it back in his jacket pocket. "Thinking I should drive you around. Whatta' you think?"

Surprised at the words leaving her mouth, Margot said, "Is that a proposition, Gusztáve?"

"Indeed it is, Ms. Margot, indeed it is."

"In that case," she smiled and said, "I accept."

Margot thought the night had turned very black—despite all the twinkling stars. She walked Gus out as far as the edge of the deck, then watched him get into her rental Cadillac and drive off. For a moment she wished for her Chicago lake front view. Her city skyline.

Camille joined her and linked arms. "I can't believe it. You're in town half a day and you have a beau already."

"Beau?" Margot teased back, "Rather an antiquated word don't you think?" After a moment of companionable silence, she added, "He's not exactly what he makes himself out to be."

"What do you mean?"

"The old coot talked about the Bobs, saying the road to his house wasn't as bad as the ride."

"The Bobs? The ride?"

"You're too young. But it was a rollercoaster at Riverview. All gone now. But hardly something a "desert-rat," would know about unless they knew Chicago."

Camille gave her arm an affectionate squeeze. "You are an observant one, aren't you?"

Suddenly Margot was very tired—and from the same "out of nowhere" that had started communicating with her, she felt an intense premonition she needed her derringer.

Silly airport rules.

Margot waited until Camille went into the bathroom to prepare for bed, then located her purse on the kitchen table, and retrieved her cell phone out of its special compartment.

Already fond of the deep armchairs in Camille's living room, she settled in the same one from which she'd watched the sunset with Camille and bantered with Gusztáve. Once comfortable, she pressed and held down preprogrammed button number-two.

George answered after the second ring. "Yes, Madame?"

He must be in his own quarters where he has caller ID. "Would you do me a favor?" she whispered into the phone.

"Certainly, Madame."

"Have Cook Phillip bake me a cake—two layer. Chocolate with cream cheese frosting. Place *Paladin* in a plastic bag between the layers when you frost it. Freeze it overnight, then send to me UPS overnight, or whatever it's called. Send with those frozen ice packets."

"I'll have him start right now. And I know what office to take it to."

She smiled and blew out a small breath of air. *She could always count on George.* He'd probably be on the phone or internet immediately, finding out how to legally ship a firearm from state to state—*and illegally.* Probably a lot of rigmarole, but he'd figure it out and get it to her. She doubted it would *actually* be in a cake, but would come with a lot of paperwork.

"Thank you, George."

"My pleasure, Madame."

What a silly game we play. Sure, they played a game, but this time, she also thought—more like sensed—there were several more ominous games being played around and with her. With very high stakes.

"Madame?"

"Yes, George?"

"What is it like where you are?"

She described the storm that morning, the Mercedes breakdown, the horrible road, the Quonset hut, and Gusztáve.

"The auto rental agency I used is one of the best," he said.

"It's not your fault. You wouldn't believe that road. And the wind and sand."

She was feeling better talking to George, being reconnected to Chicago, her anchor. Indeed, Margot thought she heard jazz music in the background, but low. George was fond of what he called "the American music," and she smiled imagining him reclining in his suite's armchair listening to music and reading an American thriller novel, which he was also fond of.

"Can this Gusztáve gentleman be trusted?" he asked.

"I don't know."

Oscar couldn't stop crying. *What the hell was going on?*

He'd parked his Honda far off on the shoulder, and turned off the headlights. When he became coherent enough to know where he'd headed, and where he now was, Oscar realized he was sitting in the dirt next to his car on National Trails, peering into the desert. His view—sparse but twinkling runway-lights of Barstow Daggett Airport to his immediate north. *Somebody must be coming in for a landing.*

What sounded like a pickup truck bumped down the road, dim headlights passing him unnoticed in the dark; but he didn't look, or try to hail them. He could feel it was getting cooler, the wind was picking up, and he thought he tasted sand in the air.

"Faye-Anne, Faye-Anne," he called out into the night—though he didn't expect anyone to hear or care. This section of Route 66 was seldom used except by a small group of locals.

I need to escape. In a Cessna, a Beechjet, a Learjet—maybe a helicopter? He'd pay for or beg a ride. But where? *No, no,* I'm not thinking right—and what good was all his medical knowledge now when *he* needed it. At first he wasn't afraid, but two days had passed, and his emotions were starting to catch up with reality—almost.

The night was Mojave Desert dark, his future looked even darker—and Oscar thought this must be the saddest point in his life.

Chapter Four

Monday

Parker chose to ruminate with his morning coffee at the end of a dirt road that ran out on the southern edge of the Cady Mountains. From there, he had not only an easterly view of the sunrise, but to the south, he could also look down on Route 66 and I-40, and even farther, all the way to the Newberry Mountains.

He was out earlier than usual, the horizon barely lighter than night. Whether it would be a fair or cloudy day was still unknown. He hadn't slept well, and was sure he knew why. Even though his prime suspect, he certainly didn't *want* to put Oscar Lewis away—*if he ever returned or was found.* He hadn't believed Ann yesterday afternoon, and he'd called her several times that evening, and again early this morning. Oscar was either supposedly sleeping, out in the yard, or in the bathroom.

But what could he do, really? Another APB wouldn't fly since Hollist had already interviewed Oscar, and hadn't held or charged him. No warrants had been issued. *Cheating on your wife and acting goofy aren't criminal offenses.* And, Ann hadn't reported him as missing.

Then there was the matter of Camille's aunt. "Margot Madison-Cross," he said her full name out loud as if that singular act could exorcise a growing uneasiness. Once again, he wished for Dogue to talk to. *Dogue has a good home.* Even if things went south with him and Camille.

The thought of Dogue, then Camille, returned him to his apprehension regarding Margot. It was like the woman looked right through him—into that spot he liked to call his soul. *So disconcerting.* A lot was in her eyes, laughing and scrutinizing at the same time.

He knew his spaghetti was the best, and their luncheon had gone well enough, but she'd been so inscrutable. Not only with him, but also with Ann Lewis. There was a back-story there, and he was guessing it involved ill will of some type. Indeed, surviving the scrutiny of "Ms. Margot"—as Gus had started calling her—was indeed nerve-racking.

Eventually, Parker's thoughts returned to Oscar. He expected toxicology and autopsy reports today. And hopefully a forensics reports would be faxed to him tonight. Or maybe he'd get lucky— they would all come in one packet and be waiting for him in his one-room office behind Deel's plumbing.

Surely, Oscar wasn't at home sleeping. *But where the heck was he?*

"Yes," Margot said to the quiet kitchen, "this is the heart-and-soul of Camille's new home."

Dressed in another of her Lenwood Mall purchases, a silken robe and knitted slippers, she'd instinctively made her way from the guest bedroom to the one place where she could start her morning with a touch of familiarity. A spot where she felt comfortable performing a daily ritual—standing in front of a window to the world with a cup of tea—albeit an oleander hedged garden view. Looking outward, orientating herself to the new day.

As planned last night, Camille had gone into the clinic early, leaving Margot to fend for herself. A smart move, she thought. Her niece needed to do some work, and she needed some quiet time by herself. By her standards, Sunday had been quite eventful.

As she'd noticed yesterday, Camille's kitchen was modest, and a tight squeeze for four adults. The window, however, was expansive. Above a double stainless-steel sink, it allowed desert-bright sunlight to flood the room.

She hadn't been in her own kitchen in Chicago in over a month; it was "behind the stairs" so to speak, at the back of the penthouse. Yet, here she stood, across the country—almost at the other end of Route 66—in a far more modest kitchen, sipping tea she'd made herself.

She could picture Camille looking out this window, taking in the seemingly unending Mojave expanse. Just like she did every morning, almost mesmerized by the lake front.

And possibly with similar thoughts about life, similar questions about the world? Tonight when she called George, she would have to tell him about surviving on her own.

How pampered I've been.

She'd easily found English Breakfast tea in the pantry, and fresh lemons in the crisper. Camille had probably taken the time to shop for her. Margot's heart swelled with warmth for her niece yet again, but the tiles below her feet felt ice-cold as she took a slow sip of steaming hot tea—savoring its aroma, enjoying its warm massaging of her scratchy throat. This tea she'd made by herself felt particularly soothing.

She heard the padded footfalls of Dogue as he entered the kitchen and walked over to her side. "I know we aren't friends, yet," she said, as she looked down into his wary eyes. She lowered her right-hand for him to sniff. "But I hope we will be." She smiled into his eager face. "Soon."

He barked once in response, and licked the back of her hand.

She returned her attention outside, to the beginnings of the morning. The intense morning light showed the windows were streaked and dusty, a condition Barisa would never tolerate. Margot chuckled aloud, and Dogue whined a little, as if he wanted to understand.

Meredith hated housework. "Daughter, like Mother," she informed the canine. "Nurture winning out." Her words led her thoughts back to the horrible task Gray had dragged her out west to do. He'd been so insistent, and right, though she hated to admit it. Who better to tell Camille about her father? And what good was family if you couldn't rely on them?

From seemingly nowhere, the face of a young Oscar from their school days appeared in her mind. She wondered again if he was at home in the main house, or had Ann been lying like she thought earlier? If at home, shouldn't he have gone back to work like Camille? She certainly hadn't heard any cars, but wasn't sure if she would have anyway—given all the oleanders and pine trees around the property. With his face came the question she'd never been sure of, and too afraid to ask. *Had he loved Leila before she died?*

Camille looked up to see Oscar entering her office just as she pressed the "send" button on her laptop. Emma Kent's prescription was on its way to the pharmacy. Always a stickler in the past for how he looked, she was surprised to see him dressed in beat up jeans, an equally distressed jacket, and a faded work shirt. Dark stubble was beginning to cover his cheeks and chin.

"I was sure I heard somebody come in the back," she said, trying very hard to keep her tone calm and non-accusatory. "But I thought it was Deirdre."

Indeed, it had crossed her mind that maybe he'd hopped a plane somewhere, or the police had come back this morning and dragged him off. Maybe taken him to jail in Victorville. She was sure Ann had been lying yesterday when she said he was at home sleeping.

His actions were so weird, and very upsetting, and she hoped her face wasn't reflecting her thoughts. Oscar was her mentor—*yes*, as Parker annoyingly teased, her 'Doctor Kildare.'

"There's yellow tape across my door," he said sadly, then picked up a stack of patient records from the seat of Camille's visitor armchair and cradled them in his arms. "They won't let me in my own office." He turned and placed the folders on the corner of her credenza behind him.

"Please, sit down." Her words sounded so formal, but she didn't immediately know what else to say. They certainly needed to have a frank talk. But how to start? After the conversation at the hospital, she was looking at Oscar with different eyes. A circumstance she found extremely disconcerting—and unpleasant.

He dropped heavily into the padded chair. "They haven't charged me yet." He seemed incapable of looking directly at her—shifting his eyes from ceiling, to floor, to door—disconnectedly talking to the world in general. "But I know they will."

Maybe he was experiencing an Acute Stress Reaction? *Oh, it could be so many things.*

"Oscar," she said firmly. He still wouldn't look at her. "Oscar!" She needed to get him to focus. "Look at me."

Finally, she seemed to have his attention.

"You asked for my help," she said. "And for me to do that, I need the truth." He was the older, seasoned doctor, yet she felt like she was talking to a child. "Did you kill Faye-Anne?"

"Of course not," he snapped angrily. "How could you think that? Didn't I make that clear to you and Parker yesterday?"

She had to ignore how fond she was of Oscar. If she was going to help him, she needed the truth. "The police think you did."

"And you do too?"

"No." Indeed, it was hard to imagine Oscar killing anyone. He was a dedicated physician for goodness' sake—once her Uncle Harvey's peer. To her, a kind and gentle man. But what did she really know about him besides his professional persona and his relationship with her uncle? Little. She'd *just* learned he was having an affair with an employee. A dead employee. A *murdered* dead employee.

She wanted to scream at him, but couldn't. *Not at my dear Oscar.* Instead, she asked, "What was that wink about yesterday? And does Ann know about your affair with Faye-Anne?" Camille could hear censure in her voice, but didn't care. Chastising was better than yelling at him.

"What wink?" he demanded. Then from seemingly nowhere tears rolled down his cheeks. He swiped them away. "You think I'm awful don't you?" Oddly, his voice suddenly seemed calmer, more focused.

"Things happen." If he had killed Faye-Anne it must have been an accident. "Unintentionally sometimes."

He rolled his head, rubbed his neck, and continued to avoid eye contact. "I've really screwed up."

Camille assumed he meant the affair, but had to be sure. "In what way?"

"Damn it!" His voice was suddenly loud, petulant, and slightly mean. Clearly angry again, he stood up abruptly, and in the process knocked the stack of folders off her credenza to the floor. "How could Faye-Anne put me in this position?" His tone was incredulous, his expression confused.

Accusing the victim? This was another facet of Oscar's personality she'd never seen. Was he mentally ill? She held her composure while her mind searched for explanation--medical and psychological.

"Oscar, what do you want me to do to help you?"

"Nothing," he shot back.

She started to get up, "But you asked for my help."

"Leave me alone." He stormed out into the hallway, his breathing heavy and audible.

In a matter of seconds, she heard the clinic's backdoor slam.

Camille fell back in her armchair, mystified and alarmed. *I sure didn't see that coming.* She blew out an exaggerated puff of air. *Maybe I should have.*

She hated admitting it, but Oscar could have murdered Faye-Anne. But even if he was innocent, something else was going on. Was he on drugs, had he suddenly become bi-polar, or developed anger management problems? The possibilities were many. *Another complication.*

Selfish of me. But maybe it was time for her to accept a new position. *Move on.* Escape the mess she felt closing in. Of course she couldn't do that immediately. *First I have to help Oscar.*

"Uncle Harvey," she demanded across the greatest of all great divides. She'd become a doctor because of him, and accepted this position partly because of the two doctors' past friendship. "What did you get me into?"

After leisurely enjoying her tea and English muffin, Margot showered—greedily long—then dressed carefully in what she considered stylish jeans, a long sleeved Liz Claiborne cotton shirt with a hint of a flattering flare, and laced Bjorn walking shoes. All the time, getting ready under the watchful scrutiny of Dogue—even in the bathroom. Evidently the shepherd knew how to push open the bathroom door, twist-knob notwithstanding.

Margot had tucked away the few pieces of jewelry she'd brought along in a jewelry box atop the guest bedroom chest of drawers— including her precious ruby ring. She had paused to look at it off her finger when tucking it safely away. The ruby was not gigantic, but a Burmese "pigeon blood red." Quickly, she banished the image of pigeon's blood, and wished she had not remembered its provenance. *Well, the ring is now out of sight, out of mind.*

The Asian styled jewelry box had two drawers below the main glass-inset compartment, and she thought the piece was lovingly finished with a deep coffee-colored lacquer, and ornamented with several tassels. Glancing at the box this morning, the thought of her ruby inside reminded her of the difference between home and here. She needed to figure out how to survive this desert, and fast. How she dressed, and what she didn't wear was part of that survival learning curve.

Still, some old interests could not be squelched, and she wondered if Camille realized the unpolished chest she was standing in front of was possibly a genuine 1830s Early American Empire chest. She smiled to herself, her mind trying to conjure up early American homesteaders and entrepreneurs—both in the earliest of times, and later in Route 66 migrations—trekking across the country, settling here-and-there, building homes and businesses. Bringing with them their cherished possessions like this chest.

"I just can't imagine," she said to Dogue. They were cut from different, and clearly stronger stuff than her. *At least I once cruised Route 66.* For a second, Margot saw herself again in Father's Mustang, venturing out into the world beyond Chicago with her brother.

Out of the blue, maybe from thinking about the past—she was overwhelmed by an apprehension-laden sense of urgency. It hit Margot the hardest in the pit of her stomach, then quickly sent a wave of anxiety throughout her body. *Why?* What was so important now?

Was her niece in danger from Faye-Anne's murderer? Or did Gray have another accident?

Oh dear, oh dear.

Three short beeps from an auto horn announced Gusztáve reporting for chauffeur duty. Margot quickly gathered her things to go out and meet him. It didn't pass her notice that despite her feelings of anxiety, there was also a smidgen of excitement surrounding what she was doing in NewTown—something she hadn't felt in a long time.

True, she wasn't eager to tell Camille that Harvey was her real father. "Darn it, Meredith," she admonished uselessly. "Why, oh why, did you tell Graham about Harvey?" *As if a half-truth would make everything okay.*

To her question, Dogue barked an explanation and trotted ahead.

"I'm sorry we can't take you," she informed him. "Camille said you should stay at home." She was sure she could have broken Camille's rule if she'd wanted, but she still wasn't one-hundred percent on Gusztáve, and certainly didn't want to put her niece's dog in harm's way.

As she locked the front door behind her—Dogue staring at her pathetically through the French door lights—Margot realized she missed having George to open and close doors for her. *What maudlin sentimentality.* Ridiculously, she looked at her cotton covered arm, *When did I start wearing my heart on my sleeve?*

Once standing on the front deck, but before going to Gusztáve, she stopped to take in the morning outside, and was surprised how warm and dry the air was—not the chilly damp air rolling in off Lake Michigan. *No,* this was not home. Maybe for Gray after all these years. But she couldn't imagine living here all the time.

She looked directly at Gus and smiled—then hesitated and gave a little wave instead of proceeding immediately. Apprehension again? *Maybe a little.*

Margot could feel a wind coming from what she thought was the west; though clearly, after the sand-storm incident yesterday, her desert directional legs were not yet reliable. No reason to be wary, however. Today she would go hand-in-hand with her niece to find out who killed Faye-Anne Miller. And she had a chauffeur—no fear of getting lost.

Still, she stood immobile a few more seconds, took in a deep breath for fortification, and smelled smoke in the air. She had stayed up awhile last night after talking to George, watching the L.A. news channel a bit. They'd reported a large fire in the Palmdale area, and that this blaze was an unusual and significant occurrence. Was that what she was smelling? The air certainly didn't look smoky.

Gusztáve was standing by the passenger door, ready to assist her. He had on his cowboy hat, and in the clear morning light, she thought it might be an actual Stetson. This morning, he looked like her mind's image of an old time comic book cowboy.

He nodded his head crookedly, and made a clicking sound out the corner of his mouth when she got close. His caricature image was oddly endearing. *Old fool.* She thought of Cook Phillip's Louis L'Amour paperbacks and CDs so proudly displayed on a kitchen shelf, and was unable to hold back a smile. Cook Phillip, Harvey, and Gusztáve —kindred cowboy spirits.

Margot also thought she remembered Parker making the same head gesture, the same sound, and in the same way. *Oh dear,* she cautioned herself. She needed to be careful and not disparage the western-ethos. Such snobbery was charming worn by George, but doubted the same would hold true for her.

"My, my, Ms. Margot," Gus said after giving her a thorough and slow once-over. "You sure dress down well. Now, if you could talk a little more folk-like." He smiled wickedly.

She wasn't sure if he was still mocking her attire, or bestowing praise. She decided to take his comments as a compliment and smiled back.

"No time for dilly-dallying," he said, opening the passenger door for her.

Dilly dallying?

Most of their drive was spent in silence. Except somewhere along a two-lane road called National Trails which Gus explained was the old Route 66, he asked seemingly out of nowhere, "Don't drive much do you? Road trips, is what I'm talking about."

"No," Margot answered. "But, I have in the past."

"Route sixty-six?"

"Once."

His voice was solemn, reverential. "When you do again, take the time to pay attention to where you've been."

She guessed he wasn't talking about a good driving habit, but about driving The Mother Road. Nonetheless, and despite both possibilities, she had the oddest feeling Gusztáve's enigmatic admonishment was a key to solving Faye-Anne's murder. But that would be too bizarre, and before she could further contemplate her sudden insight, *or* premonition, *or* craziness—she wasn't sure what to call it—he turned off National Trails and pulled into a driveway.

Her initial thought was, *this can't possibly be the place.* Gusztáve must have made a mistake.

"Here we are," he said pulling into what she could now see was a parking area. "Give me a second and I'll come around and let you out."

Margot thought she caught a grimace flash across his face—*must be his leg*—and rushed to say, "No problem, Gusztáve, I'm

112

perfectly capable of opening my own door." She cleared her throat. "Are you coming in also?"

"Not right off." He turned and looked at her, a smile replacing his look of discomfort. "Need a little stretch first. And, yes, this is the right place." His smile morphed into a chuckle. "You wouldn't believe the expression on your face."

She ignored him.

Once out of the car, and standing at the front door, she knew he must have gotten the directions wrong. Nonetheless, the sign on the painted-over front window clearly said, "NewTown Clinic." She turned a wobbly knob on a faded tan door which was marked "Entrance." The door stuck a little, forcing her to give it a fairly good push.

Surely sick people aren't expected to be so strong?

Once inside, there were only a few feet between the door and a tall counter that overpowered the small area before her. A woman, her head bowed and barely visible, was sitting at a lower level behind what seemed to be a reception desk. All the walls were light blue, low volume music played from all directions, and a pleasant scent Margot couldn't immediately identify filled the air. Such was the contrast to the building's exterior—Margot was taken aback for a moment.

She heard someone cough to her right, and as she looked that way, a middle-aged man with a lot of uncontrolled black hair—head and face—brought a cloth handkerchief away from his mouth. He gave her a curious once-over look, then smiled and nodded.

Margot smiled in return, and relaxed a little. He was sitting in the second of three plaid-upholstered chairs lined up against the wall. An overflowing magazine rack sat at the end of the minuscule waiting area. *A sick person and magazines. Must be the place.*

She stepped forward and noticed several clipboards and tumblers holding pens with fluffy-ball tops sitting on the counter.

"Hi," the woman said without looking up from her computer keyboard. "If you'll just sign in."

Margot thought her voice was pleasant enough, but weak. Almost as if she were on the verge of tears. "I'm not a patient," she said.

The receptionist looked up—and with her round face, deep-set and swollen brown eyes, small but puffy nose, and tight-lined mouth—Margot thought her plain, "indeterminably" young-looking, and probably suffering from allergies—or had recently been crying. Her name badge read, Deirdre Lorrie R.N.

An expression of surprise flashed across Deirdre's face—followed by a lengthy, comprehensive, and undisguised appraisal. "Are you looking for directions?" She reached into the area underneath the countertop and pulled out a thick folded paper. "I have a map."

"I'm looking for Doctor Metoyer-Madison." Margot still half expected this wasn't Camille's workplace.

Deirdre's eyes widened. "Do you have an appointment?"

Margot cleared her throat, came closer, and laid both hands flat on the counter.

"You said Doctor Madison...," Deirdre stammered.

"I'm her Aunt." Margot smiled graciously. "I believe she's expecting me." Then she recognized the scent filling the office. It was the same aromatherapy oil they used at her day-spa in Chicago. The one Camille liked so much. *Pomegranate*, if she remembered correctly. And the music—*Spring* from Vivaldi's Four Seasons.

Okay, this had to be where Camille worked, but before she could firmly get her bearings, Margot saw Oscar charging down a short hall, then out a back door. She hadn't seen him in years, but recognition was instant.

"Oscar," she called. "Wait, I'd love to talk—"

He was gone—outside somewhere. And his exit from the darker inside of the clinic into the blazingly bright morning—captured as it was in the distance at the end of the hallway in the seconds the back door opened and closed—was quite dramatic. *Eerie actually*, as if he'd stepped from this world into another.

114

She blinked, and the essence of her experience vanished. The memory, however, remained.

"How weird," Margot said out loud.

After Deirdre took Margot back to Doc Madison's office, she took a detour into the break room on the other side of the hall. It was turning into a long morning, especially with Faye-Anne's murder hanging over their heads. She hoped *she* had one more energy drink in the refrigerator. *Might not be any more in the future either.* Hard to think Patricia would have the heart to keep the practice up. She certainly wouldn't blame her if she stopped.

She really needed a pick me up, and was glad a drink with her initials on it remained on the refrigerator shelf. She must have two empties at home, which reminded her she needed to wash and bring them back to Patricia's return crate by the plastic bottle recycle tub. Even if Patricia didn't keep the energy drinks coming, she wanted her to have all the stainless steel containers back. She thought they were nice, and probably pricey.

Deirdre took a moment to lean back against the refrigerator and take a long deep breath. Calm her mind and body. Unconsciously, she tried to flatten her back against the door, then she brought her sport-bottle to her chest with both hands. It was cool, reassuring.

It still bothered her she hadn't seen Faye-Anne's murderer. She closed her eyes, trying to remember Friday evening again. *Nothing.*

She opened her eyes, looked into the refrigerator again, and checked. *No,* Faye-Anne's last bottle was gone. She thought they must have taken it. Evidence—but of what, she wasn't sure. Clearly, Faye-Anne had been bludgeoned.

Deirdre sighed and headed back towards the front counter. As she passed Doc Madison's office, she could see Mrs. Madison-Cross sitting at the Doc's desk, and Chief Parker and Mr. Martinez standing in the doorway. She'd heard both men come in the backdoor, and hoped they wouldn't be chatting long. Mr. Carter had arrived right before Mrs. Madison-Cross, and was waiting. *Yet another hyphenated name to deal with.*

She wasn't a classical music buff, would have preferred if they played Country Western through the speaker system—Johnny Cash in particular. She could listen to him all day. But she'd heard so much of the stuff now, she recognized Vivaldi—and for once she liked it. Seemed appropriate for some reason.

Not only was missing Faye-Anne's murder a cloud hanging over her self confidence, but Deirdre had been surprised by Mrs. Madison-Cross's visit this morning. *Should have recognized who she was.* Deirdre didn't like being caught off guard like that.

She flipped open the top of her plastic sport-bottle, took a healthy swallow of concoction, and made the same face she always did. *This stuff is horrible.* She'd talked to Patricia several times about some kind of cover up flavor, but they had yet to come up with anything. Well, the bottles were nice at least, a smoky-gray-black finish, with their initials printed on them in big white letters, no mix-ups that way. No passing of germs either—not that she thought any of her co-workers were carriers of anything. Nonetheless, hygiene and sanitary guidelines needed to be adhered to.

Once back sitting down at the front counter, and after a quick look to make sure Mr. Carter was doing okay, she let her thoughts wander again.

The aunt woman certainly was an oddity. Okay, it had taken a bit for her to get used to Doc Madison, she talked a little different, and was prissy sometimes, but all and all, pretty much a regular person. But her aunt was a definite oddity. She wasn't familiar with many cultures across the country, but for sure she didn't talk like a westerner, much less a Southern Californian.

And looks-wise, she was tall and thin, almost like a model, but not quite. And she looked like she'd just stepped out of a fashion magazine—even at her age, and even in jeans. She knew a little about designer clothes—Faye-Anne was always bringing in those kinds of magazines—some were on the rack in reception. Though the woman was dressed casually, she clearly wasn't a WalMart shopper.

"Good that Doc Madison has family." Deirdre didn't realize she'd spoken out loud until she heard her words come back to her.

She believed in family. Without family what were you anyway? Good, or bad, family was what counted. Faye-Anne had always been going on about friends, and how you couldn't count on family. Deirdre doubted that.

And she did see a family resemblance, around the eyes. Well, odd looking and acting or not, prissy or not, it would be good for Doc Madison to have a relative around. Heavens to goodness, *who knows what might happen next.*

She took another healthy swallow of energy drink. She shook her head, and said out loud, "Ugh." A quick look in Mr. Carter's direction showed he hadn't heard her.

Margot didn't like the look of concern on her niece's face. *Worrying about Oscar?* Or maybe just tired? She wished she could do something to help, and almost gave away her thoughts with a frown. If Gray had his way, about now she'd be confronting Camille with the fact Harvey was her biological father. *Just what she needs on top of a murder.*

She also didn't like the way Gusztáve was giving her "the eye" from the doorway. Margot even thought Parker, leaning nonchalantly against the doorjamb next to Gusztáve, had an insolent curl to the corner of his mouth. With further thought, Parker's expression seemed charming, while Gusztáve's was most irritating.

Trying to ignore both men, she said, "You know I recognized Oscar immediately. And it's been hundreds of years." Maybe small-talk would lessen Camille's distress. "And you've decorated your office very nicely." She was sitting in the same chair Camille had explained Oscar vacated in a huff.

"Thanks." Camille smiled and her frown lessened. "We can talk for a bit after I see Mr. Carter. He's having pains in his chest on a regular basis." She patted the area on her own body right below her throat. "I'm pretty sure it's GERD, and I'm going to refer him to a gastroenterologist this morning to schedule an endoscopy. I've already given him some dietary suggestions and prescribed a proton pump inhibitor, but I just want to make sure." She paused for a second, then added, "Glover just had his heart checked out, so I'm not too worried on that front."

Glover, what a nice name, Margot thought. "Of course Mr. Carter changed his diet immediately," she said, and laughed lightly as she remembered how Harvey was amazed and delighted when a patient actually followed his advice. Especially when it came to diet. "Is it just you and Deirdre here this morning?"

"Patricia's here too, checking stock." She made an exasperated sound. "As you know, Oscar was here earlier. I hope he's okay." She looked away for a second, then said, "Jeez."

"He drove his own car?" Margot hadn't paid attention back at Camille's place.

"I guess." Camille looked back at her. "Not surprisingly, everyone but Mr. Carter canceled. Word gets around fast, and who wants to come to a doctor who kills off his patients? May get out of here early today."

Harvey's office came back to Margot. It was still there, a three story "Graystone" in the Northwestern University area. It was a unique property— freestanding, with its own parking lot where the previous next door building had been demolished, and in a prized location. Nowadays, directly next to their building was a courtyard surrounded block of townhomes; and next to the parking lot was a brand new "Brownstone"-inspired medical complex. *I remember how much Camille loved it there.* Tears almost came. Not for the buildings, or the way of life they had embodied—but for Harvey. Seven years now, and it still hurt like hell.

"Well," she said. "Should I go away for awhile? Come back in a couple hours and we go out to Faye-Anne's husband's place?" She wasn't sure if Parker or Gusztáve suggested they go, but the trip certainly sounded intriguing. *Almost like being a detective.*

However, milliseconds after the words left Margot's mouth, she heard, "Help, Help!" A frantic male voice—from the front of the office.

Parker rushed out into the hall, Gus a few steps behind.

Camille jumped straight up from her chair and said, "That sounds like Mr. Carter—my next patient."

In the hallway just at the entrance of the intake area, Mr. Carter was feebly attempting to shake Deirdre by the shoulders as she lay slumped, almost gracefully on the floor. "Nurse Lorrie, Nurse Lorrie," he was pleading. "Are you alright?"

Camille pulled Mr. Carter away, and Parker put his arm around the shoulders of the eighty-five year old man, guiding him farther away, while simultaneously calling 911 on his cell phone. Camille could hear him taking care of the obvious, and was grateful. She could focus entirely on Deirdre, who she could see was still breathing—and a quick check found a pulse in her arm. However, like Faye-Anne, spittle was building in the corner of her mouth.

Camille called out, "Gus, do you know where the cardiac crash cart is?" She didn't wait for an answer. "In the file room. Patricia is there and can help you. Auntie Marg knows what one looks like." Just with her hand, she could feel Deirdre's heartbeat was irregular.

On the crash cart, besides a defibrillator, there was Ipecac and activated charcoal in one tray. She needed to do what she could with what she had in the clinic—but Deirdre really needed to get to emergency immediately.

Camille's thoughts raced. She wasn't an expert in gastric lavage, or cardiac pacing—and hadn't done the procedures since Cook County Hospital. At a minimum, Deirdre's vital signs needed immediate monitoring and control. Hopefully she wouldn't have to resuscitate, or worse. *Her breathing is definitely labored—getting worse.* Camille prayed a tracheotomy wouldn't be needed. *Hate doing them.* And again, it had been a long time.

While Patricia, who'd come running with the cart, sorted wires and paddles in case they were needed, Camille's hand didn't leave Deirdre's chest—intuitively monitoring as best she could—without benefit of equipment. "Where's my stethoscope?" she murmured, then realized it was hanging around her neck.

Eventually—minutes actually—she heard sirens. "Thank goodness," she whispered to herself. The medics were volunteers, she now remembered. *But damn fast.* A few more minutes, and she could hear feet running—coming closer—and cart wheels clanking against the clinic's ceramic tile floor.

Camille's next "medical" action was to take Deirdre's cold but shaking hand into hers.

Margot said a silent prayer Deirdre would make it as she turned the polished brass knob of Gusztáve's Quonset hut. Unlike the knob on NewTown Clinic's entrance door earlier, this one moved easily, and with precision. The door, evidently well hung and balanced, swung smoothly and silently, opening into the interior, and revealing to Margot yet another world to be reckoned with. *A world of darkness.*

She moaned under her breath. Gusztáve was only feet behind her in the world of brightness, and she certainly didn't want to offend him. Nonetheless, she recalled her apprehension from yesterday when she first saw the building. She'd subsequently reconciled her premonition to "dust storm" stress. She almost smiled at her thought—so many syndrome's these days, and she'd just created another. But why not a Mojave malady?

Genuine amusement, however, would not come.

Margot did understand a little about what was going on with her emotions. She had recently realized, and commented to George, that quite a number of recent movies and TV shows, especially the police drama and science fiction types, used a blue-gray or verdigris color palette. She found the "look" unpleasant, ominous even. It wasn't that she only liked bright colors and light—indeed she loved her nighttime view of Lake Shore Drive. It was the emotional baggage that came with the dark steel-blue or patina-like colorings. Depressing—and no doubt the producer's intent. Here in her non-celluloid reality, it was as if the darkness ahead in the Quonset hut would surround her, pull her into a black-hole of sorts. *What silly and fanciful thoughts.*

Gus said behind her, "Watch your step."

He was too late with his warning. The threshold was three or four inches higher than the floor inside, and she stumbled going in, and even though protected by a Bjorn walking shoe, pain shot through her right big toe, and she wanted to yelp in an unladylike fashion.

Now, besides being afraid, she was also in pain—and irritated.

Why did I let Gusztáve talk me into this? Of course it wasn't his fault, not really. It was her not wanting to hang around Community Hospital's emergency room. Since Harvey's death she hadn't been back in a hospital—not once. The longer that situation lasted, the better.

Barely an hour earlier, she had stood with Parker and Gusztáve under the hospital's outside canopy. It had been an odd moment, the wind silent, and the air hot—momentarily stifling, causing her to feel as if she couldn't catch her breath. For a millisecond, panic had flashed, then dissipated just as fast. Fortunately, Camille volunteered to go in with Deirdre's gurney stretcher alone.

Parker had also made a move to go in with the two EMTs urgently wheeling Deirdre in, but Gus had pulled him back. "Got a minute?" Gus had asked, grabbing Parker by the arm, and turning his head so Margot couldn't see his face.

But her ears were sharp, and she caught his every word. "Deirdre doesn't look good," he whispered, pulling Parker further away from her. "Don't need a doctor to tell you that."

Parker had nodded, and Gus continued, "Oscar, Patricia, and maybe even Ann were in the clinic this morning." He waited for Parker to nod again. "Could be attempted murder."

"Don't you think I've thought of that?"

"Both our gals need some protecting here."

Our gals? Margot turned her back on the two men and walked to the back of the canopy. "Insufferable," she said out loud. Nonetheless, despite Gusztáve's annoying presumption, she had come to the same conclusions. Actually, she wasn't concerned for herself—she didn't live in NewTown or work at the clinic. But Camille did.

Maybe she'd made a very big mistake coming to NewTown. She could have had Camille come see them in Palm Springs. She was sure her niece would have come, even with this murder thing—and consequently she'd be out of harm's way.

Too late now.

She'd turned back, and watched Parker leave Gus and rush into the hospital after exchanging knowing looks. *Who am I kidding?* Parker would protect Camille much better than she ever could.

Gus then walked over and asked if she wanted to go back to NewTown. "Could be hours," he'd cajoled. "Parker will make sure Doc Madison gets home okay." He'd smiled wickedly and said, "Like to show you my stuff. Keep your mind off Deirdre."

"Stuff?" Instinctively she knew this was a circumstance to be avoided.

"Got quite a collection."

Still, she had agreed to see his "stuff." *Anything not to go into the hospital.* And now, half an hour later, she was standing in darkness in Gus's Quonset hut with a very sore toe.

From the world of brightness behind her, she heard some kind of bird screech. *A warning, no doubt.* And as she stepped forward, she heard the door close behind them—and Margot couldn't ward off the feeling of being entombed in a haunted Halloween mystery world.

She willed her heart not to race. "No," she said aloud, and tried to also force her emotions to be like steel.

"What did you say?" Gus asked.

She turned to see him, but couldn't. With a final click of the door, it went black. She stood perfectly still, hoping that given a minute, her eyes would adapt. Outside it was barely afternoon, but here, it was the dead of night. Along with her apprehension, the off-putting darkness, and her still aching toe—the simple matter was, she was afraid of the dark. Yet here she was, and once again alone with Gus wishing for *Paladin.*

On top of all that, she suddenly had the most intense urge to sneeze.

"Are you always on duty?" Camille asked Doctor Carol Kubiak by way of greeting.

Carol had just left the side of Deirdre's cubicle bed. "Sure seems that way sometimes," she said from behind a small smile, and in a weary sounding voice. "I think we pumped her in time."

Camille hoped the gastric lavage worked, and she quickly took in Deirdre's vital-signs on her ICU monitor. "I think she didn't drink that much." Margot looked to Parker for confirmation.

"I have her sport-bottle bagged and tagged," Parker said. "And I'm running it down to BFS as soon as I'm finished here." He rubbed his hand over his mouth then clicked out the corner of his mouth. "Only about a fourth of the bottle gone."

As usual, Camille found his mannerism annoying, but was very glad he was immediately getting the sample off to Riverside's Bureau of Forensic Services.

"You think," Carol asked, "the poisons will match up? Oleander is what I assume based on symptoms and your input." She shrugged and shook her head. "But you know as well as I, symptoms are similar for so many things…"

As her voice faded, all three turned to stare at Deirdre—tubes in her nose and mouth, and a catheter and IV line attached to her arm. Camille wondered if there was something more she could or should have done at the clinic. It was often like that, hoping you did your very best for your patients.

Memories and images from her stints in Cook County Emergency wanted to resurface, but she pushed them back. *Baggage.* It was a great hospital, a great place to learn, but some things no hospital or doctor could fix.

Again she thought about her L.A. offer—an attending physician for internal medicine residents. Pay was good, with benefits. Hours would be long, though not as long as the interns. But ER management rotation was involved. Did she really want that again? Constantly bombarded by stress filled conversations and sounds of pain from surrounding cubicles—she thought not.

Margot heard a click, then a hanging light bulb came on, illuminating Gusztáve wearing a smart-aleck grin on his face—and somehow, now standing in front of her with his hand just then letting go of a string pull. *A string pull he'd somehow found in the darkness.* She willed her eyes to adjust quickly so she could deal with this man and his Quonset hut from hell.

"Spooky, ain't it?" he said. "Darned dark in here, Ms. Margot. Don't come in here unless you have a flashlight. I knew where the string was, but had to flap my hand around a bit."

"Couldn't you just put a switch by the door?"

"That would take all the fun out of it, now wouldn't it?"

Something about Gusztáve was intriguing, but the man's personality was becoming quite annoying. She drew herself up to her full height. "I would like to go back to Camille's now, Mr. Gusztáve

Martinez." Hopefully her voice sounded commanding and haughty. Superior even. *He's earned my ire.*

And as the seconds went by without him responding, she felt herself getting angrier. He had looked surprised for a second, but then hadn't immediately responded. Finally, his expression turned apprehensive and he asked, "I didn't really scare you, did I?"

She was in turn surprised he cared, and her emotions flip-flopped. *He sounds genuinely concerned.* "It was rather dark for a moment," she said. But Margot did not share, that after stepping into his beloved hut, she'd felt for a second—on top of everything else—a sensation she couldn't yet put a name to. *Déjà vu? No,* just the opposite. More like a vision of something to come.

Oh dear.

She seemed to be morphing into a different woman under the Mojave sun. Silly, anxiety riddled, and psychic. Or had she been that way in Chicago too—just insulated, protected, and without occasion to feel or experience? Isolated since Harvey "up and left her" —*as if he had a choice about dying.*

Well, on the opposite end of the spectrum, since landing in Palm Springs, it certainly felt like she'd boarded a rollercoaster ride where the rises and dips were getting steeper and deeper. *Her own personal Bobs.*

He smiled, and took a wide-legged stance. "Well, now that you have light, look around." His tone was prideful.

She stepped a few feet farther into the first room of the Quonset hut. That was odd in itself—the building seemed to be broken into rooms instead of one long expanse. From where she was standing, still close to the door, Margot could see several compartment-like areas ahead of her. She couldn't see the far end of the hut, not only because of the darkness looming ahead, but also because of the optics of looking into a black infinity. She wondered just how long the darned thing was.

But here, in the lighted area, it didn't take Margot long to see she was standing in Gusztáve's personal homage to Route 66.

She took a deep breath and coughed from dusty stale air. Nonetheless, now more relaxed, Margot took her time taking it all in. What lay before her was what she would have easily called "junk" if not tethered by Gusztáve's presence. Most assuredly in his eyes, she was surrounded by treasure.

The light Gus had pulled on was dim, consisting of a shade-less single-bulb fixture—yet it felt like a beacon. One part of her wanted to flee to the closed doors behind her, pound on them and yell until she escaped back into the real world of brightness—and sanity. Instead, she took several more steps forward.

To her left, dust coated fifties-style display shelves were crammed with items juxtaposed in no particular fashion. Recognizable among the clutter were a collection of pie pans, a woven-wooden basket filled with railroad spikes, an aged and yellowed milk shake machine, several punch bowls which she liked, and multitudinous rocks of various sizes and shapes—some volcanic, she thought. No signs or labels were visible.

And there was more.

Leaning against the shelves, stuck in corners, in piles on the floor, in barrels, and piled on the seats of matching faded avocado colored recliners. So much, she couldn't take it all in and turned her head away—only to be bombarded by more directly in front by the archway to the next room.

A wooden airplane propeller blade. A wringer washing machine and a Coca-Cola tub-style vending machine. The soda machine's paint, still a surprisingly vibrant red was chipped in places, but to her uneducated eye looked original; Margot guessed the coke dispenser to actually be a valuable antique. Maybe the washing machine too.

Okay, so not all "junk."

Indeed, one odd item leaning lopsidedly against the curved wall caught her eye. "A hammered dulcimer?" she asked quietly. Louder, for Gusztáve's benefit she said, "You have some remarkable pieces here." *How interesting.* "Is that a dulcimer?" she asked, while touching what she thought a beautiful, but negligently uncared-for instrument. She felt grit from the piece on her fingers, and dusted her hands against each other.

"Well sorta, kinda," he answered. "That's a cimbalom, at least that's what Gypsy-Jake told me."

Margot touched the clearly broken instrument again—and an odd sensation shot through her, causing her to shudder. *Most peculiar.* She remembered the Gypsy storefronts that populated Chicago in the forties and fifties—some homes, some fortune teller businesses, some both. She even remembered wanting to have her future told, but her mother and father had vehemently refused.

"Should be cleaned," she said.

Gus humphed and said, "That thing ain't really mine. Should be in the next section. Belongs to Ann and Oscar." He made a head movement toward the area ahead of them. "Asked her several times to move *their* stuff to *their* area." He chuckled. "Guess Ann does the buying, and Oscar does the moving part—and she ain't nagged him enough."

Margot bristled at his words and his underlying world view, but let it pass. *This man will soon be out of my life.* So why bother setting him straight?

She took another step forward and unintentionally brushed against the cimbalom, revealing another item tucked away under its edge.

Gus continued, "Rescued that Coke machine from a gas station in Oklahoma when it closed, and that propeller blade came from Barstow Daggett Airport—right down the road—circa 1939. Mahogany, I'd say. Oscar thinks otherwise." He strode over to the shelves and touched a piece of volcanic rock. "From Amboy crater, don't you know." His eyes were alight in a way she hadn't seen before.

Margot smiled. Couldn't help it. "Do you do that a lot?"

"Do what?"

"Regale your listeners with tidbits of Route Sixty-six trivia?"

"Do you always talk like that? 'Regale' for Christ's sake?" His tone was teasing, not really critical. "Who do you think you're talking to? A bunch of effete intellectuals?"

"Effete?" She was hoping for a verbal standoff. "Now who's using fancy words?"

"You're right." He laughed "I should have said 'snooty.'"

She laughed too, and for a moment, her sense of apprehension lightened. Still, even with being more comfortable with Gusztáve, she involuntarily shivered yet again. *What's going on?*

"You want to see more?"

"Certainly," she lied. "But while we're here," she pointed to the item under the cimbalom that had caught her attention. "What's that?"

He squinted and gave her an appraising look. "You seem to have an 'eye.'"

"It's under the dulcimer—I mean cimbalom," Margot said. Even in the dim light, it seemed to gleam from its crevices. *Ruby jewels?*

He closed his eyes, and tilted his head toward the ceiling. "Give me a second, it's got a fancy name. Just a sword handle..." A few seconds passed before he smiled, opened his eyes, and said, "Scimitar."

She recognized the word once he'd said it, and knew its roots went way back in history —but couldn't remember specifics. She found it interesting, Gusztáve knew the name. *Another mystery, this man.* Most of the scimitar's blade was missing, broken near the handle, and she doubted it was worth very much. Still, she would like to come back and examine it up-close and personal-like.

Despite the lovely dulcimer, and impressive scimitar, almost glowing in dusty dimness, Margot wanted to turn around and leave. She hated the place on a visceral level, and her urges to sneeze hadn't stopped. As she followed Gus forward into the next room, which seemed to be European furniture, she wondered what George, Cook Phillip, even his wife Bari were doing in her spotlessly clean and well lit penthouse back home; while she proceeded farther down loony-lane behind a man she simultaneously distrusted, relied upon, found interesting—and immensely irritating.

"How long is this 'hut' of yours?"

"Eh, only about a couple thousand feet or so."

Oscar started walking home from the clinic, then after half a mile or so, realized his actions were absurd, and dropped into a sitting position in the dirt by the side of the road. "How humiliating," he moaned, then cradled his face in his hands.

Hadn't I been driving a car?

After a couple moments, he was able to look around and try to orientate himself. Seemed like he'd just left the clinic—but for the life-of-him, he couldn't remember what he'd done in the time period between leaving the clinic and now. He didn't want to call Ann, but his car must be at home. *Or had he left it somewhere along National Trails?*

Besides, how could he possibly face his wife again? Sure, she'd been wonderful this morning when he showed up after being gone almost a day. He wasn't sure about the time, but she'd made him tea, tried to get him to eat—all the time staring at him like only she could do. He shook himself seeing her face again—knowing her, knowing her icy-cold nature.

"How can she ever forgive me?" He knew she couldn't— *wouldn't*— even though she claimed she had. *Why should she anyway?* "What a horrible position I've put her in." He knew he was talking out loud, but couldn't tell if at a whisper, or shouting. *I just need to relax and think for a moment.* "How to get my car, how to get my car?"

For a moment, his vision blurred, *then* he felt a pain shooting through his left buttock. A rock. He tossed it away and noticed how rough his hands were, *then* for the oddest second didn't recognize them as his own appendages. *Then,* he noticed all the sticker-bugs on the ground surrounding him. He sighed and said, "Good thing I dressed in these old thick jeans."

Fumbling around in his jacket pockets, he found a Baby Ruth. It was fresh and moist. "Just what I need." His having the bar and relishing it were strange because he couldn't remember ever being much of a candy person—or even buying this particular bar. Nonetheless, the chocolate, peanuts, and caramel all tasted wonderful. "The sugar will give me energy." *Why am I talking like there's someone to hear me?*

Still, Oscar continued to talk to the world in general as if it were an interested friend.

"I'll use my phone." He fumbled some more, inside pockets, outside pockets, finally locating his cell in his jeans front pocket. He put his right hand on the ground to push himself up, yelped with pain, then fell back onto his butt. It only took him a second to pull the sticker out of his palm, but falling back, he'd stirred up the dirt around him and was overcome with a coughing jag.

In the distance, he heard the faint sounds of an auto approaching.

That's it, "I'll hitch a ride." He nodded his head as if his desert surroundings had voiced their approval of his plan.

Oscar tried standing again, and was successful on this second go around. He shook himself, then smiled. The answer had come to him. Once home, he would get his car and drive to the perfect spot to hide.

"Why hadn't I thought of that before?"

After Margot finally convinced Gusztáve she'd had enough, it was well into afternoon, and she was not only feeling a tad traumatized, but also tired, hungry, and in much need of a shower. She figured he must have seen signs of distress in her face, because as soon as she escaped out into daylight—and for her, the land of sanity—he offered to take her to lunch at the Bagdad.

After a little explaining, she realized he was referring to the Bagdad Café of cult movie fame. Oddly, she had actually seen the movie, and was pleased she and Gusztáve could share a joint interest. Nonetheless, she was in no mood for more of his companionship, Mojave Desert talk, or Route 66 treasures. Indeed, if she had her way, she'd be catching a flight back to Chicago. *Maybe.* Margot certainly didn't want to abandon Camille in her time of need. And now there was poor Deirdre, and Harvey's old friends Ann and Oscar—with Oscar under suspicion of murder.

Eventually, after a lot of verbal sparring during a gut-jarring ride back down Tappy Road, Gus agreed to take her to Camille's and call it a day.

"I want to be there when my niece gets back from the hospital," she'd explained.

"Yeah, probably tough on the Doc losing two nurses like that, one right after the other."

Margot hadn't picked up on the "nurse" aspect, and didn't think the fact added much to catching a murderer. "Well, Deirdre isn't dead yet," she said, and without thought made the sign-of-the-cross over her chest.

"Catholic? Episcopalian?"

"Please keep your eyes on the road, Mr. Martinez." She certainly didn't want him knowing her thoughts or her religious perspectives. "I don't want to explain to the rental agency why their Cadillac is dinged and rattling." *Two damaged cars would be a little much.*

"Did I tell you how much you're paying for this rental? Don't think they'll be complaining about much." He laughed with gusto, before adding, "So now it's *Mr. Martinez* again?"

Margot gave Gus a tired goodbye wave after she closed the chain-linked gate behind the departing Escalade. Then turning to walk to Camille's doublewide, she fancied she got a glimpse through the oleander hedge of Ann watching from her porch. It was just for a second, and through the tiniest of openings in the stiff intertwined leaves. But she remembered Ann had wanted to have lunch—hopefully today was not that day.

Once inside, Margot gave waiting Dogue a pat on the head, then on further reflection, squatted and managed to give him a good hug even though her back hurt. He rewarded her with a slobbering ear lick. Tired and achy as she was, it was nice knowing they were now buddies.

She stood up with a groan, then told Dogue, "That Tappy Road is just awful." He barked, and she took it as understanding and agreement. He didn't act like he wanted to go out, and she figured he'd used the doggie-door in the laundry room.

Her body wanted to head to the guest bedroom, snuggle in with Dogue, and take a nice long nap. Her mind however, insisted she get out of her current Quonset hut-infested outfit, take a shower, and stay awake.

"Some quiet time to think."

Dogue barked again, and started toward the bedroom before she did. Whether for nap or shower, she wasn't sure, but guessed nap. Once there, he jumped up in the middle of the bed, stretched out, and closed his eyes. His intentions were clear.

Despite wanting to join him, Margot forced her body to keep moving and showered, then dressed in a comfortable looking lounging suit Camille had hanging in the guest closet. She also slipped into a favorite pair of ballet-styled slippers. After today, her Bjorn walking shoes were now symbols of change and adventure—good and bad; while her slippers represented, comfort, her past, and the status quo.

Purposefully, she ignored the cheval mirror in the corner. Didn't want to see how she looked now, preferring to retain the image reflected back from her "truth teller" mirror in her penthouse foyer. *Only days ago.*

Dogue didn't stir, so she decided to make a cup of tea, then hunker down on Camille's comfy loveseat with its desert expanse view.

The phone ringing in the kitchen, however, ended both her and Dogue's plans. When Margot touched the receiver in its cradle, she knew, "without knowing," this was a pivotal moment. Once again, unexpected foresight overtook logical thought—and she found herself struggling to comprehend.

The caller was Ann, asking if she'd like to walk across the yard for lunch at her house?

"I'd love to," Margot lied into the receiver.

From Ann's front door, Margot followed her college friend into a spacious, skylight-lit, and tiled foyer that after a few feet, opened on her right into a wrought iron railed step-down living room—and into a formal dining room to her left.

Everything Margot could see was perfect. *Unnaturally so*, she thought. The contrast to Gusztáve's Quonset was so startling, she paused a moment in awe. Then for a fleeting introspective moment, she wondered what impression visitors had when they entered *her* penthouse foyer for the first time?

Thoughts of her own home's image were quickly pushed aside by college day memories flooding in. Indeed, standing where she was, Margot remembered how Harvey had not thought well of the "Ice-Queen's" personality. But her brains and classical looks he'd certainly admired, and wondered what he'd think of her now. Age had treated her looks kindly—*but this obsessively clean and neat house.* She smiled, remembering some of Harvey's rather slovenly habits.

She heard Ann saying ahead of her, "I'm so glad I saw you and Mr. Martinez arriving."

Margot made her body move forward to catch up with Ann. It wasn't just the orderliness and memories that had momentarily immobilized her, but the perception of an aura of pristine perfection. The idea Ann's house had an aura was a stretch; nonetheless, the impression remained.

"If you don't mind settling in the kitchen," Ann said. "It's much more cozy."

Cozy? The furnishings she was seeing were modern, probably top of the line, and well coordinated—but certainly not cozy. Admittedly, Anne's crème and pastel decorating pallet was soft, but there was no feeling of warmth—*maybe because there was no clutter?* A sterile showroom of sorts. Most notably, she didn't see—and consequently hadn't inhaled one speck of dust. Margot took a deep breath, and realized with pleasure her breathing had immediately relaxed. In tandem, her eyes felt less scratchy and irritated.

Eventually, she found herself standing next to Ann in a spotless kitchen with its own off-kitchen dining-entertainment area. In the kitchen proper there was a center island, commercial quality stovetop, hidden away appliances, top of the line cabinets—a kitchen Margot thought even Cook Phillip could work in. And marvelous as Bari was, *well,* Margot doubted even Bari could produce such gleaming surfaces.

And like in the foyer, light streamed in from above. Through tube lights this time.

Margot straightened her back, shoulders, and neck into her full correct posture. "You must have some kind of air filter," she said. "I'm in awe, Ann." She took in a long, dust-free breath of air. "Not just at your lovely home and furnishings, but the quality of your air." She paused a second for emphasis before finishing. "Marvelous."

Ann laughed, took Margot's hand, and patted it affectionately while leading her to the area off the kitchen—furnished with deep-pillowed seating, small eating tables, and a wall encompassing television at the far end. French doors opened to a back garden where Margot thought she spied just-beginning-to-bloom roses, and more oleanders for sure.

There was even a game table, which brought back another memory. This time playing pinochle in the student union, and the occasional, almost idyllic times when they moved the game to a makeshift blanket-table on the lake front. During the school year,

Lake Michigan weather was dicey—making such times few and memorable.

Margot gently extricated her hand from Ann's, walked over, touched the table's leather edge, stared down at its green felt surface, and asked, "Do you remember those pinochle games we all used to play?"

"How could I forget?" Ann came over and stood by Margot, also touching its leather edge and looking down. "I think I always lost, no matter who my partner was."

Fascinating, *what* and *how* one chooses to retain the past. Her own recollection was Ann, a sharp and skilled bidder, would *let* Harvey, then Oscar after him, win. In fact, thinking back, as smart as Ann was, she never seemed to have the need to shine. *But then, neither had I.* In that same line of thinking, Ann had chosen not to go to medical school—picking nursing instead. At the time, Ann's career choice hadn't seemed a significant item—but in retrospect, another instance of her not wanting to outshine Harvey and Oscar.

Margot could feel Ann look up and turn her gaze on her. Then, as if reading her mind, Ann asked, "All those years, married to Harvey, did you ever regret not going to med school yourself?"

Margot was surprised, partly because they were mentally wandering down similar paths, but more by the intrusiveness of Ann's question. They hadn't seen each other for decades, and hadn't actually been that close way-back-when. *Rather pushy*, she thought, and afraid of what her face might reveal, Margot didn't look up immediately, but when she did, she was again surprised to see the intensity of interest in Ann's eyes, waiting for her to answer.

"No," Margot answered simply. She wasn't about to share with her how wonderful her life had been with Harvey. Not after all these years; Ann was a stranger, really.

"You were so smart…" Ann let her voice trail off and an ironic smile spread across her face. "Never know where life will take you, when you're as young as we were then."

"How true." Margot straightened her shoulders once again— and another memory came. Youthful silliness—her wanting to slump down to meet the height of her friends. And here she was eons later, the ridiculous habit returning next to Ann.

"So nice of you to invite me for lunch," Margot said. She looked around the room, wondering if she was expected to sit in this family area, at the kitchen center counter, or around a real kitchen table currently hiding behind one of Ann's cabinets. "It was amazing to find out you and Oscar are Camille's landlords."

Again Ann stole her hand, and led Margot toward the main part of the kitchen. "Come, sit at the counter-bar while I prepare everything."

Like a kid being led by a teacher, she followed Ann to one of several wrought iron high back barstools with cream-colored seats and back padding. The counter eating area was set with one tan cloth placemat, a tan cloth napkin, a water glass, a wine glass, and sparkling silverware—not stainless steel. An also cream-colored marble surface below their place settings was nicely marbled and streaked, and designed to accommodate an eating area on one side, and a gas burner stovetop and small stainless steel sink on the other.

Ann freed Margot from her friendship-grip, and said, "I don't cook much these days." She went a few steps to her left and reached up to a cabinet above another small sink. "Minestrone soup is already in the microwave." She opened the cabinet door and pushed a button. "The oven is already warm, I'll just pop the baguette in."

Margot sat in the high back barstool at the place setting, then watched in amazement. All appliances seemed to be behind cabinet doors, even the oven—which was only visible after Ann pushed an accordion kind of wooden curtain into what seemed to be a pocket door-frame. *A kitchen that doesn't look like a kitchen.* And minestrone and fresh bread she couldn't smell?

Once again jumping into her mind, Ann said, "Downside of the air filter is you can't smell anything. Not even bread baking."

When Margot had reconnected with Ann the day before, something odd had struck her about her hair, and today—in bright kitchen light and from the rear—she realized what it was. Ann was wearing a wig. Now she noticed a portable oxygen tank, the lightweight kind she'd read about in a recent pharmaceutical ad, sitting unobtrusively at the counter's end. Next to it was what looked to her like a small backpack, for the cylinder no doubt. *Poor Ann.* She wouldn't survive a minute in Gusztáve's dustbowl hut thing. Unfortunately, a sad bit of speculation came with those pieces of information. The heavy duty air filter was needed because either Ann or Oscar had a comprised immune system. The wig made her think it was Ann.

Margot didn't dare ask.

Even with the air filter, now that their soup was warming, Margot thought she caught a whiff of tomatoes, and basil, and garlic, and more.

"You know everyone thought Harvey was the star of our little clique," Ann said.

Once again, Ann surprised her. "What are you talking about?"

"That he was going places." She smiled coquettishly. "He was the catch in our group."

Margot, truly flabbergasted, just stared at Ann—momentarily unable to comprehend or speak. Had they been in two different worlds? Her Harvey, the shy plodder—a "catch" for goodness' sake? True enough, she'd always thought his heart was the best of them all, including herself. *But really.*

Finally Ann said, "Leila always said you didn't know that. But I never believed her. I guess you really didn't."

Ann remained on the cooking side of the counter, evidently planning to serve then watch her eat. *How odd.* From somewhere underneath, a hidden wine cooler she guessed, Ann produced an unopened bottle of a California Merlot.

While Ann deftly uncorked the wine, Margot said, "Well, sure I thought Harvey was great." She felt herself chocking up, but willed herself to recover immediately. "I was in love, didn't think about anything else." *I was so young then.*

Ann looked away for a moment, then turned back and raised her wine glass. "Here's to Harvey."

"And Oscar." Toasting a possible murderer was strange, but seemingly appropriate given Ann's tribute to Harvey.

Ann hadn't mentioned Deirdre, and Margot wondered if she knew the poor woman was in the hospital. Maybe she should tell her—but something held her back--and almost immediately, she knew what. *Parker.* He wouldn't want her to reveal anything, and the realization she wanted to please this desert sheriff reinforced how much she loved her niece. She didn't want to upset Parker because Camille liked him.

The loud ring of a telephone somewhere in the kitchen startled her, and she watched as Ann rushed to a floor-to-ceiling cabinet behind her. Margot wondered at Ann's penchant for hiding everything functional. Indeed, upon opening the cabinet door, she revealed a built-in desk, neatly arranged, and like everything else, sparkling.

She heard Ann say with relief, "Oscar!" She kept her back turned to Margot, and lowered her voice. However, Margot could hear every word. "Where are you? I've been so worried." Then after a moment, Ann said, "I'm on my way."

Ann turned toward her, and Margot saw her expression— relief and fear. *Odd bedfellows,* she thought.

Ann grabbed what looked like a purse and keys from the desk, and said, "I have to go." She looked around quickly. "Will you lock up and close the gate behind me? Oh yeah, and turn off the oven?" She laughed nervously, still looking around as she rushed toward the front door, then, as if trying to make sure she was thinking of everything, called out over her shoulder, "Please help yourself to soup—take it with you if you want. Containers are in the cabinets." She almost ran outside, letting her beautiful entry door silently close behind her.

For Ann's sake, Margot certainly didn't want Oscar to be Faye-Anne's murderer. She certainly must care about him. Why else would an otherwise intelligent woman rush out and leave a virtual stranger in her house—doors unlocked, oven on? They hadn't seen each other in years—Ann knew nothing about her.

"All very peculiar," Margot said aloud.

When she saw the taillights of Ann's red GMC Terrain go through the gate, she went over to the cabinet doors that concealed Ann's refrigerator. She opened both cabinet doors, then both refrigerator doors. *Won't hurt to take a little peek, now will it?*

Neither Oscar's Honda nor Ann's GMC had returned — but the UPS delivery truck had come and gone. Paladin, Margot's beloved derringer, was now safe-and-sound with her. The box was surprisingly small, tan, corrugated, and contained a lot of official looking papers that Margot paid little attention to — except for a second to note some business names she didn't recognize, and to amusedly wonder at George's connections. She was well aware he was not above subterfuge if needed. Bullets were in a separate box. She'd had to sign for the packages as the representative of another company she didn't recognize. Margot already knew her own capacity for deceit and duplicity.

Psychologically, having Paladin with her went a long way in calming her rising apprehension. *George came through yet again.*

Dogue had barked fiercely at the truck's arrival, but then let the driver — a very pleasant and agreeable young man — pet him, then returned to barking aggressively as the truck took off and was well out of doggie earshot. Now, the UPS excitement just a memory — Dogue's eyes intent and ears straight up and alert — he sat silently watching Margot and Camille from his post under the arch between the living room and kitchen. He was so still, Margot thought you might not notice he was there. But she knew quite well he was.

"You wouldn't have believed it, Sweetheart," she said from the loveseat. "That hut place went on and on and on..." Paladin was tucked into the cushion next to her, and both women had glasses of wine in hand as they took in the blazingly-bright late afternoon horizon. Margot was tired, but very glad to be finally relaxing and going over the day with her niece.

Camille chuckled. "And really dusty too, I bet," she said. She was sitting in the armchair to Margot's left—and while carefully balancing her wine in one hand, she brought her legs up and underneath her body. "How are your allergies holding up? This desert can be hell on nasal passages. I've seen a lot of cases of sinusitis." She turned and looked at Margot. "Is that medicine we stopped and picked up helping you?"

"Extremely fast acting and working great."

"I'm glad to hear that. Often my patients go straight to an infection, which requires an antibiotic and a nasal spray." She tsked. "But I have one patient who's allergic to sprays."

"Prescribing is so complicated these days," Margot said. "Drug interactions, over prescribing antibiotics, new drugs all the time, keeping up on the literature—" She stopped herself. "My goodness, what a litany of complaints."

Both women laughed. Then Margot sighed, shook her head, and returned to the topic of Gus's Quonset hut. "You wouldn't believe how far back we went in Gusztáve's dust-bowl hut-thing before I insisted we turn around."

"I guess you can't see how long it is from the road."

"Heaven's no." Margot's mind was weary, but she wanted to try to explain what she'd seen and experienced to Camille. Having someone to share with was nice. Thinking back, the place had been so bizarre, so alien to her sensibilities. "Have you been in there?"

"Only once, with Oscar and Ann. Helping them take an old *armoire* there." She laughed briefly. "I remember thinking it was a piece of junk, not much better than that thing in back of us." She did a quick head-motion toward the dining area near the arch Dogue continued to guard. "But Oscar and Ann said it was an antique. Wish I knew more about that stuff."

"I'll start your antique education by telling you that 'thing in back of us' is possibly a Louis the Fifteenth *armoire*. The carvings make it special. Though it does indeed need some finishing work."

Camille's eyes lit up, and she said with fondness, "Oh Auntie Marg, you're amazing."

She sounds like an adoring child. Margot was caught off guard for a moment by how much she and Camille cared for each other. She cleared her throat and said, "I'm a lucky woman," and hoped her niece understood what she was trying to say. Quickly, she went on, "It's room after room, sort of. Each little section is different."

"Yes," Camille said. "Like in an antique mall kind of thing where there's different people renting spaces." Her voice picked up a bit. "It's coming back to me now. Ann did explain the layout to me. Gus rents each section for storage, though I don't think he's actually collecting any rent. And the plan is—well *was* to have antique shows or sales there."

"But it's so dark, dusty, and dingy."

Camille laughed. "Such alliteration." She turned her gaze outside.

Dogue stood up, sauntered over to the loveseat, jumped up next to Margot, positioned himself just right for the maximum snuggle-benefit, and plopped down against her. Margot saw dog hair fly in the air, and smiled.

Thank you, Gray, she mentally whispered. The Lenwood Mall had the types of clothes she'd needed to purchase; just like Camille's washable lounging suit she'd changed into before going across the yard to have lunch with Ann. *I'm learning from Gray and Camille about desert living.* True enough, on her way out of Palm Springs, she'd also picked up a wonderful pair of James Perse handmade Repetto ballet slippers. A pricey purchase and an indulgence for sure, but they were for home—to wear in the confines of her penthouse.

The thought of walking around in French ballet slippers in NewTown—Gusztáve's hut in particular, was an amusing incongruity that made her pause. She was willing to poke fun at Gusztáve and his hut, even denigrate her afternoon adventure. Yet, she'd been genuinely apprehensive much of the time—but *darn it,* she'd enjoyed the experience. *Titillating even?* She said, "I don't really know if I trust Gusztáve. Yet."

Camille asked softly, "But you *do* trust George?"

What an odd question. "Why, of course." She almost added, *"Don't you?"* But caution held her tongue. Indeed, Camille wouldn't understand. He'd only been around a year. Phillip and Bari were already accepted members of her household.

"He's certainly good looking." Camille brought her eyes back to her aunt for a few seconds. "And he's good to you, Auntie Marg. That's all that counts." Her smile was broad and warm.

Margot was again overwhelmingly pleased. "And so are Cook Phillip and his wife Bari." *I'm a lucky woman.* "Good to me, that is."

Camille laughed again. "What is her name again? Unbelievable."

"Barisa Callas Garcia de Cooper." It was indeed a mouthful, and she'd had to memorize it early on. Barisa was her full first name, Callas her father's paternal-line surname, Garcia her mother's paternal-line name. The 'de Cooper'` was for Phillip's benefit.

"Does she still stay in her room all the time when she's not cleaning your house?" Camille rolled her eyes. "As if your place is ever dirty."

Margot felt herself flush. "I should be doing more."

"Housework? You mean for the exercise?"

"No, no. Bari's English is poor." She tsked. "I should talk to her more, maybe have a tutor come in."

"Well, her husband could help."

"True enough," Margot said through a staccato laugh. "But I really don't want to take him away from the cooking he loves so much."

"The food *was* good when I last visited."

"And thinking back, I can't remember Phillip talking about anything but food since they've been with me." For a moment, Margot was struck with how little she actually knew about the couple. True enough, their references had been outstanding—she wouldn't have let them into her home if they weren't. But she'd had so little interaction with them. *My fault entirely.* At least she knew a lot more about George.

Margot balanced her wine glass in one hand and stroked Dogue's head with her other. *So this is what it feels like to have a daughter. Share her life.* "What did Doctor Kubiak say about Deirdre's condition?"

Camille drained her glass and sat it on the end table next to her. Then she sighed, uncurled her legs, sat up straight, and turned toward her aunt. "At least she's not going to die." She shook her head sadly. "But you know as well as I do, lack of oxygen to the brain—" Camille spread her hands.

Margot also sat her wine glass down, but hers was still half full. "She wasn't unattended that long," she said. Actually she couldn't remember if she knew how long it had taken Camille to get to Deirdre after Mr. Carter started yelling for help. "Oh, Sweetheart, you don't think she's going to have brain damage?"

"I just don't know. She never stopped breathing while I was with her. But I don't know after they took her away."

Margot almost said, *"But you're a doctor, you must know."* No, she'd heard too many patients complain to Harvey *and* herself—using those exact same words.

Both women surrendered into the padded comfort of their chairs and fell silent. Margot let her mind relax and wander where it willed. Out the picture window she was surprised to see a sunset developing like none she'd ever seen before. Afternoon had disappeared in what seemed like a blink. Topping a low ridge of distant hills, the panorama before her had filled itself with brilliant streaks of red, orange, and a yellowish color akin to gold. Early sunset moments, and beautiful.

What really brought awe to her senses was its breadth, feeling more like she was in a bowl—and the vibrancy of the colors, so outlandishly bright. Garish even, if compared to her only point of reference—Lake Michigan sunrises. Margot wondered if she was witnessing an anomaly, or just an everyday occurrence. The same question she'd wondered about the dust storm. *Strange place, this Mojave.*

She hadn't known Deirdre or Faye-Anne. The thought, however, that one of her niece's trusted nurses might not ever appreciate such a sunset again, and that Faye-Anne Miller, would never appreciate *anything* again in this life—was sad, and made her quite angry.

Good grief. She was not a woman easily consumed by anger. *Another anomaly.* Indeed, there was something very strange in this NewTown desert dust. Not only was it clogging her Midwest sinuses—but also messing with her brain.

Once again, Margot was happily talking on a "regular" phone.

"Are you eating right, Madame?" Tonight, George's voice sounded particularly comforting. She laughed, and he rushed to explain, "Cook Phillip wants to know."

"I made my own tea this morning," she said proudly. "But you can tell Cook Phillip I'm suffering immensely without his cuisine." The sunset had faded to night, and she'd lingered on the loveseat after Camille headed off to her bedroom, cell phone in hand, talking to Parker.

Margot continued, "That should give him pleasure, knowing how much I miss his gourmet treats." Phillip was indeed an outstanding chef, even by Chicago's high and eclectic standards. She then proceeded to describe the day's happenings.

After she tried to describe Gusztáve's place, George said, "Madame, I certainly think you should not reenter that place." His voice was his most stilted and ultra dramatic, one of his favorite affectations.

But it's fun, playing our games. She even felt herself relax a bit more—even though they were discussing the most irritating Gusztáve Martinez.

When trying to explain Oscar's shenanigans, she said, "He's not the man I remember." *A zillion years ago.* "His actions, as Camille has explained them to me have been extremely bizarre." She didn't go into details about Ann and their clique's college day melodramas. "And he acts like he's lying about something. Or trying for some type of misdirection." She hadn't said that directly to her niece, but even Camille must realize how weird he was acting, no matter how much she admired him as a mentor.

"Madame, everyone lies."

Even you? "How cynical you are, George."

"Yes, Madame."

The front windows rattled a bit, and outside she heard the ominous whoosh of unseen but approaching winds — sounding almost like a train rattling across the terrain.

After George hung up, he sat thoughtfully for a few moments. He was in his own suite, ensconced in the burgundy leather lounger Margot had presented to him as a birthday present a couple months back. With his remote, he turned up the sound on his CD player — a Miles Davis Quintet recording of "My Funny Valentine."

From the odor of rising bread wafting its way to his quarters, he knew Phillip was probably in the kitchen — oblivious to all things non-culinary. His wife, Bari, was no doubt in their own two-room suite behind the kitchen, watching the soaps she recorded all day. *What a silly woman,* he thought. She was pretty for sure, and Phillip was a lucky man in that respect, but he didn't think she had a working brain cell beyond what was on TV. He'd even heard her talking back to the TV. Still, she seemed happy enough with Phillip.

All the better.

Now, Margot, she had a brain — a real challenge.

He brought his mind back to his next task. It was Monday night, time to call home. Margot had called him on the house phone. He picked up his cell and started to press button three — then stopped. *No,* he'd wait until Miles finished. No hurry to call overseas.

* * * * *

145

"It's been a long time since Chicago," he said from across the world. Doctor Kenneth Melon's voice was as deep and rich as she remembered, and still resonated with a flat Midwestern accent, with a little nasal vowel emphasis, much like her own. "Glad I finally caught up with you."

Margot had answered her cell phone without looking at the caller's number. Now she awaited his next words with apprehension, and prayed Camille was asleep in her room. The last thing she needed was for her to hear—even if Kenneth was six-thousand miles from Los Angeles. He wasn't a dangerous man, but his call was certainly cause for alarm.

"You, know," he continued amiably, "I came back and retired in Barcelona."

She took a deep breath, willing her voice to be calm. "Yes, I'd heard."

"You need to know I'm on a cell phone, and it's not a good connection. If I lose you, call me back. Okay?"

"Of course," she said, knowing she would not, and hoping he'd lose his connection right then. Whatever he was about to tell her could not possibly be good news. "I'm surprised to hear from you."

He hesitated a few seconds before saying, "I wouldn't have bothered, but I needed to tell you two things."

She held her breath.

"First, your brother Graham called, wanted to know if I knew anything about any goings on between Meredith and Harvey." He waited, and when Margot didn't immediately respond, he added, "Don't know why he called me. Why he'd think I would know something like that."

Meredith. That's how.

"I told him I knew nothing, nor had I seen or heard anything to make me think there was anything "untoward" going on."

Margot unexpectedly heard herself laugh. "*Untoward,* Kenneth?" She wondered for an instant if that was how she sounded

146

to Gusztáve? Pretentious—using an esoteric word when several plain ones would do. In this case—*having an affair*. "You sound like me."

She heard him laugh too, then he said, "And the other item was—"

His phone went silent. She didn't call him back. In fact, she muted the ringer. Margot wished she could do the same for her building anxiety—and the winds outside.

Graham was sitting on his balcony, enjoying the night. A congregation of sparrows once again had decided to visit—possibly expecting a late night snack. Unfortunately he hadn't thought ahead and brought anything they would like.

A soft breeze was flowing through his deck. *Very nice,* he thought, and yet again, he reminded himself how lucky he was. For a second, he was in his Cabriolet again—*still breathing, and giving thanks* he wasn't dead. He'd have his car back tomorrow—his amazing machine, like himself, had suffered little actual damage. And he again reflected the doctors had wanted him to stay for more tests after the X-rays—MRI, CT, blood tests—he couldn't remember the whole list; of course he'd been smart enough to refuse. *Completely unnecessary.* He wasn't hurt, and had just wanted to go home. The accident had caused an *epiphany*, not serious physical damage. A few headaches— *everyone got them*—came with life.

He had at the ready on the side table, a small saucer holding a small round of gouda and paper-thin sliced peppered Italian-salami. There was also a snifter of Remy Martin XO Cognac Brandy, and a Cabaiguan *Belicoso Fino* cigar. As with driving, he had his sunset accoutrements. Graham considered Palm Springs sunsets the best of the best. Tonight's color display wasn't the "best" he'd seen, but still pretty darned nice, and definitely worthy of brandy and a cigar.

He said aloud, "Maybe I should tell Margot she's adopted." Voicing his question to the world caused him to physically shake. *Why think of doing it now?* The answer was quick and obvious. Other secrets and lies were being revealed. The onion, so to speak, was being peeled; could one and only one layer be revealed? He doubted it, and feared there would be more tears ahead. *God knew*, he'd cried enough over Meredith's infidelity before taking action.

Did Margot need to know? She clearly didn't remember anyone but Harlow and Martha, and they never saw fit to tell her the truth. He'd only found out by accident himself, overhearing snatches of one of their whispered conversations. *Many years ago.* Maybe he should have told her then, when they were children.

Past history. Dead history.

With a weary sigh, he took his snifter in hand, raised it to his lips, and again wondered why Margot had not been more upset about his revelation Harvey had fathered Camille?

His sparrow friends flew away, and out of the blue that horrid man was sneaking on his property again. *Darn it!* He'd installed motion sensor flood lights, and there the intruder was, clear as if it were daylight.

"Time to bring the police in," he said and took his cell phone from his pocket. Graham knew the mayor and he'd met the Police Chief just the other night at a cocktail party. *I'll call him directly. This was private property for goodness' sake.* The trespasser had definitely outgrown his welcome.

Part Two

Into the Darkness

Chapter Five

Tuesday

Parker began Tuesday standing outside his jeep, leaning against his back tailgate—wanting to feel the desert air on his face. Inhale his Mojave. Taste the new day.

Margot was getting under his skin, but not necessarily in a bad way. Heck, he was beginning to like her—*sort of*. But it galled him her personality was not one he could easily identify and catalogue. She was snooty *sort of*, cordial *sort of*, naïve *sort of*, wise *sort of*, but for sure, intelligent and well educated. And he could tell from the way she looked at him—he was definitely under scrutiny.

Clearly, spaghetti alone would not be enough to woo Camille's sophisticated aunt. Unfortunately, or maybe fortunately—he wasn't yet sure—Parker knew on all levels of his being that if he wanted to win over Camille, he needed to also win over her Auntie Marg.

The implication of his need to impress Margot hit him with a clarity and intensity he couldn't ignore. "I must love Camille," he murmured. *Well, not exactly love.* Of course, mentally eating his words wasn't the same as refuting his underlying emotions. *Oh yes,* Camille was clearly filling a gaping hole in his heart.

He forced his thoughts away from Camille, and back to her aunt. She seemed warm enough for someone who was loaded and lived in a Michigan Avenue penthouse. Objections, even though she hadn't voiced any, were to be expected. Camille was her only niece, and comparatively young, while he was clearly older, and consequently would have some baggage.

This morning he'd parked at the end of what was barely a footpath at the point where Riverside Road faded into the Cady hills. He'd turned his car around right after the last sign of humanity, a pistachio field—then backed up as far as he dared.

The view that lay in front him was one of his favorites, and well worth the backwards maneuver of not trying to run into the ditch.

He let the predawn air hypnotize him, pull his mind away from personal matters, then go where it willed—landing expectedly on Faye-Anne. Thinking about her, and the way she looked Friday night dead in Oscar's office, brought a flash of anger. It swept through him quickly, and for the first time since her murder, went deep to his core, and was surprisingly powerful in its intensity.

He wanted to slam his fist into the tailgate, but knew from experience his hand would be the loser in the knuckle versus car encounter.

Sure, he was always angry when faced with needless death. But this was personal. He'd known the woman, talked to her, heck, even asked her out once. His anger faded a bit, remembering with a touch of humor how she'd turned him down.

"Why Chief Reed," she had said—her words wrapped in a half-laugh, a coquettish tilt of the head, and a slight lifting of her chin. "I couldn't think of dating *anyone* in law enforcement." She'd slowly moistened her lips. "I'd find myself in constant," she held the last word until the timing was perfect, "trouble."

He'd been foolishly flustered at the time, but remembering now, it seemed humorous, and so obviously contrived. Maybe a little sad.

Poor sap Oscar had evidently succumbed to her feminine wiles. He laughed out loud, and said, "Feminine wiles, no less." *How outdated. And clichéd.* The effects of that Madison-Cross woman no doubt. She seemed from a period that had seen its day. And for a moment, an old pang of past regret resurfaced, then as quickly disappeared. *I should have gotten my Masters.*

Yet, he liked being a cop. He didn't think a Masters in criminology would help him catch the bad guys any faster—a thought that led to the partial toxicology report laying on his Jeep's front seat. He allowed himself another loud and weary sigh. He'd seen so many of the darned things. *Too many.*

An autopsy report would follow, hopefully soon. But Thompson clearly had connections, and this request had gone to the top of the pile. *Curious for someone so young and inexperienced.* As to the report itself, very importantly, a sample of Faye-Anne's heart blood, peripheral blood, and tissue samples from her brain, liver, and kidney had been expedited to Toxicology. So the ME had also jumped-started their request. *Connections and politics*—Thompson, somehow, knew the right people. He wondered who knew who, *or was it whom*? He decided he didn't care—neither grammar nor politics mattered in figuring out who killed Faye-Anne.

The two-page report stated all tests had not been completed, and that per the DA's request, this was a preliminary analysis for murder investigation purposes. But they could say Faye-Anne Miller Jones had first suffered from oleander poisoning. Parker noted the signature on the report and mentally gave the technician high marks for a footnote that clearly said they would not have detected the toxin unless alerted by police officials. It was not in their standard panel.

Margot also seemed quite knowledgeable about medical matters—seemingly able to keep up with Camille. He guessed that was what happened when your husband was a doctor.

His life-misspent regret returned, but this time, he philosophized a lot of education certainly hadn't helped Oscar Lewis. A doctor, yet here he was, probably in an unhappy marriage, acting crazy, the number one suspect in a murder, and again, nowhere to be found.

Where the heck was Oscar? He thought he'd better try the hospital and Ann again.

* * * * *

Graham was forced awake by the sun pounding on his eyelids with a ferociousness he didn't understand. Usually, he loved waking up to the first light. Didn't have drapes or blinds, just a beautiful 180º view of the Santa Rosa Mountains. This morning the light felt like a harbinger of something.

The phrase, *a darkness to come,* popped in his mind, and he didn't have a clue where it came from. He shook his head. *Still dreaming?* He flexed his hands—*no,* he was awake alright.

"What the hell?" he said aloud.

A darkness, for goodness' sake? If anything, truth telling was all about letting the light in. And even with that, as far as he knew, no secrets had yet been revealed. For sure, the obvious one, the one Margot was supposed to tell Camille, was still untold. He would have heard back from his sister otherwise. Still, his whole being somehow *knew* that today was pivotal—but he didn't know for what or why?

He sat straight up in his second-floor bedroom—afraid. He hadn't liked the fear he'd felt during his car accident, and this—more of the psychological foreboding variety—Graham found even more distasteful. Worse, he thought, because it wasn't connected to something concrete like almost dying.

Then, and much like the sun's assault on his eyeballs, the blinding realization came forward into his consciousness that the world had shifted in a way he was yet to know. One mule deer in the middle of the road had started it all—changed everything. And now his sister Margot was in the center of whatever was about to happen.

Damn, damn, damn.

Her bed was comfortable, the air temperature perfect—and outside the night had after awhile returned to quiet. The wailing winds disappearing as abruptly as they'd appeared. In fact, an all encompassing silence reigned—except for several early morning interludes of talkative owl conversations in an aged pine tree right outside her bedroom window.

Nonetheless, despite the peacefulness surrounding her, Margot's night was fretful. She woke up several times, jittery and anxious from a fear she had yet to put a face on, much like she'd felt in Chicago before leaving. Specifically, she never felt physically comfortable, didn't think she ever fell into REM sleep, and indefinable anxieties caused her to continually toss and turn.

Actually I know where some of this is coming from, she thought, sitting up in bed. She was *angry* at Meredith for spinning a half truth to Gray: she was *angry* with Gray for expecting her to tell Camille: and she was *angry* at herself for letting Gray manipulate her. Pile on top of that, her beloved Camille was in the middle of a murder investigation, and she couldn't think of one thing to help her. Then there was the premonition of something yet to come with its attendant fear Camille might also be in danger. And again—how could she help her?

It was unacceptable she would let anything happen to Camille. *I need to shake this and do something about it.* Today she would figure out who killed Faye-Anne and sickened Deirdre. With new-found conviction, Margot proceeded to get up and shower, all the while trying to reset her perspective.

And just maybe, she actually owed Ann and Oscar her help. They'd been close friends way back then. For a second, a picture of them all resurfaced, so young, so optimistic—their lives still ahead of them. Lounging on blankets, eating cheese and drinking wine disguised as sodas at a free Grant Park Orchestra concert in the summer, or a Chamber Music concert in Ida Noyes Hall at the University of Chicago—Oscar often with Leila, and after her death, whoever was his latest conquest. More pictures flooded her mind's eye—spending a Saturday hanging out at The Art Institute, or Oak Street Beach, or Lincoln Park Zoo—where Ann and Harvey had that awful row. She forced her mind back to the present. *The past is the past—can't be changed.* And she prayed Faye-Anne's murderer was not the unfaithful Oscar.

By the time Margot finished her ruminations she was dressed—this morning in a rather plain but sturdy polyester no-wrinkle "travel" suit she'd brought from Chicago. Thinking about her choice of attire brought back even earlier memories with her mother—spending hours in Marshall Fields—shopping, having lunch. Pleasurable times.

Dogue was sitting outside her bedroom door. Waiting. She wasn't sure if he was there to guard, or to keep her in. Nonetheless, when he did an unusual mouth and lip movement upon seeing her — she took it as the equivalent of a doggie smile.

Accompanied with a head pat, Margot said, "Today, doggie Dogue, we help Camille clear her—correction, *our* Oscar." He barked in return, and they made their way amiably through the house to the kitchen. Once there, she found her cell phone and made a quick call to George. No answer, but she left a short message.

Margot was becoming fond of the window over her niece's kitchen sink. Besides being expansive, she loved the wonderful view of a mature line of fuschia and double-white oleanders. The tall thick hedge formed a privacy barrier and small garden between Camille's doublewide quarters and the Lewis home. Margot thought the prolific flowers and garden wonderful. And calming. Just what she needed to get past last night's sense of apprehension.

Indeed, as she loaded their few dishes from last night into the dishwasher, it was rather pleasant "helping out." Especially while watching sparrows, finches, and humming birds at play—*or was it actually work they were doing?* She smiled thinking about what might be going on in the little birds' brains. *Nice of Camille to maintain so many feeders.* She was like Meredith in that way. Nurturing.

She was so taken with the bird's fluttering chatter, she considered for a moment asking George to set up some bird feeders on her rooftop patio at home. *If these little ones even fly that high.*

On the counter, her cell phone rang—breaking her almost-found sense of serenity and calm. She wiped her hands on a kitchen towel and answered, "This is Margot." As she spoke, she thought she heard a car pull into the yard on the other side of the hedge.

"I received your voicemail," George said. "Is this an appropriate time, Madame? I assumed you wanted an immediate return call."

"Perfect time." A few minutes later would have been better. Right then, she wanted to know who was coming to see Ann behind the oleanders. Her attention divided, she continued, "I need you to look something up for me. This afternoon if you can."

Events in the Lewis yard held her curiosity. Camille had told her yesterday there was a break in the foliage near the end of the hedge. *"And if you really stretch,"* she had claimed. *"You can see into the main yard."*

"What information would you like me to gather?" As usual, George's tone was proper, stiff, and respectable. "An item on the Internet?"

"Yes, and maybe talk to that private-eye gentleman." If he could get Paladin to her in a day, she was sure he could get information equally fast.

Margot thought she'd give Camille's peek-a-boo claim a try, and took a step to the left of the kitchen sink while continuing her instructions to George, "What was his name? Mr. Thomas, or Tolman—something like that." She leaned forward as far as she could over the sink, then stretched her neck—her entire upper torso actually—looking to the right for a break in the hedge. She found the stretching maneuver hard as it required quite a bit of physical determination even with her statuesque height. "There are three people I'd like you and the detective to research for me."

"Of course, Madame."

She gave him Ann, Oscar, and Parker's names, Camille's address, Parker's position, and the approximate ages for all. "Just being careful," she explained.

Back on the oleander hedge front, Camille's spying trick had worked. Margot could see her rented Cadillac had pulled in.

George's voice lowered, and he abandoned his deferential tone. "I need to tell you something." He near whispered, "You received another call today."

She stretched once more across the kitchen sink and saw Gusztáve get out of the SUV as Ann came to meet him. Margot returned to a normal stance and asked George absently, "Who called?" Gusztáve handed Ann something—something so small she couldn't tell what it was.

"Doctor Melon." George hesitated before finishing, "From Barcelona I think."

Her stomach churned, apprehension returning—and aggravation from George's curious tone. She should have called Kenneth back last night, *but darn it.*

Margot felt her body stiffen, but she tried to force her neck and back muscles to relax. Whatever else he wanted to tell her last night, she could handle today. "Did he leave a message?"

"No, just that he'd call your cell again."

Behind her, from the kitchen archway Camille called out, "Are you ready to go and talk to Nealy Jones?" Then evidently seeing Margot on the phone, she added, "I can wait—"

Margot turned around and held up her hand. "No, no, Sweetheart, we need to go." To George she said, "We can talk again tonight." She wanted to say more to him, but it would have to wait. She disconnected, and as soon as she did, realized she'd forgotten to include Gusztáve on her investigations list.

"Was that Father?' Camille came into the kitchen, dropped her purse on the counter, lounged against a counter barstool, and peered curiously at her aunt. "No, it was George, wasn't it?"

Again Margot stiffened, and felt her heartbeat involuntarily race. It was not good her face was telling Camille some kind of story. "Yes," she said simply, and hoped she wouldn't press for details.

Fortunately, her niece answered her own curiosity. "George is getting lonely, isn't he?" She smiled mischievously. "Doesn't know what to do without you giving him instructions. Am I right?"

Margot laughed. "You certainly are perceptive."

Seemingly satisfied and pleased with her answer, Camille stood up and grabbed her purse. "Ready to go interview some suspects?" She started walking toward the kitchen door. "Front's all locked up."

Margot nodded. "I'm ready." If they left immediately, Gusztáve and Ann might still be talking—and just maybe, she'd find out what his visit was all about.

"We've got a murderer to catch. Oscar is counting on us." Camille sounded excited.

"Indeed."

Camille stopped mid-step and turned back to Margot who was in the process of checking her new Gucci handbag. Another Palm Springs purchase.

"I sure hope Oscar didn't kill Faye-Anne," Camille said. "But, darn it, where the heck does he keep disappearing to? And why?" Then with a wave, Camille indicated she was finally ready to go.

"Wait," Camille said, stopping in her tracks again, and pointing past Margot toward the front window. "I think that's your Escalade pulling up out front. Gus must have come for us. We don't have to drive."

Margot didn't mention he'd only had to drive around the oleander hedge.

It was turning out to be a clear blue sky day. *Very nice,* Margot begrudgingly conceded. *Perfect day to catch a murderer.* The winds were calm, the air fresh, and for a moment, her thoughts wandered to Ann's super air filter. At least today, there wouldn't be many nature driven challenges to the poor woman's immune system.

"I don't have to talk to you about anything," Nealy Jones snapped as he got out of the passenger side of his red twin-cab pickup. He slammed the door behind him, pushed his wraparound sunglasses on top of his shaved head, crossed his arms across his chest, then glared at Margot and Camille—seemingly ignoring Gus leaning on the Escalade behind them.

Nealy's the one, Margot decided immediately, and for the moment, forgot about Ann and Oscar. *He certainly looks the part of a murdering philanderer.* She almost humphed aloud.

Camille stepped forward toward Faye-Anne's estranged husband and said, "You're right, Mr. Jones, you don't have to talk to us."

Nealy was of average height, and muscular thick—mainly in his upper torso. It was his face, however, that told the story—broad and long, with prominent nose and cheek bones, small lips, and a puckered and petulant curve to his mouth. In bizarre contrast, his eyes were dark brown, big, liquid, and gorgeous.

After taking in this strange looking man, Margot found herself stepping backwards—while her niece moved forward again.

She wanted to grab Camille by the arm and jerk her back. She also wanted to turn around and see what Gusztáve was doing behind them. Hopefully, he was stepping closer, coming to their assistance. He should have warned them before driving out to see this man that he was dangerous.

Camille said, "Don't you want to help find your wife's murderer? I'm just looking for the truth."

Gus must have walked around where he could be seen, because for a second Nealy looked beyond both women. Margot prayed Nealy remembered who Gusztáve *had* been.

But Nealy demanded, "Go away." His eyes were challenging. "Don't care if you are a doctor, and you," he gestured toward Gus, "the old Chief. I got rights." He focused his gorgeous eyes on Margot. "And I don't give a rat's-you-know-what *who* you are."

Margot wasn't sure if she wanted to sputter with laughter, or slap him as she watched Camille step forward again, almost close enough to touch him—or worse, him to touch her.

"Faye-Anne," Camille said, "was asking for everything in the divorce. You have a live-in girlfriend you want to marry, and you don't have an alibi."

"Now how would you know that?" A lascivious smile curled the corners of his small mouth. "Pillow talk with Reed?"

This time for sure, Margot wanted to rush in and slap him. How dare he insinuate her niece was sleeping with Parker Reed! Camille hadn't been raised that way. But fear, cowardice—something held her back. She heard Gus clear his throat behind her as if about to speak. *He'll have the guts to do what I can't.*

"Did you kill your wife, Mr. Jones?" Camille asked before Gus could intervene.

Or, Margot suddenly thought, *had Camille and Gusztáve planned this out?*

"See those horses?" Nealy asked. He looked out toward a fenced area to his left where five or so horses were grazing. "And those dogs?" He jerked his head in the other direction. "Don't you hear those cats out back?" His tone softened a bit. "Have their own cattery, don't you know?"

Then he took a long deep breath, and his face also softened. "They don't have anybody. Dumped in the desert like trash…or worse…mistreated." His eyes moistened, and he looked away. "Peaches and me take care of 'em. Otherwise they'd be sick or dead."

Suddenly Margot heard footsteps to their side, and turned to see a woman approaching—a rabbit cradled in her arms. She'd been so engrossed in the workings of this strange man, she wasn't sure exactly where the woman had come from. The house, she thought.

Then she recognized Tina "Peaches" Paxton from the picture Gusztáve had shown them driving over. The photo hadn't done justice to the dark-haired beauty walking over to Nealy.

"This one's sick," Peaches said in a throaty voice that made her complexion and near perfect features even more alluring. "Been to the vet. She'll make it we think." When standing next to Nealy, Peaches shifted the rabbit's weight into one arm, and rubbed her free hand back and forth across Nealy's back. Lovingly, comfortingly. "Nealy takes care of me and them. He's not a murderer. Look somewhere else."

Nealy blushed, looked over at the rabbit cuddled in Peaches's arm, and his face morphed into that of a child. "Let's go inside, Sweetheart," he said in a soft and caring voice. "I've got Nibble's medicine in the car. It's time for another dose." He slid his sunglasses down over his eyes.

Okay, Margot conceded. *This man with gorgeous eyes, living with a gorgeous girlfriend, and surrounded by rescued animals couldn't have murdered Faye-Anne.*

"I was completely wrong," she murmured to herself. Indeed, Camille turned to look at her, and the mystified look she saw on her niece's face reflected and affirmed her own confusion. She didn't think Nealy had killed Faye-Anne either. But then, who had? Unfortunately, suspects were turning to dust and disappearing into the Mojave winds.

Then Margot looked back to see Gus, still behind them, arms crossed, an inscrutable smile plastered across his face. He hadn't said a word the entire time.

What an insufferable man.

But most disconcertingly, out of seemingly nowhere, Margot was hit with the most horrible feeling in the pit of her stomach — accompanied by the notion that they, all of them — had started down a long dark tunnel. The imagery was so vivid, its intensity startled her.

Most distressing, since she couldn't see a light at the end of that tunnel.

Where the heck are these "pictures" coming from?

After leaving Nealy's place, they decided Gus would drop them both back home, then Camille would go back to the office to do some paperwork she'd left undone Monday.

The day was still desert-bright, calm, and a nice temperature. Around seventy-five degrees, Margot guessed. If every day was like this one weather-wise, it made sense why people liked the area. She however, had felt the Mojave Desert winds, tasted its dust.

At Camille's insistence, Margot was sitting up front next to Gus, and had yet to decide if she wanted to spend any more of her day with him. Mentally reappraising Gus yet again, his smug, holierthan-thou demeanor was wearing thin. She knew she was reacting like a silly teenager, but for some reason, he seemed to bring out an immature side of her personality she wasn't proud of.

"It's a funny day today," Camille said, trying to project her voice into the front seat, and sounding like she was talking to a patient with an inadequate hearing aide. "With our new Saturday hours," she continued, "we close the clinic on Tuesdays."

"Like Chinese restaurants," Margot murmured, again remembering college days—and Chicago's wonderful Asian offerings. They'd had their favorites, of course. Out of the blue, she remembered how much Ann had loved Moo-Shu Pork, with the delicate wrappers, bean paste, and thin sliced scallion strips. She found herself salivating over remembered meals. *Harvey and his Peking Duck,* Ann always insisting on *"Just a little taste."*

Camille's cell phone rang, and brought Margot back to the present.

"Doctor Kubiak, good hearing from you." Camille's voice sounded cautious. "Hope you're not calling with bad news."

Margot heard distress in her niece's voice and turned around so she could see the expression on her face.

Camille tsked, then said, "Gosh, Carol, seems like there's always some kind of pile up on the freeway—"

Then after a moment more of listening, she answered, "No, I haven't seen Deirdre, yet. As soon as I know she's home safe, I'll give you a call."

Margot watched her niece intently as she said, "No, I haven't seen Oscar either." Then Camille quickly added, "Is Chief Reed there?"

Margot wanted to smile, but didn't. *She wants to know where her sweetie is.* The thought that Camille was in love made her heart swell, and additionally brought along the realization that she must accept Parker Reed. He was *"good enough,"* as her grandmother Thelma Edison-Hall would have proclaimed of a prospective suitor, *"for my daughter."'*

Camille closed her cell phone and sighed heavily.

"Problem?" Gus asked without taking his eyes off the road.

"Yes." She didn't elaborate, but Margot guessed what was going on, and figured Gus had too.

Margot asked, "Gusztáve, do you think we could go to your house, drop you off, and Camille and I will take the rental to her house?" She had no idea why she wanted to have the Escalade available, but she did. *Odd that.* The desire to have a car had come from nowhere.

He grumped, but said, "Sounds good to me."

After watching Margot and Camille pull out of his yard, Gus locked his gate as was his habit, then went inside—to the delight of his dogs. He wasn't a napping man, but he would take the occasional "sit down" thinking break. This was one of those few times.

He'd been in law enforcement for thirty years. Of course, he'd been a rookie once, but he'd left police work a seasoned—and he thought savvy—Chief of Police. Sure enough, NewTown, his final landing spot, was small—but he'd done his stint in LA, then San Bernardino, and garnered a couple commendations along the way.

But darn it, as sharp as he thought he was, he had yet to see any hard evidence indicating who killed Faye-Anne Miller. Nor had his infamous "gut" led the way. He didn't like that. Always in the past, he'd prided himself on sussing out the perp right from the start. Heck, gathering evidence was usually easy, once you'd figured out where to look.

Not this time.

Making matters worse was the fact Parker didn't know either. Sure, he'd latched onto Lewis as the obvious suspect—boyfriend always gets a *numero uno* position, especially if he's married. But they'd talked several times since the murder, and hadn't jointly figured out squat. The thought had entered his mind that maybe their closeness to the people surrounding Faye-Anne—all possible suspects if you're doing your job right—was putting blinders on their eyes.

163

Indeed, Parker couldn't seem to move his attention off Oscar. Sure the man was rumored around NewTown to be a "chaser"—even he knew that. But Oscar just didn't hit Gus as a killer. As for Deirdre, he knew she had a spiteful streak, but he couldn't put her in the picture as a murderer either. Petty and insecure maybe, but cold-blooded killer? He didn't think so. Besides, she'd been poisoned too.

Faye-Anne's sister Patricia, well she was his neighbor, and a darned good one. No way she'd killed her. And Nealy—just too darned goofy. True enough he wouldn't now have to get a divorce—just slide into his new life hassle free. But being a murderer just didn't fit the Nealy he knew. Puffed up and emotional sometimes, but murderer? Still, divorces were messy and expensive. And he sure hadn't seemed that concerned Faye-Anne was dead.

And the method of her murder—that was also strange. There were poisoners, and there were bludgeoners. Poor Faye-Anne had received a double whammy.

"Jeez, fellas," he told his dogs who were all splayed across his large great-room in their favorite spots—either snoozing, licking some part of their bodies, or watching him. "The meekness of poison, and the fury of bashing another human being's skull in." He shook his head. "Doesn't make sense." Or speaks to a more complicated motive than they were thinking.

Unfortunately, he reminded himself, he'd seen a lot worse done for meager amounts of cash by don't-give-a-damn lowlifes. This however felt different. *Personal.*

Then there was Ann, maybe she'd just had enough? Maybe, but like all the rest of the suspects, he knew her. Let her and Oscar store their antiques in his Quonset. And once again, he just couldn't put her in the picture.

"Tell you the truth," he said, and shook his head. "I've gotten too old for this job." His largest dog, a lab-mix named Prince barked as if he agreed. Gus laughed, and said, "Is that a comment on my age?"

Well, maybe he was a little off his game, but Parker was a young pup, and he sure seemed like he was floundering too. And he didn't want Parker to fail. Heck, he'd recommended him, helped him with connections, thought of him almost like a son. Well, not exactly a son—but he sure did like Parker—and thought him a perfect fit for NewTown. Most of all, Parker was a good cop. Gus also knew even though it wasn't Parker's case, he's the one who would carry the shame if it went unsolved. Not Hollist, and not Thompson.

When his phone rang, Gus was thinking about his Quonset hut. He wasn't sure exactly why, but something was bothering him about it. What had that snooty Margot woman said on their tour— something about it being a good place to hide something you didn't want found? Seemed silly at the time—just like the woman herself— *everywhere* in the Mojave was a good place to hide things.

He retraced his thoughts. *No,* the woman was not silly. But she certainly didn't fit. So why was he so concerned about how she acted? He sighed thinking about her—causing Prince, now the only dog still awake and paying attention to him to turn his head sideways. He'd almost given himself away to her—knowing about the Bobs at Riverview—that he was born in Chicago, lived there through high school.

Jeez. After all these years you'd think I'd know better. He was a Mojave desert-rat now, and he wanted it to stay that way. It was a minor lie, but it was *his* lie.

He picked up the receiver on the third ring as was his practice. Never wanted to seem too eager. Whoever was calling was local, knew his home number. Strangers called on his cell phone. A cell phone with the best provider in the area, and he probably should tell Margot about the company—not that he thought she was staying. He kind of went a little far on the "old coot" bit and phone reception.

"Yeah," he said into the receiver.

"Come quick!" The voice on the phone was throaty, and spoke in a low hiss. A woman he thought. "He's got me," the voice sucked in air as if in distress. "Please, please…help me."

It was a woman, Gus was sure of it. Deirdre? *No,* she was probably still in the hospital. Doc Madison? Sounded more like Ms.

Margot. "Oh, no," he moaned out loud, then demanded, "Who is this?"

The voice lowered, a barely audible whisper. "He's got me in the empty mobile east of the Bagdad." The line went dead.

In minutes he was in his truck proceeding toward the Bagdad Café on National Trails—only taking the time to make sure his dogs were locked safely inside the house, but leaving his gate wide open. As he drove off he could hear them voicing their complaint. He was leaving without them, and why was he going anyway this time of day?

It was illegal to use a cell phone while driving in California. He did it anyway. He might need the younger Parker. *Hell of a thing, getting old.* No reception—*emergency calls only*— his phone mocked his prior superior thoughts. *He,* evidently also needed a new provider.

Chapter Six

Tuesday Still

Oscar was sitting in the dark on some stool-like thing, he thought—his arms wrapped around his body—and more scared than he'd ever been in his life.

But something within had brought him here. An unknown compulsion he couldn't control. *Someone* had told him to come here, hadn't they? *Someone* using him as a pawn—bait in a trap. *Someone* he trusted. *Someone* who knew his state. He felt his body shudder uncontrollably.

His state? Good God. Even he didn't know what his "state" was. He remembered his friend Harvey had often used the term, starting his notes with, *The patient's state of health.* He sure wished Harvey was here now, he'd know what was going on. Harvey had been a great doctor, in capital letters. And he could see that same intelligence, same dedication in Camille. Probably because Camille had so often looked to her uncle for advice.

Good old Harvey hadn't even objected when he'd wanted to marry Ann all those years ago—claiming there really hadn't been anything between him and Ann. Well, maybe not from Harvey's perspective, but Ann, well he'd never been completely sure she'd gotten over Harvey. *But Ann married me.*

"And I've failed her." He could hear his voice quiver on dank air. Even sounded like a whimper. He released one arm from his vice-grip around his torso for a second and swiped his eyes to make sure he wasn't crying. *Dry.* At least he hadn't turned into a blubbering fool.

He wasn't even sure how he'd physically gotten here. Driven himself? But here he was hidden out in the back of Gus's dirty old hut. And *once again*, he tried to fathom why his body had followed his mind's incomprehensible and silly lead.

"I'm not in control," he whispered. This time on hearing his own voice, he didn't recognize it—*some stranger is sending words out through my mouth*.

He felt like he was shaking again, but when he looked down at his arms, they were tight, but still. Was he here for a purpose? *Of course I am*. And if so, what could he possibly want or need here? Then he remembered his earlier conclusion. He was a pawn in *someone's* game. *Someone* he trusted, *someone* who knew what was going on with him.

"Wish I did." This time Oscar's voice seemed to echo for miles through the hut stretching before him. *The world's longest Quonset hut.* He laughed. It wasn't, he'd looked it up once.

Now he really did want to cry. Even though he couldn't see much, Oscar knew the place was dirty—and it smelled awful. Full of other's people's discards they hoped were treasures. Mostly remnants of failed ideas, and lost dreams.

Again, he questioned how he'd gotten here. Must have driven—but he couldn't remember driving, arriving, or parking. At last, a picture flashed across eyes—his Honda, dusty and scuffed-up a little—parked half-skewed in scrub-desert at the very back of the hut. He'd come in the back door.

"But I still don't know why I'm here." This time his words were a plaintive whimper into what felt like an all encompassing darkness. But then again, for a brief moment, he gained control of his mind and remembered bumping across the landscape—not really on the road—but with a destination. *Here.*

He managed a steadying deep breath, but the dust in the air remained heavy, and he coughed—the sound of his discomfort disappearing into the blackness ahead—finally dissipating somewhere between him and the front of the hut. Then he remembered the rows of small compartments—endless, it had seemed, when looking down from the front.

"Okay, okay," he said, shaking his head. The Quonset hut held his thoughts, and this time he squinted hard into the darkness. A *darkness* shrouding barely-discernible shadows of piles and stacks of stuff—boxes, furniture, equipment—and making them seem like blurry floating apparitions. All in front of him. *And me, last in the row of discards.*

With another long breath, followed by another cough, he made himself unwrap his arms from around his body, then clasp his hands tightly on his lap. He could barely see his own appendages, but he could *feel* himself squeeze his fingers together to the point of pain.

The darkness ahead was soundless. *Wait, did he hear something?* Somewhere in front of him, further toward the middle of the hut? Sounded like a chair, scraping against concrete? No, couldn't be. Who else would possibly be here tonight? Next he heard distant thunder—deep and rolling. Couldn't be either. Never rains in NewTown.

Oscar dropped his head into his hands, and rubbed his face as hard as he could. But he just couldn't get his thoughts to make sense. Or *make* himself stand up, *make* himself leave this awful place.

He wished for a Baby Ruth—for any kind of candy bar.

And he still hadn't figured out why he'd come here.

Was it to die?

Deirdre felt she was trapped in the middle. *Story of my life.* Funny how things turn out, but here she was once again—maybe experiencing the last moments of her life—between a "star" and a "cherished one"—never successfully escaping the sibling dynamics of her childhood. *In the middle,* with nobody paying attention. Nobody to care. Admittedly, she was still woozy, possibly hallucinating a bit from hospital drugs, but *oh yes*, she'd heard Doc Lewis, the "cherished one" speak behind her, and the "star" in the front section.

169

What a devastating day this had turned out to be. First, passing out at the clinic—then waking up in the hospital connected to tubes with her stomach aching like hell. Then she'd been sprung out of the hospital, only to be gagged and tied up in a chair chained to a post or beam in this horrible place. She couldn't yell, or wiggle around—and *oh my God*—she prayed, she wouldn't have to go to the bathroom before she was rescued. *Or died.*

Just because it finally came to me, there were four Faye-Anne cups, not three like everyone else had. She shouldn't have said anything, but she would have never guessed she was placing her trust in the murderer. *A complete surprise.* And me, a trained nurse—supposedly observant.

At least she hadn't been blindfolded, and at first, it had been black as tar she'd seen poured on roofs. She'd lost track of time, but eventually her eyes had adjusted ever so slightly, even in this all encompassing darkness. But it had taken awhile.

She tried licking her lips around the gag—some kind of material—and found her bottom lip was raw from somehow unconsciously chewing on it underneath the horrible cloth. She needed to stop doing that immediately. *Hah!* What difference did a bad habit make if you're dead? Who'd care if she'd chewed on her lip? The Medical Examiner?

Suddenly a wave of nausea swept through her—so intense that it made her head swim. *If I could just yell out and cry.* She hadn't eaten anything since her gastric lavage. *Psychological*, that was what it was. Time spent in her Drug Therapy and Poison Treatment classes came back—and for the first time in her life, Deirdre felt regret. Regret she hadn't gone on to become a psychologist, or a shrink like her smart older sister thought she should have. *Too late now.*

She was barely breathing, and it was heard to swallow—but both nostrils were wide open. It was this place that was freaking her out, causing her physical reactions. Her eyes had adjusted to her surroundings—but it was so dark, so smelly—and she felt what she guessed were spiders crawling on her foot. Though spiders didn't really bother her. But the scratching sounds she could hear in the distance she was sure were mice. And mice she didn't like one darned bit. If she could just wriggle around a bit.

She was imprisoned somewhere in the middle of Mr. Martinez's Quonset hut—unable to talk or move. Her body tried to laugh out loud, and she almost choked. *That was her life alright, always somewhere in the middle.* Never the star, or the dullard either. *The one in the middle.*

She felt her emotional pendulum swing, swooshing from wanting to laugh, to crying in self-pity—then she saw Doc Lewis's face in her mind's eye—how kind he'd been to her. At least for a little while someone had cared—respected her credentials and abilities. He realized how important her RN training was. Well, in this her death knoll, she would forgive him his dalliance with Faye-Anne. A nice man like that, so easily swayed by her coquettish ways.

I'm going to die tonight.

Deirdre hadn't been to church in years. Her excuse had been the hassle of driving into Barstow, the closest Catholic Church around. Though, a lot had to do with the mass nowadays. It just wasn't the same without the Latin.

Somewhere in the recesses of her memory, the words came, *Pater noster, qui es in caelis, sanctificetur nomen tuum. Adveniat regnum tuum. Fiat voluntas tua, sicut in caelo et in terra—*

A sound? A door opening? Thunder?

Couldn't be. It never rained in NewTown.

Parker was sitting at the side of her desk, and Camille could feel his stare.

"Okay, okay," she conceded, turning away from her monitor and meeting his eyes. "It says there's a possibility of rain in NewTown." He was smiling smugly back at her. "But," she continued undeterred, "that doesn't mean squat. Often when they claim it's going to rain, we don't get a drop." She cleared her throat and raised her chin. "Even I know that, and I'm a newcomer." Indeed, her patients had repeated over and over, in various ways, *"It never rains in NewTown."*

"I'm telling you," he said, and leaned back in his chair. "That was thunder I heard."

It had sounded like thunder to her too, but she wasn't about to give in. She was fighting a foul mood, and as despicable as it might be, Parker was getting the brunt of her irritation. "Could have been a mining blast," she said, knowing it wasn't. "Or a sonic boom."

"I can tell the difference." He shook his head, then tsked through his teeth and out the corner of his mouth. "Why are you being so obstinate?"

She blurted out, "Because we don't know where Oscar is and *you* haven't figured out who killed Faye-Anne." Seeing the expression on his face, she immediately apologized. "Oh, Parker, I'm sorry." Camille stretched her hand out toward him. "I know you're doing everything you can." She saw his expression soften. "And you've been wonderful about sharing information, and with Oscar running off..." She forced a smile. "You want to go for that drink we missed Friday night at Velma's?"

He sat up straight and laughed out loud. Then he took her hand, gave it a long but gentle squeeze, finally letting go with a caressing motion. "You sure know how to wound a man, then swoop in with ER care."

She liked his medical analogy, and smiled to herself. "I'm just worried." *He needs to understand.* "Something is going on with Oscar." She held up her hand. "And I mean medically." She paused. "Something's not right."

"Don't tell me you're starting an insanity defense for him already?" His tone was teasing.

But Camille thought there was some truth-telling in his words. "I mean, physically," she explained.

He stood up and said, "Hmm."

"Are you leaving?" She wanted to talk more.

Parker stared at her for a moment before saying, "Meeting Hollist in town. He has a ME report for me." His expression told her he was expecting some news. "And they've had a power outage. Can't fax or email. Called me on his cell." Then he smiled warmly, and added, "I'll call you as soon as I get back to town. I *would* like to have that drink."

"You think we'll find out what killed poor Faye-Anne? Poison or the blow to the head?" she asked.

"Yep. Maybe even a murder weapon."

"You've already decided on cause?"

"Yep."

Camille shook her head, but knew she was also smiling. She walked with him to the back door, wanting to make sure it was locked behind him. Faye-Anne's death had definitely made her cautious.

In mental lockstep, Parker said on leaving, "Make sure you keep this door locked. And call nine-one-one if you hear anything strange." He leaned forward, almost as if to kiss her. Instead, he stared hard into her eyes. "Then, you call me."

Camille nodded. "First nine-one-one, then you." Somewhere in her heart, genuine caring advanced a step, and she said softly, "I'm looking forward to tonight."

"Me too," he said, then released her from his piercing stare — and before she could say more — he was gone.

After she watched him pull out of the clinic's back parking lot, Camille locked up and went back to her office, intending to finish her paperwork. But thoughts of Faye-Anne, Oscar, and Deirdre — even Auntie Marg, just wouldn't go away. Patient ailments, for once, were pushed aside.

Back sitting at her desk, she switched her computer off, turned slightly toward the wall, and stared at her R. C. Gorman 'Navajo Indian Pottery Keeper' print. She'd purchased it in Old Albuquerque, at some little shop in the square. She'd thought the print lovely, and oddly calming. And that's what she needed right now. Calm.

Deirdre came front and center in her mind. Not that she and the Navajo woman looked alike, but because of the subtle understatement, even with the strong dramatic lines of the painting.

Deirdre was the steady one, the one nobody paid attention to. A plain-Jane everywoman. Camille suspected there was passion there, nonetheless.

She tried calling Deirdre's number for the third time since arriving back at the clinic, but no answer. She left a quick callback message. Camille also wanted to know if anyone had seen Oscar. So, she also gave Ann a call. No answer there either—but with Ann, she didn't bother leaving a message.

Then there was her aunt and her old college friends. So strange that—Ann, Oscar, Uncle Harvey, and Auntie Marg going to school together. She'd known and stored somewhere in her brain the knowledge they'd all gone to Northwestern, but clearly had never connected the dots.

She closed her eyes, willed her brain to float, and realized she had the same feeling about Faye-Anne's murder and Deirdre's attempted murder—that she was failing to connect the dots.

"Because I don't like where the dots are leading," she said opening her eyes and taking in Gorman's painting again. There was no one around to bounce her thoughts off, but speaking out loud felt good. "Oh, Oscar," she bemoaned. "I like it here." It was the first time she'd admitted that fact, but wasn't surprised by her self-revelation. *And now I think you've gone and killed a lovely young woman, and attempted to kill another.*

Camille felt rising within a sadness she feared might become uncontrollable, making her feel helpless and vulnerable. In fact, she *was* helpless, as a combination of disappointment, sadness, grief, loneliness, and even guilt swept over her like an ocean wave—leaving her momentarily awash in misery—with salty tears stinging the corners of her mouth.

She didn't cry often, didn't like how it left her feeling. *I think Auntie Marg is like that too.* "Cold fish, the two of us." Her spoken words and the picture of her mother Meredith helped her push back her emotional ocean—at least for the time being. Meredith, she remembered quite well, would tear-up at the drop of a hat. With a long deep breath and the memory of her mother's exciting and volatile personality, Camille thought she might even feel a smile tugging the corners of her mouth.

But darn it. Her heart so much didn't want Oscar to be a murderer. On top of that, she was also concerned he was in the middle of a physical ailment of some kind. *And he's all alone out there somewhere.*

She stood up and said, "I need some tea."

As Camille headed down the hall toward the break room—she remembered something else that was bothering her. Did she notice there were one too many insulated cups with Faye-Anne's name on them? But before she could reach their break room, she heard her phone ring. She managed to get back to her desk before the call went to voicemail.

The voice on the other end was deep, low in volume, and hurried and anxious almost to the point of a hiss.

"This is Gus. I'm at my hut."

Camille didn't think it sounded a lot like Gus, but it certainly could be. Before she could respond, the voice continued, "I've got your killer corralled and Parker's here with me. Parker asked me to call and make sure you're okay."

"I'll come there right away."

"No."

"You can't stop me—"

"If you insist." His voice was now barely audible. The phone reception was deteriorating.

"Where's Auntie Marg? Aren't you driving her?"

"She's here too."

Poor Auntie. "I'm coming now!" Camille could hear near hysteria in her own voice. *I have to calm down.*

She hung up, made herself take a moment, then take another long slow deep breath. She needed to lead with her logical mind, not her emotions. She had left her aunt at home to rest a bit, have some time to herself. Quickly she found her cell phone and dialed her home number. It rang until her answering machine kicked-on. She left a short message to call her cell. Next she dialed Margot's cell phone. No answer. She left a voicemail.

Why doesn't anyone answer their phone for goodness' sake?

Camille didn't pray often, but she heard herself say, "Dear God, please don't let Oscar be the murderer Gus and Parker have in custody—and please, please, let Auntie Marg be okay."

Silly kind of prayer. Camille grabbed her keys then rushed out the back door—thinking how just last Friday, she'd come through that very door, Parker only steps behind her—scared to see Faye-Anne's lifeless body. Death by illness was one thing. Death by foul play, quite another.

"Dear, dear Faye-Anne," she said. "I'm so sorry you were murdered." She fought down the lump in her throat, and swiped an escaping tear with the back of her hand. "And I'm very sorry I wasn't nicer to you."

If Oscar murdered Faye-Anne—there was nothing she could do about it now—except maybe wish God would send her mentor straight to hell—no matter how fond she was of him.

Oozie just wouldn't stop howling no matter how much Patricia tried to cajole her beloved Saint Bernard. Something horrible was going on, and Oozie knew it. Her pup had made the same woebegone, ear splitting, and heart-wrenching moans the night Faye-Anne was murdered.

Thoughts of her sister coupled with Oozie's canine proclamations broke through the barrier she'd so carefully set up to control her grief. The memories, the surprise, the regrets—all overwhelmed her at last.

In the distance she heard thunder—first as a clap, then a rolling boom—but paid no heed. It never rained in NewTown.

Woman and canine friend huddled together as one, sat on the cold tile in their entryway—with Oozie's snout raised and Patricia's arms around her. And while Oozie complained morosely to the heavens over *events* about to unravel, Patricia drenched her thick coat with salty tears over an *event* she couldn't understand or undo. Her sister's death.

The sky above was dark, like it was about to rain. But Margot distinctly remembered Gusztáve proclaiming it seldom rained in NewTown. She had just risen from what Harvey called a cat-nap, and was once again at Camille's kitchen window taking in her oleander-edged garden.

She suspected Camille had left her home to have some time alone. She *was* rather tired after this morning's confrontation with Nealy, and it must have shown in her face. *Camille is so thoughtful. Like Harvey.*

Not that she needed or wanted time away from her niece. No matter how this visit turned out on other fronts, one thing was sure. She now realized with every fiber of her being how much she needed Camille's love—and in turn, how much she loved her. And on another level, this visit had caused her to realize Camille thought of her as representing the "older generation." Meredith and Harvey were deceased, but for Camille—she, Gray, and Oscar were clearly life-anchors as she started her adult working life.

Margot warmed, remembering how before Camille headed back to the clinic, she had hugged her and whispered, "I don't know what I'd do without you and dad." They'd held that hug for several long moments.

She breathed deeply, and tried sneaking a peek through the hedge. The contortionist maneuver was easier this time, but she saw nothing. In fact, it didn't even look like Ann was home. She'd guessed Ann had picked up Deirdre at the hospital—but now with second thought, she wasn't so sure that was correct. Camille hadn't actually said.

"Could something have happened to them?" she asked Dogue sitting in his usual under-the-arch watching spot. "Well, worrying won't help."

He barked his agreement.

All in all she was glad Gray had dragged her out here, and on an impulse, she retrieved her cell phone from the bedroom, Dogue following, and returned to her window view.

When Gray answered after only two rings, the reception was scratchy and he sounded out of breath. "Are you all right," she yelled into the phone.

"No." He sounded breathless. "Terrible headache, Marg. I'll call you back—"

"Gray, wait." She was suddenly afraid—and not her recent apprehensions. Something else.

"On my property again…" His voice faded.

"Who's on your property?" She heard scraping, maybe thrashing. "Are you at home?" No answer, but she thought she heard Gray cough, then groan. Then only static. "Gray!" she demanded. The line was dead. Quickly she redialed, but no signal.

Now on top of everything else, something horrible seemed to be happening with her brother and she was well over two hours away. *If I leave right away.*

"Dogue, I need to call Camille." The German Shepherd came over at the mention of his name.

Camille's home phone rang, and she rushed over to the kitchen desk to answer.

"Doc Madison?" the caller asked. Margot recognized Patricia's voice.

"No, Dear. It's her Aunt Margot."

"Oh good." She sounded relieved. "Do you know where Gus is?" She snatched a breath, then rushed on, "I can't reach the Doc or Gus."

"What's the matter?" Margot asked trying to keep her voice level and calm, but she could feel her heart start to race, the blood pound in her ears.

"It's Oozie. She *knows* something horrible is about to happen."

Patricia's words were crazy. Nonetheless, she didn't dismiss them.

A boom of thunder made her jump, and phone in hand, Margot turned and rushed back to the window, almost tripping over Dogue in the process. Then she saw lightning shoot downward through the sky to the east, followed by another boom, this time rolling and ear throbbing.

"It's a big storm," Patricia answered her unanswered question. "It's all over the area." She sounded a little calmer.

Margot tried to gather her thoughts. "What do you think Oozie is trying to tell you? And what do you think Camille or Gusztáve have to do with it?"

"I don't know." Suddenly Patricia's voice sounded worn out— emotionally spent. "I shouldn't have called."

"No, no," Margot rushed to assure her. "Tell you what Patricia—I have a car."

"Oozie thinks," quickly Patricia took her words back, "I mean, *I* think it has something to do with Gus."

Margot's decision came easy. "I'm coming your way." She felt she now knew where she was directionally. NewTown as it turned out, wasn't that complicated. "I'm only maybe five miles away, right? You're at the end of Tappy road, and Gusztáve's place is before yours." Sunday morning came back to her in a flash. *Just a couple days ago.* "Right?"

Inanely, she noted her travel-suit was turning out as durable as advertised—no need to change.

Another rolling peel of thunder made her look out the window. Once again, she'd missed the preceding lightning.

Parker realized he'd stayed in town too long. *Damn it.* He could feel the blood pounding in his temples. "Camille probably has some medical term for this," he scoffed into the interior of his jeep.

His strobe was on, but no siren—I-40 was almost empty except for a few eighteen-wheelers.

For him, the best way to overcome fear, was to realize and accept the worst he thought was about to happen. Didn't help this time—made it worse. He was now very much afraid.

Afraid I'm too damn late.

Alone in his Jeep, Parker almost slammed his fist against the steering wheel, but in the last millisecond remembered the last time he'd done that, his knuckles and wrist hurt for a week afterwards. Instead, he cursed again, loudly.

Back in Hollist's office, it had taken him forever to actually hand over the reports so he could read them. He couldn't really blame Hollist. If you get two code-3's in a row, a 10-15, then a 10-71, you deal with them first. The NewTown cop, though an impatient "brother," would just have to wait. A shooting and a prisoner in custody came first.

Finally, the two men were able to read Faye-Anne's autopsy and forensic reports, courtesy of the San Bernardino Coroner's office and the Bureau of Forensic Services. Poisoning was oleander, toxicity not enough to cause respiratory failure, but brain damage for sure.

Remembering, he caught his breath, sniffed, and shifted his weight in his seat. Hardened as he was to dead bodies, reports, the aftermath of murder—he'd known Faye-Anne a long time—and the lump rising in his throat was very real. The image of her on the ME's table was not pleasant, to say the least. *A woman I once wanted to date.*

There were dark ominous clouds crowding the sky above Barstow, and he could see through Hollist's dingy office window it was getting worse east on Route 66. He guessed at the time—that just about where NewTown was—it was either about to rain, or already coming down.

Now heading back to NewTown, the interstate was still wide open. He pushed his speed; it wasn't yet raining where he was.

"Never listens to me," he said about Camille and his rain forecast. Nonetheless, his mind was still dealing with images of Faye-Anne—in Oscar's office, and in the morgue.

Cause of death was from a blunt instrument—a very odd-shaped blunt instrument yet to be determined. But Parker knew what it was, he'd admired it before. And he knew who it belonged to—and *now* that he knew, it all made sense.

Camille had not answered her cell. Neither had Margot. Even Gus wasn't picking up. *Where the hell was he?* Maybe Gus figured it out too—knew who'd murdered Faye-Anne? Maybe *he'd* get there in time.

Thunder in the distance. Then he saw the lightning—but that didn't make sense. Didn't the lightning and thunder happen at the same time? But sound was slower than light—if I'd gone to grad school. No, he knew perfectly well about the speed of light and sound—he'd just missed seeing the earlier bolt.

Why was he thinking about thunder, lightning, and grad school? This time he did slam his fist on the steering wheel. And as expected, it hurt. People he cared about were in mortal danger, and here he was, at least half an hour away from helping them.

He switched on his multidirectional siren—irrationally hoping its ear-piercing wails would get him there faster. He remembered occasionally picking up Jerome's Kingman, Arizona pursuits, and weird as it was, Parker remembered his exact thought Sunday morning. *Often the way with catching the criminals—too far away.* This time, however, he wasn't talking about just catching a criminal. It was also about saving a life.

As a bolt of lightning shot through the sky to his east, Gus slammed closed the back door of the dilapidated fifth-wheel trailer hard enough to cause one of its two rusted hinges to finally give way. As the dinged and rusted door collapsed and sagged, a momentous clap of thunder marked this latest indignity.

Gus remembered when the property owners had parked their gleaming new possession on this parcel fronting Route 66, with I-40 as its backyard. They planned on living in the camper quarters while building their dream house. Turned out, after just a few months, the couple realized the Mojave was not their "cup of tea." Now, only five years later, the trailer stood as a monument to the power of sun, sand, wind, and unchecked vandalism—its faded green color barely recognizable, its windows broken, tires flat, the inside stripped almost bare.

The now down-and-out camper shell was empty. Mocking him.

He'd been tricked—sent on a wild-goose-hunt. He'd worn his Stetson, the brim and crown shaped just the way he wanted. But he took it off, and after slapping his forehead with the heel of his hand, he threw his beloved felt cattleman-styled hat to the ground—causing sand and dust to fly up around his feet and mix with the building storm winds, swirling and spinning eastward. He was darned mad, and on top of that, a very big storm was coming.

Still, he immediately regretted his anger, and quickly retrieved his Stetson before it headed east, too.

"Fooled me like a new born baby." It didn't matter his words were taken by the wind, and no one else was around to hear. *Someone wanted to get me away from the house.* Then he realized where he should be. "My hut."

At last, his "gut" had kicked in, and he thought he knew who'd been on the phone—who'd suckered him. Gus sure hoped he was wrong, but figured he wasn't. As he rushed to get in his truck and head home, he also realized how worried he was about that silly Margot woman.

With a flash—more like a jump—Camille returned to the conscious world, and her first realization was she'd been chloroformed. For a moment, nausea and dizziness almost sent her back to unconsciousness, but she forced a rush of rapid breaths to keep from passing back out.

What had happened?

Slowly, her symptoms and accompanying panic decreased a little, only to be followed by a jumble of medical concerns rushing through her head. *Has my central nervous system been depressed? My exposure was probably not high enough—but then there's cardiac arrhythmias. I do feel dizzy, my head hurts like hell, I'm still slightly nauseated. Oh my God, do I have kidney damage?*

She tried to speak, *to calm* herself, *to organize* her thoughts, *to minimize* her fears—but she couldn't speak, her lips wouldn't seem to move. *A light anesthesia drug too? Versed, Propetol?* Her hands wouldn't move either.

Auntie Marg, Auntie Marg—her mind screamed. I'm in Gus's hut. How she knew that, she wasn't sure. *It was that awful road.* Yes, even in her semi-conscious chloroform dream-world, she must have felt the effects of Tappy Road.

Camille took a string of long, deep breaths—in and out, in and out. At least her respiratory functions were working.

Then she tasted "it," even felt it crawling along her arms. *No mistake,* Evil was in the air. She'd seen its handiwork in Cook County Hospital, in the morgue in San Diego—in Oscar's office looking at Faye-Anne's body.

She couldn't fight "it" though—immobilized with drugs. She even thought she heard Auntie Marg talking, and she knew that couldn't be. *Could it?*

Something beyond her life experiences told Margot to stop at Gusztáve's. *Do not* go all the way down to Patricia's.

After she made the turn through Gus's open gate, lights off, she drove slowly past his house to within fifteen or so feet of the hut's entrance. Through the storm, she couldn't hear his dogs bark, but knew they were around somewhere. She hoped the sound of gravel crunching under her wheels had been lost in the light and sound show from above, and they wouldn't start barking. Or worse, howling.

She was scared beyond what she could imagine. Maybe she *should* go on to Patricia's. *No*, she was being pulled here—*here to Gusztáve's Quonset hut.*

In minutes, dark thick clouds, heavy with rain had turned late afternoon into night, and she could see puddles were forming in Gusztáve's driveway—all the way to his hut.

Never rains in NewTown.

Margot wanted to sit and wait for a moment—gather her thoughts, prepare. She couldn't. *Time is of the essence.* Without further thought or hesitation, in quick succession she patted Paladin in her right suit-jacket pocket, checked her cell phone was in the other, left the keys in the ignition, and stepped down out of the SUV. The door seemed unusually heavy, but Margot guessed that was fear—*trying to hold me back.* Immediately her feet became soaking wet, and also heavy. The ground was mush; nonetheless she crossed the ten or so feet from the car to the hut's entrance quickly and sure footedly.

In seconds, she was drenched—and chilled to the bone.

The huts front door window was dark. *Darker than before—if that were possible.* And now, she could hear Gusztáve's dogs barking—and even thought she heard a plaintiff canine howling in the far distance.

Oozie?

In seconds she opened the unlocked door, and watched it swing inside—again with precision—and took the step down into what Margot perceived as hell. Her heart was racing, seemed like she could feel it beating in her throat, but knew that was impossible.

No toe stubbing tonight.

Ahead was darkness. *A soundless darkness.* And all-encompassing. At least it was dry, and warmer. She dared not speak, though—couldn't actually. Faye-Anne's killer was present, and every fiber of her body knew it.

A soundless darkness, except for the killer's labored breathing.

Slowly Margot stepped forward—each footfall a life transforming event as she felt herself become a person she did not know. She was no longer walking on the compressed dirt in Bjorn walking shoes. Instead, she felt as if she were walking on air, and inexplicably knew where the light-pull was—and that somehow her hand would find it. *I know I will.* She saw on a never-before tapped-into part of her mind's eye, exactly what was going on in Gusztáve's Mojave Quonset hut—albeit in muted gray tones. *No Technicolor second-sight for me.*

All her premonitions, anxieties, psychic glimpses were culminating in these few moments. *Moments that matter more than anything else in my whole life.*

She remembered her awful nightmare in Gray's casita bedroom the night before heading to NewTown. *I will not let Camille be harmed.*

Margot found her voice. "I know you're there," she said, with a new and different version of Margot in control.

"I've been waiting."

Margot, laughed, once—and harsher than usual. "Thirty plus years." She took a silent step forward. The light pull was near, but she needed to be exactly underneath. There was no light source—it would take awhile for their eyes to adjust to this darkness—but eventually they would. Now was her only chance.

"Camille," Margot said into the blackness. "If you can hear me sweetheart, I'm here for you."

"You can't possibly see her."

"Did you drug her? I know you have a gun pointed at Camille's head."

"You don't know anything."

"I know you can't see me," Margot said. "But I know about past, present, and future," She heard a sharp intake of breath from Faye-Anne's killer. "The past—Oscar—is way at the end of this miserable place. Deirdre, the present, is somewhere around the middle. And my niece, the future—is but a few feet away."

Just a few inches to my right—so close. Margot slipped her right hand into her pocket and wrapped her fingers around Paladin and prayed she wouldn't need her trusty friend. She would have to find

185

the light-pull with her left. This version of Margot Madison-Cross was not only intuitive, but also ambidextrous and confident.

"You were always the smart one." Ann Lewis took a deep breath. "You and that arrogant husband of yours."

"You can't stay here for long." Margot took a half step to the right. She had to be in the perfect spot. "Even with the oxygen. Too much dust."

Now! She reached up, the string was there—and she pulled on it—hard. The light was not bright, barely a sixty-watt bulb, but the contrast and the suddenness made the now visible Ann—with a .38 pointed at Camille's skull—blink, and move her arm.

Margot released her hand from Paladin, rushed at Ann and pushed her backwards against a table of "treasures." Ann's gun went flying, but Margot took no chances, and yanked the plastic oxygen cannula from her nose.

She pressed close against Ann and felt again for Paladin. *I'll shoot her dead.* It took all the will power Margot had to fight against an almost unstoppable compulsion to bring justice to Ann. Kill her dead for what she did to Camille's nurse and poor Deirdre. But she couldn't. This was not Margot Madison-Cross—not even this version, not *any* version.

Ann was gasping for breath.

How can I shoot someone who needs tubes in her nose and an oxygen tank to breathe? Then she looked back and saw Camille's sweet face— her eyes closed, her condition unknown, and within a blink her fingers were wrapped around her little derringer. At that moment, she hated Ann.

Before Margot could bring the gun out of her pocket, Gus charged through the door, a rifle in his hands—rain seemingly dripping from all parts of his body. It took him a moment to take in the scene, then proclaim, "Good God, woman, I was scared half to death." His words were heavy with relief.

Margot pulled herself off Ann, and stepped back. She looked to Camille slumped in a huge dining chair and went to her side. She sat on the chair arm, pulled Camille in to rest against her chest, and checked for a pulse on her wrist. She thought it should be stronger. She could smell chloroform, and took that as a good sign—better that, than poison. Through all her raging emotions and thoughts, she heard Gusztáve talking to 911 on his cell phone. *Reception, thank goodness.*

Ann was still leaning precariously against what Margot could now see was a decrepit wooden display case. She had dropped her head, cupped her face in her hands, and was now brutally rubbing her eyes with the heels of her hands. Her breathing sounded awful.

Gus lowered his rifle, and mumbled looking at Ann, "And this is why you wanted me to bring a key to your house?"

Ann stopped rubbing her eyes, and cried out in a scratchy voice, "My air, my air."

Margot refused to even look at her. Gus found the plastic tube and carefully handed it to her.

When Ann was able to speak, her voice sounded defeated. "Do you know how lonely it is to never fit in? Always being the odd one out." She shook her head miserably. "Even in kindergarten, I was the one who had to wear leggings, the one with aching ankles. The one who didn't like graham crackers and milk."

Margot thought, *who cares?*—and was surprised at her own harshness and lack of empathy. After a couple seconds of thought, she said, "You're a crazy, deluded murderer. You were never the odd-woman-out, but the center of attention. The beautiful one everyone envied. If you felt lonely, it wasn't because you didn't have friends that cared." Margot shook her head in disbelief. "You're absolutely..." The right word would not come.

"Looney tunes," Gus said.

Camille's eyes fluttered and she said, "Auntie Marg?" Her voice was barely audible.

Quickly, Margot felt for a pulse again, this time at Camille's carotid artery with her left hand, while continuing to caress her head in her right arm. Her pulse was strong and regular. She heard herself sigh from relief, and looked to Gus, whose face indicated help was on the way.

Camille's eyes opened, and amazingly she smiled — then said groggily, but with joy, "I know what's wrong with Oscar." She wiggled her body around, and sat up straighter. "I think he's in the back of the hut."

"What?" Gus demanded, looking back and forth between the two women and Ann as she slid to the dusty floor in defeat. "Oscar?"

"I know," Margot said, her voice calm and knowing. "And Deirdre."

"What the hell?" Gus looked incredulous, but immediately flipped his phone open again. Margot waited until she heard him say, "Send three rigs instead of one."

"And Harvey," Ann was muttering. "We belonged together. He was my world, you know." She tried to push herself up, but fell back. "We had the same tastes, liked the same foods."

All of a sudden, it came back to Margot how much Ann had loved Moo-shu pork, with *the delicate wrappers, bean paste, and thin sliced scallion strips.* So had Harvey. *Especially Harvey.* Then Gusztáve's words also returned — *'Take the time to pay attention to where you've been.'*

"Hypoglycemia," Camille blurted out. "Oscar has hypoglycemia. The symptoms all fit." She dropped back against Margot. "And he didn't kill Faye-Anne, he didn't kill Faye-Anne." She smiled. "My Doctor Kildare."

Margot took her attention off her niece for a moment and looked at Ann. *I should have seen it right off.* Ann had loved Harvey, and she — Margot Madison-Cross had taken him away from her.

"What are you looking at?" Ann whimpered.

Margot said, slowly, softly, and with genuine sadness. "I'm sorry you have cancer."

"How do you know that?" Ann demanded half heartedly.

"Your wig, your compromised immune system."

"Always so smart." Ann laughed, sounding unhinged, almost hysterical. "And Oscar cheated on me. Again, and again. Knowing how ill I was."

Margot looked around to see if Gusztáve was noticing Ann's behavior—*I really don't want to handle her alone, maybe have to shoot her.* But he had disappeared. Then a light came on further down the length of the hut in what she thought was the next "room," then another, then another—*four lights maybe?*

He was searching for Deirdre and Oscar. Taking care of them. *Lovely man.* Before she could think further about the ramifications of what she'd just thought, she heard sirens in the distance.

"The cavalry is arriving," she told Camille, and stroked her face. "Or is that too old-fashioned a saying?"

Camille smiled up to her. "Not if you watch the old movie channels."

To Ann, Margot said, "Do you remember *Primum Non Nocere?* Father Timothy repeating that at the beginning of every Latin class?"

"Ha," Ann scoffed in return. "*You've* done a lot of harm in your life. You're by no means an innocent. You, you, you…"

Margot heard Ann break into sobs. She couldn't look. In the distance, down from Gusztáve's seemingly infinite tunnel, she thought she heard Deirdre's voice. *Thank God she's alive.*

To Ann she said, "How could you poison two young women in the prime of their lives?" Margot felt her anger returning. "And bludgeon Faye-Anne?" The picture Camille had painted of her nurse's body lying across Oscar's desk had not been pleasant. "And manipulated Oscar in his sickened state?"

The meager light *blinked*, and a clap of thunder rattled the hut. For Margot, time also *blinked*, and she understood about Gray— without knowing how. An insight, she figured, like Camille on Oscar's condition. Based on the accumulation of bits-and-pieces finally fitting together into a recognizable picture. A puzzle, *fait accompli.*

Ann hadn't moved, but the thunder seemed to have energized her a bit. "You can't prove a thing," she said.

Weariness with Ann and fear for Gray replaced Margot's ire, and she said in a tired voice, ""I think Chief Reed will want to look at that scimitar over there. I'm guessing there's blood on it." *Not precious* rubies. But Faye-Anne's life blood. *And there was a .38 around in the junk— and treasures—with Ann's prints on it.*

Ann murmured something she couldn't hear, and Margot added, "I'm guessing Deirdre remembered something about the drink cups. That's why you tried to kill her." She blew out a quick short breath. "I should have known it was a woman from the start. Poison first, to subdue before the fatal blow." She needed to remember to tell Parker about the slimy-looking green colored bottle of "something" in Ann's refrigerator. Her hunch—oleander juice. *Killer nectar.*

"Can't prove anything," Ann repeated, her voice trembling. "This has all been about you, little miss privileged Margot Madison-Cross. I hate you," she hissed. "Always have. You and Harvey—could have been me," she said. "No, I got left with Oscar. And that was only because Leila died on him." She paused, as if lost in memory.

"You knew who Camille was from the beginning, didn't you?" Ann had always been smart. "That she was my niece and a pawn to get to me." So sad this is where Ann's abilities took her. "You murdered Faye-Anne, getting rid of the latest in Oscar's string of infidelities and assuring my arrival on the scene to rescue my niece. But after I got here, you decided Oscar and Deirdre, with her harmless crush and knowledge about Patricia's drink cups, needed to go too." She sighed. "Empty the world of everyone who ever wronged you." *All lined up in Gusztáve's Quonset.*

Without warning, Margot no longer cared what the crazy woman was saying, what she thought, what misconceptions and emotions she'd carried around for thirty years—even what she'd done. *Hell with Ann.* She pulled Camille in tighter—her niece and her brother—they were all that mattered now.

Chapter Seven

Betwixt and between

It was still raining, and snatches of thunder and lightning still punctuated NewTown's improbable weather reality. Yet, Margot, Camille, and Gus stood outside getting drenched and chilled to the bone as they watched Parker, EMTs, Thompson, and a forensic team do their jobs. But neither could they make themselves stay in the hut and watch evidence gathering, nor were they willing to be pushed into vans or cruisers. So, in the rain they stood.

Margot thought it an eerie scene, flashing strobes streaking through sheets of rain and bolts of light cutting through the horizon. And the sound of the thunder when it broke was deafening. Indeed, she'd never experienced anything like tonight, and felt like she was visiting another world. A world where the past, present, and future were converging in ways even crazy Ann couldn't imagine.

Camille said to Margot, "You know you've helped save three lives tonight." She was standing in the middle between her aunt and Gus, and looking and sounding like nothing had happened to her tonight. "Oscar, Deirdre, and me." The rain dampened her voice, but it was strong and clear. "I knew you were in the center of this, Auntie Marg. I just didn't know what 'this' was."

Margot pulled herself tall, and as usual, rubbed her hands down the front of her thighs. Her travel-suit trousers were slick with rain—and cold and clammy against her skin. The EMTs were finally closing the back doors on the ambulance about to carry Oscar and Deirdre to the hospital. She inhaled—deep and long—preparing for what was still to come.

It's not over yet.

Despite the miserable circumstances, she almost smiled remembering one of Harvey's favorite sayings — *"The fat lady hasn't sung yet."* She never thought it a kind quip, but Harvey had usually been talking about a patient hanging-in-there against medical odds. So over time, she'd accepted the saying for what it was — his expression of optimism and hope.

"I'm going with them," Camille said. "Oscar needs me." Her words conveyed a sense of urgency. "Since I know what's wrong with him. I need to tell Doctor K what tests —"

"Your father needs you more," Margot said with her own sense of urgency.

"Father?"

"If you're feeling strong enough, we need to go to Palm Springs." Her words and tone were unequivocal. "Tonight. Now."

She was no longer worried about Camille, and it was a heck of a time, and heck of a way to do it. Whatever was going on with Oscar was important, but Margot knew that for Gray, *time was of the essence,* yet again. Wind had joined the rain, and seemed to now want to take their words and pummel them into oblivion. But the three of them were standing almost shoulder-to-shoulder, so she guessed Gusztáve could hear their words — despite Mother Nature.

Margot was past tired, emotionally drained, and soaked. She closed her eyes and lifted her face skyward for a few seconds, letting the rain pelt her eyelids,

Gus turned and stepped in front of the two women. "I'll drive you."

"No, Gusztáve." It warmed Margot's heart he wanted to help her without a clue to what was now happening. But Camille was right, Oscar and Deirdre needed support; for the time being, Gusztáve and Parker would have to supply that handholding. She could barely see Gusztáve's face, and rain was pouring off the brim of his soggy Stetson, but she reached out, touched his arm, and softened her tone. "I appreciate the offer. I really do. And I certainly don't want to drive in this storm — but someone needs to stay with Deirdre and Oscar."

"Cajon Pass can get nasty in this kind of weather." He took her hand from his arm and enclosed it in both of his. "And in the dark." He shook his head. "Not going to be fun." Then he leaned in closer, squinted his eyes, and peered into hers. "This has been a long night."

"I have to go to Palm Springs."

He glanced quickly at Reed and Hollist a couple hundred feet away. "Not even sure they'll let you go."

"I'm not asking." His hands were large, warm, and comforting—especially in the cold wind-driven rain. Nonetheless, Margot pulled her hand away, and grabbed Camille. "Come on Sweetheart. Gray needs us."

After they'd turned and started walking away, Margot fumbled in her pocket and found her cell phone. No signal. *Oh well,* once on the road, back closer to "civilization" they'd get a signal, and she'd have Camille call George. Even though he was in Chicago, he could make some calls for them. Get everything set up. *George is my treasure.*

She remembered she'd left the keys in the car, and before Gus could further complain, or Parker could figure out what they were up to, she again took Camille by the arm and pulled her the remaining few feet to the car. "This is serious," she insisted as they finally reached her SUV. "A matter of life and death."

Camille said, "I'll drive, you ride. Maybe you could call the hospital and give them the details on Oscar's condition? Carol Kubiak heads up Emergency, and she can communicate with the EMTs behind us."

"Of course," Margot said. Her niece was right, Oscar needed to be diagnosed quickly and correctly. As she rushed around to the passenger side, she prayed they'd get to Palm Springs in time, and as Camille backed up and turned around, Margot looked back at the scene still playing itself out at Gusztáve's Quonset hut. Even through the darkness and rain-streaked window, she thought she saw a wry smirk on Gusztáve's face, and it looked like Parker and Hollist had yet to notice their departure. Was that Patricia and Oozie on the periphery, getting drenched? *Patricia must have seen all the lights.*

Their "escape" would have been humorous, if she wasn't so tired, cold, and wet—and the circumstances so dire.

"Gray," she whispered across the Mojave. "I'm coming, I'm coming."

The night was equally dark in Palm Springs, with dense clouds blocking the stars and moon, making Gray's hillside treacherous. Thorns and piercing stickers seemed to be on every plant, bush, or tree she tried to grab hold of, and the water-soaked sand and clay below her feet felt like mush.

Once again in the same night, Margot was scared beyond what she could imagine.

At least they had two meager flashlights Gus had evidently stuck in the glove compartment, *and* the storm had already passed through this area. But she was now beyond soaked—and feeling like she was swimming in dirt and sand-colored mud—struggling to find Gray, but so afraid they wouldn't reach him in time.

Camille was twenty or so feet ahead, and seemed to be faring a little better as they searched the hillside below her brother's hacienda. *I just need to keep Camille in sight.*

Until Palm Springs, the storm had mocked them, swirling its mischief around them, making visibility horrible, and the usually dry roads hydroplane-slick. Margot was grateful Camille had driven through Cajon pass—though going faster than she thought advisable.

To keep their minds occupied, Margot kept talking about all the latest developments in brain surgery, skull based surgery techniques, Intraoperative Guidance Systems—whatever medical developments came to mind. *Anything to keep our minds off Gray.*

She didn't want Camille to know how scared she was, but internally Margot prayed they'd make it through the night. She'd stopped Ann, hadn't she? Rescued Camille, Deirdre, and Oscar? Indeed, somewhere around Beaumont, for an eerie but significant moment in time, she realized she was a different woman. *Certainly not the Margot Madison-Cross who'd left Chicago just a few short days before.*

"We have to find Gray," she called out, knowing Camille couldn't possibly hear her. In frustration, she complained to Graham's hill, "I should have seen it earlier." The headaches, the voices, the mule deer accident, the mysterious trespasser that only he saw. *Hallucinations.* Camille had agreed on the drive over. *A brain tumor.* It had been the memory of Leila's death from college days, and the study in the medical monogram she'd skimmed on the airplane flying in that had brought it all together.

If he'd only had tests done after his accident. Thank goodness he'd insisted she fly out. She caught her breath loudly, and Camille must have heard, because she turned and called out, "We'll find him, Auntie Marg, we'll find him."

With those words, Margot saw Gray, barely feet in front of Camille. She pointed her flashlight toward him and cried, "Over there! Over there!"

In seconds, Camille was at his side. In another moment, Margot was there too—on the ground in the hillside slush—watching her niece cradle Gray's head in her arms.

"Oh, Daddy, oh, daddy," Camille cried. "You're alive, you're alive." Tears streamed down her young face.

It was in that moment that Margot knew she would *never, ever* tell Camille that Gray was not her natural father.

In the distance she heard the siren of what she thought was an approaching ambulance. Though thousands of miles away, George had come through yet again.

Chapter Eight

Graham spoke with both of them. The best sign of a life still to be lived that she knew of. She'd heard Harvey admonish many times. "Get them to talk to you. Don't just rely on the damn machines."

Still, Margot was not yet convinced the worst was over. Evidently, neither was the hospital staff. She was trying to make herself inconspicuous next to the door while two nurses were doing their checking-vitals routine. Camille was in the room too, but only inches from his bedside, watching everything, and unabashedly putting in her unrequested medical two cents.

It was a side of her niece Margot was unfamiliar with, and seeing her "being a doctor" was interesting—though the dynamics were a little different in this case since the patient was her father.

Gray looked like he'd been to hell and back. He was alive, nonetheless, and Margot was surprised how full her heart felt just guessing he'd make it. It had only taken him two days to come around enough for her and Camille to explain what had happened Tuesday night.

He still didn't know about Ann and Oscar. *Later.* A little at a time.

The pre-op team had been competent, the neurosurgeon was a young doctor Camille had never met but said had excellent diagnostic skills, radiology had acted with a sense of urgency, and the OR theatre team had been great. She couldn't have asked for better. Nonetheless, no matter how "perfect" the medical team, you don't just pop out of surgery to remove a craniopharyngioma like a pop-tart—benign status notwithstanding. Gray's recovery so far was remarkable, given his age, but some things could wait. Like the knowledge his sister and daughter were almost killed just a couple hours before finding him wandering around his property looking for a nonexistent trespasser.

Poor Gray. "He could have died," she mouthed the words, then shivered in her corner, letting the images of that night come back for a moment. Gray did know they had come looking for him—found he wasn't in the house and the front door open, and guessed he'd gone hunting for his trespasser.

Eventually the nurses left, and from the look on Camille's face, Gray was progressing okay. Margot closed her eyes for a moment, and tilting her head toward the ceiling, took a couple seconds to be thankful. For a moment she expected her eyelids to be pelted with rain—just like Tuesday night. When she opened them she found Camille staring at her, now only a couple feet away, and a slight smile caressing her face.

"You've been scared, too," Camille said. "Haven't you?"

Hearing the relief in Camille's voice, she also smiled. The words and thought, *so many lies,* forced itself through her consciousness. Followed by, *first, do no harm.* "Of course, sweetheart." She reached out to take Camille's hands into hers. "Your father means a lot to me."

Camille let her take her hands, and said, "I'm so glad you're here…" Her voice broke, and she looked away toward Graham. When she returned her gaze to Margot, her eyes were moist—and their handholding morphed into a long embrace.

When her niece finally allowed herself a restroom and cafeteria break—Margot went over to Gray's bedside where Camille had so diligently stood watch—then took his hand into hers. Unlike Camille's warm moist hands, his skin felt dry and cold. His eyes were closed, and she thought he was sleeping.

"I'm not going to tell her," she whispered. *No.* "Camille is happy."

"Everyone deserves the truth." His voice was also a whisper, and his eyes remained closed, but the clarity of his words were as if he'd shouted from the roof tops.

She leaned forward and stared at his profile. "Why? So there can be more misery, more uncertainty, more disappointment in her life?"

"Harvey was her father." He opened his eyes, staring into the space straight ahead.

Margot spoke slowly and with emphasis. "*You* are Camille's father, *Graham*." She moved so she could capture his gaze, look into his eyes. "Harvey sacrificed little on her behalf. It was easy for him to mentor her—he had all the fun part. You and Meredith—you were the ones that gave her everything—did the hard part of making her the woman she is. The parenting that counted came from the two of you."

Graham was silent for a long while. Finally, he said, "You're right."

"You know," she said, her heart full. "Before I go back to Chicago, do you want to go for a drive?" She thought he smiled a little. "You have some lovely hills all around your hacienda." In truth, she knew it would be awhile before Graham would be on his own. She and Camille would stay with him a few days, but plans were already in the works for him to stay in NewTown with Camille until he could manage on his own.

She felt her cell phone vibrate, but ignored it. These moments with Gray were too precious.

When Camille returned, Margot stepped out of the room, went down the hall to a general waiting area, and found a quiet spot. The second before she flipped open her cell phone, she had the oddest sensation in the pit of her stomach. The only time she experienced anything akin was during a Mt. Shasta hike on her first trip to California. *Decades ago.* At the time, Harvey had "clinically" diagnosed the sensation as vertigo. *So much a doctor, so much of the time.*

She looked down at her phone expecting the worst. 'Missed call,' it read. 'Doctor Kenneth Melon.' Her mind instructed her to call him later—much later. Nonetheless an inexplicable force from within took hold of her index finger and pressed the green call symbol. The guiding hand had her bring the phone to her ear and wait through three ring tones.

The time of reckoning had come.

And again, she felt the self she knew as Margot Madison-Cross was not in control. Fear sent ice-shivers down the back of her neck to accompany her increasing queasiness. Margot felt as if an interloper version of "Margot" was continuing to overrule her safe and preferred mental state of control and stability.

"Margot!" From across many miles and an ocean, Doctor Kenneth Melon's voice sounded inexplicably familiar—but ominous nonetheless.

"Kenneth," she heard herself say.

"Do you remember when we last talked? I said I had two things to tell you."

"Yes."

He hesitated, before continuing, "I wanted you to know I was asked to submit my In Vitro records for a comprehensive study report in Spain. Coverage was from the very beginning days in Chicago, and then here in Barcelona."

She held her breath, and felt as if her heart stopped.

"I didn't give them your records," he said.

She couldn't speak for a moment, and when she did find her voice, Margot was barely in control. "Thank you," she said in a whisper of relief and gratitude. She wanted to pour out over the phone how grateful she was to him in so many ways—for what he did several decades ago, and for what he'd just done. But the right words just wouldn't come.

"I understand," he said, then rung off.

Margot brought her cell phone from her ear and stared at it, as if the little piece of technology was somehow complicit in this most wonderful piece of news. This cell phone she hated so much.

It took her a bit to gather her mind, heart, and emotions. *Kenneth Melon was protecting the biggest lie of them all.*

Dearest Harvey had willingly endured the clinical embarrassment of supplying his sperm in an attempt to impregnate her. *He had so wanted a child.* Maybe she should have endured more tests herself, but, *no,* she hadn't wanted a pregnancy as badly as him. Oddly, her ovum were healthy and fertilizable—but clearly not within her own womb.

"Meredith," she now called out to her deceased sister-in-law across the great beyond. *Meredith had so desperately wanted a child.* Meredith the adventuress, wanting to try the great new "test tube" process. Yes, she would carry the cherished zygote in her womb.

Her and Harvey's sperm and ovum. Meredith's womb. Just the four had been involved—Harvey, herself, Meredith, and their doctor, Kenneth Melon.

Even now, Margot felt her skin warm remembering what they'd done. For sure, they'd been medical trailblazers. Had their acts been shameful? Naïve? Virtuous? Evil? Against God and nature? She'd asked those questions so many times since—and honestly didn't know. She did know the result—her dear Camille Metoyer-Madison was a precious jewel.

She would never stop calling Camille her niece. To call her daughter, even in her mind would be disrespectful to what she and Meredith had agreed to—and Harvey and Meredith had kept as a secret into death. Meredith's death did not change that—even though her half-lie had almost brought disaster on them all. Margot guessed Gray had guessed something had gone on, and Meredith had manufactured an affair rather than tell the whole truth. *So be it.* Better to leave the deceased Harvey and Meredith maligned as lovers, than hurt Camille now.

Lies of convenience. Or maybe lies of love?

Camille would always be her niece in nomenclature, in thought, and in public. Physiologically and in her heart, of course, Camille was her daughter. But words, well, words were just that. Words.

After Margot left, Graham remained conscious for awhile. He hoped they'd let up on the opiates soon. Of course, neither did he want to be in pain.

Remembering how his sister had peered into his eyes a few moments earlier, he wanted to smile, but his face muscles refused to respond. It was like Margot had peered into his very soul again—not much different than when he was babe in the world.

When he was lying in the ditch thinking about dying, he'd thought the only answer was telling Camille the truth. But here, in his hospital bed, having survived brain surgery of all things, Margot had made him understand that doing no harm was what mattered. And sometimes lies of convenience were more than just "convenient." They were necessary. Margot would never hear from his lips she was adopted. A small omission, he thought.

Indeed, Margot had saved his life. *A brain tumor for God's sake.* He would never forget. So as his sister wished, his not being Camille's natural father would remain the *biggest lie of them all.*

His fading thought before returning to pain free opiate-land was, *what a lucky man I am.*

Chapter Nine

A week later

While Graham continued to recuperate, Margot thought that in some ways, the time spent with Camille at Gray's hacienda was like a vacation. A lovely setting with plenty of time to talk to her. An activity she hadn't realized in the past could be so special. She'd settled for telephone conversations—that would not be enough in the future.

Albeit her new personal discoveries with Camille occupied her heart and mind, the wheels of justice had ground on, with both of them having to go into Palm Springs and make statements, which were then transmitted back to NewTown, and ultimately Barstow and the County.

While Graham slowly recuperated, Margot talked to George and Gusztáve daily, and she noticed Camille often on the phone with Parker Reed. After one such call, Camille shared with her how he was still very fond of Dogue, and drove her pup around with him in his jeep during his shifts. Not kosher, but he did it anyway. Didn't want to leave him at home alone.

They also found out, through both Parker and Gusztáve, Oscar had only been kept for a couple days at the hospital. They were however still monitoring Deirdre's recovery. Oleander poisoning was not something to be messed with. Fortunately, medical consensus was she'd eventually be alright.

And though Margot fought the compulsion, the week also turned out to be a time for trying to understand her past. One day she would see Ann in court—and have to relieve their early days, and that night of hell in Gusztáve's Quonset. It had still been all so clear and vivid during her deposition in Palm Springs. Painful as it might be, she needed to retain that clarity for her time on the witness stand.

In passing almost, she also noted Graham seemed to be viewing the world a little differently. She couldn't yet tell to what extent, *and only time,* she thought, would produce a meaningful answer. For now, she could see his "Hacienda" no longer mattered as much as in the past. And his sports car, his former pride and joy, now returned to like-new condition—was sitting in the garage lonely and un-adored.

Finally, a week passed, and the time came that Graham was able to travel. They loaded him into the backseat of the Escalade with pillows, blankets, snacks, and plenty of water. Camille was pampering the hell out of him, and it warmed Margot's heart she loved him so much. *Harvey would have liked it too.* She even allowed herself to romanticize the sometimes unpredictable Meredith probably would have also taken pleasure in the two's interaction.

Logistics were easy—Graham's housekeeper and her husband promised to make sure everything at the Hacienda was kept tiptop. Particularly, Graham had insisted, feeding his beloved sparrows.

Margot, Camille, and Graham arrived in NewTown after an uneventful drive in beautiful seventy-five degree weather, and under a clear blue sky.

No wind, no rain.

They met Parker and Gusztáve at the hospital where more pieces fell into place. Even Graham had wanted to stop and see how Deirdre—a complete a stranger—was doing. Hopefully she would be released later that afternoon. Their stop and meet-up involved Camille moving Graham to Parker's jeep. They would drive him to the Lewis place where Oscar was waiting for them. Patricia had taken Deirdre under her wing—*a sister substitute?*—and was picking her up later. The fact Patricia was a Certified Nursing Assistant was a bonus.

Pride swelled her chest as Margot waited patiently, watching it all—coordinated by Camille. *What a competent young woman.*

As for Gusztáve, however, Margot found him as irritating as ever.

"How are you planning on getting through security with that little gun of yours?" Gusztáve asked after Parker, Camille, and Graham finally pulled out of the parking lot. His gaze on some distant and indiscernible spot ahead of him, his hands hanging from his baggy jeans pockets by his thumbs, and his aged Stetson tilted to hide a smirk she was sure was there.

Nonetheless, she managed to keep her voice even. "Not trying to. I'm leaving it with Camille." She nodded her head once in confirmation of her words. "Every woman needs a gun."

"I ain't arguing with you about that," he agreed amiably, then asked, "Want to take a ride before going home?"

Maybe I was wrong about the smirk?

She looked out at her rental, now sitting lonely in an almost empty parking lot. "Where to?" She smiled slightly, thinking about the last two weeks. "We've gotten a lot of miles out of that car."

They were standing under the emergency entrance canopy—like they'd done that horrible afternoon only a week or so ago. Margot felt the moment awkward—not necessarily unpleasant—but anticlimactic for sure.

"Well," he said. "There's no sand blowing, it's not too hot." He turned to her and smiled invitingly. "What about giving your niece and brother time to settle in?" He waited a few seconds before adding, "Hungry?"

"You know, I never did like Ann." After she'd said the words, Margot was quite amazed that she admitted such a personal item to Gusztáve and felt her face warm from embarrassment. And, *why now?* "Yes, I could eat."

"Come on," he said and extended his hand. "We've got plenty of time to head out to the Ludlow Café. And I'll tell you all about Amboy on the way."

She took his hand for a moment as he helped her off the one step covered area into the parking lot proper, then immediately pulled it away. Not too abruptly she hoped. *Don't want the old coot to get offended.*

"You want to wait for me to pull the car around, Ms. Margot?"

She caught a tease in his tone and laughed. "Am I a senile and doddering old lady in your eyes?"

"Hardly."

Margot cleared her throat quickly and followed him to the end of the parking lot where their Escalade awaited. Now the only car there.

"So, what's so special about this Ludlow place? And who's this Amboy guy?" She further cleared her throat, and felt she had her emotions—*whatever the heck they were*—under control.

"Amboy is a place made famous by Buster Burris. Ever heard of him?"

"No, but I'm sure you're about to tell me."

He opened the door for her. "Tell you the whole story once we get going." He went around to the driver's side, and once in his own seat asked, "You ever done the whole Mother Road?"

"No," she lied. *Too many years ago to still count.*

"Hmm. Well maybe…" He let the end of his thought be swallowed into the roar of the Escalade's 403 horsepower motor turning over.

Later that evening, after a pleasant and surprisingly interesting Route 66 adventure with Gusztáve, Margot found herself standing alone "taking in" Velma's--letting the tavern's faux saloon doors snatch her thoughts and emotions. And inexplicably, she found herself overtaken by a strong sense of *déjà vu*--even though she'd never been there before.

Then in rapid succession, two more things happened. The recognition that, *"it" wasn't over yet,* screamed through her consciousness—followed by the memory of a cold and dreary afternoon in suburban Chicago waiting in the country club foyer for Graham. Wishing she could disappear, while watching as he charged into the club bar, his face contorted in anger, yelling at his wife Meredith, and chastising the bartender. She'd watched from the distance, but still, she'd been able to see Camille cringe as he'd grabbed her five-year-old hand, pulling and hurrying her away from Meredith, out through the dining area—out into the club's foyer and into her waiting arms.

But why remember now?

She'd stopped when they had arrived, letting Camille go in ahead without her—and now, Margot took several more moments to really appraise the building standing before her.

On a visceral level, she realized her mind had somehow elevated Velma's swinging double-door entry to the level of some kind of life altering portals. Once she stepped through those doors, Margot was sure her world would alter—and there would be no return. *A stone was still left unturned.*

She shook herself slightly and whispered, "Good grief." Nonetheless, for a moment, she wanted to call Camille back outside and go home, thwarting whatever was about to happen.

As was her usual, Margot rubbed the front of her Dolce and Gabana jeans along her thighs—while wondering if she'd ever rid herself of the ridiculous mannerism. Then she pulled down on the Route-66 T-shirt Gusztáve had given her as a going away present last night. The shirt was definitely not her style, *but what the heck*, she'd decided at the last moment. She so wanted to fit in Camille's new environment. Still, she'd also slipped on a Liz Claiborne linen sport jacket—her latest purchase from a revisit to the Lenwood Mall.

The building certainly wasn't ominous. It looked like it had been built in the fifties, and was styled like an old-time saloon. Indeed, the bright purple color caught your eye, and though the building sat a little back from the road, it was located on the south side of Route 66—down the road from Deel's Plumbing Supply.

She took a deep breath, then headed up Velma's entry steps—toward her unknown.

It was dark inside, as a tavern should be, and it was hard to see at first, but she heard Camille's voice, saying, "There she is now."

Her niece's voice was coming from her right, where a group of tables and a pool table occupied the space in front of a juke-box.

"Over here, Auntie Marg, over here."

Her eyes adjusted quickly, and though there were only a couple vans in the parking lot, there were ten or twelve people gathered around the tables which were strewn with pictures, and *brochures?* They were laughing, and chatting in several European languages, she thought. Indeed, the place was surprisingly crowded and alive with energy.

Parker was sitting next to Camille, leaning back in his chair, a half filled beer mug in his hand, and an expectant look on his face as he switched his gaze between her and Camille.

He doesn't know what Camille is up to. Neither did she.

As soon as Margot was in reach, Camille stood up, grabbed her arm, and pulled her in close. "Look," Camille said, and held her own hand up high, twirling it around dramatically for all to see.

Margot's Burmese "pigeon blood red" ruby was now on Camille's index finger, and the beloved stone managed to sparkle, even in tavern darkness. Margot wondered if the word "tavern" was correct? Maybe Velma's was actually a saloon because of those swinging doors? *No,* bar—that's what she'd heard Camille say. Just like at the country club—though "tavern" was often used for Chicago neighborhood establishments. Evidently the word was planted firmly somewhere in the crevices of her psyche.

I need to replace the old, with the new.

Camille was saying excitedly, "My Aunt gave this to me last night." She pulled Margot in closer, her face aglow. "It belonged to my great-grandmother Thelma Edison-Hall."

Her ruby was now where it should be—that Margot knew for sure. She said, "I'm glad you like it." Camille seemed so comfortable in this setting. Evidently she hadn't been too traumatized by her mother's bar-hopping.

Parker got up, found a chair, and squeezed it into the space between Camille and him. Once she sat down, he said *sotto voce*, "She's changed, you know." He waited, and when she didn't responded, added, "You changed her."

Surprised, Margot turned to look at him. He was smiling, and he added, "I think she dreaded coming into this place, just a couple weeks ago."

She didn't know what to say, how to feel. He was complementing her, she thought—but wasn't sure.

Someone turned on the jukebox, and Johnny Cash's distinctive voice made hearing and talking difficult. But Margot was sure Parker next said, "I knew all along, you were the center of all of this."

Inexplicably, she knew what he meant.

"Who are all these people?" Margot asked, and was relieved to hear her voice sounded normal. First, intimidated by a tavern—*bar*—then almost overwhelmed by her niece's love. "And all these pictures?

"A tour from Sweden. Doing The Mother Road." He smiled. "It's part of the experience, you know. Taking tons of pictures of the people you meet, the sights you see."

The young man sitting inches to Parker's side, said, "Hi, I'm Oskar." His accent was thick. "And this is my friend, Emma." He nodded his head toward a young woman to his left. "Sorry, wasn't eavesdropping, but we listen to you Americans good. Learn English better, you see?"

Oskar? Unbelievable. Margot smiled and said. "I'm visiting from Chicago." Then inclined her head toward Parker. "He's local."

Oskar's eyes lit up before he turned to his lady friend and said, "Ja, Ja. See, I said. Different accents."

Margot laughed outright, and Parker said, "Funny how an accent will set up a whole picture of a person in your mind."

She turned and gave Parker what she hoped was a piercing look. "You don't think I have an accent, do you?"

It was his turn to laugh. "Of course you do."

"And the picture of the person you *think* you see?" Camille's young man was sounding almost as insufferable as Gusztáve.

"I take the fifth," he demurred. And everyone laughed.

"You're right, you know," Camille said looking across Margot to stare at Parker. "George has a great accent. Makes you feel quite proper." She said to Margot, "I heard Cook Phillip call him Gregory once, and I could see he was steaming. But his anger was delivered in his British accent—made a huge difference."

This was news to Margot, but she knew George and Cook Phillip had a minor rivalry going on. *Gregory*. She lulled the name over. *Just as elegant as George*, she thought.

This time, Oskar's jaw dropped before he spoke. "We were just talking about a Gregorio—we met him in Spain a few months back. In an American-style Jazz club." He waited for Emma to nod her confirmation. "I was just showing our friends a picture of him." He closed his eyes and smiled broadly. "*Underbar*. Lots of *cava*. Too much *cava*."

"Want see?" Emma asked, passing the picture to Oskar. "He Gregorio. I call Gregory." She laughed and shook her head. "He say, NO, he George."

That's odd. Margot asked, "Can I see your 'George'?" He handed her the picture, and she looked down at the dog-eared color snap.

Margot's world died, and for several long moments, she couldn't move—was barely able to breathe. *Her George* stared back at her. Finally, after what felt like an eternity, she felt Camille's hand take hers, then take the picture away from her as she prayed her face had betrayed nothing.

"Why, it's—" Camille started, then caught herself in seeming disbelief. "This is our George," she finally stammered. "I'd recognize that look anywhere." Then she laughed. "George hasn't told you the whole truth, Auntie Marg."

Miraculously, Margot managed to compose herself and force a laugh with her niece. "Is that his family in the picture?" she asked congenially. And for the first time in her life, she did not like being Margot Madison-Cross.

Fool, fool, she screamed within her head.

Seemingly in another world, she heard Oskar say, "We're still connected on the Internet. Knows cyberspace good."

Camille passed the photo back to Oskar. He shook his head. "Don't know for sure, but think he say wife, kid, her parents." The young man gestured broadly and a worldly smile spread across his open face. "We travel lot, we meet lot of people. Some truth tellers, some not so much."

"Ja, ja." Emma agreed.

"But," Oskar said in a lower and more serious tone. "You Americans—Route 66ers—all honest. Friendly." He looked all around the bar good naturedly. "No liars."

Margot wanted to cry out, *"Oskar, there are liars everywhere."* And for a second she had to fight down the urge to pound her fists on the small bar table in front of her.

Fortunately, before she could vent such unladylike anger, Velma's saloon doors burst open allowing Gusztáve to appear on the scene in dramatic form—silhouetted in the door frame. Margot was overjoyed to see him again—and quite dismayed that she was.

"You decided to come," she said, knowing her words and delivery sounded like a school girl.

Seemingly not mindful of anyone else in the bar, he headed straight to their table, squeezed in yet another chair as close to Margot as his bulk and the chair legs would allow—pushing her closer to Camille in the process. All in all, a very tight squeeze.

"Didn't think I'd let you get away without a big fat kiss, now did you?"

She looked into his eyes and thought the crazy coot was serious. Then he winked, and she smiled in return. Gusztáve was still an unsolved mystery.

Clearly, he hadn't always been a "Mojave man," and in time, maybe he'd reveal his past to her. *Probably with a few lies thrown in.* She almost laughed, but felt too miserable inside.

It was his turn to lean close into Margot's ear, the other one. "Oscar said you're buying the clinic for Camille."

She didn't answer, and he added, "She's lucky to have an aunt like you."

It was the least a mother could do.

"Why do you think this town's founders called it NewTown?" Margot asked him out of the blue.

"Lack of imagination, I'd guess."

Epilogue

A thin line of orange illumination stretched across the lower ridges of the Cady Mountains. Camille was aware she was witnessing the first seconds of the new day. But more, it was if she was witnessing the birth of a new era of her life. What stretched before, she could only guess at. Nonetheless, with the rising of the sun, a tickle of excitement was rising in her heart.

She looked to her left at Parker in the driver's seat of his police Jeep. Dogue was was sitting up in back, looking out the window. He too, seemed entranced by the emerging sunrise. They were parked at what Parker said was the end of the road—for cars at least—past Patricia's house.

So they sat, the heater on low to ward of the early morning chill, a thermos of sweetened tea, and a box of day-old donuts at the ready.

They were on a slight hillock, and though faced with rising hills fairly close, they still had a panoramic horizon view. She thought Parker must have spent time here before, picking this perfect spot to sit and think. For sure, this was a spot for contemplation.

Silence enveloped them, and it was nice, comfortable actually. A good sign, she could be with this man and not have to talk—even though they'd gone through a lot when her aunt had been in town.

What Oscar must be going through now was horrible. He'd taken one of those extended stay places near San Bernardino. Ann's trial process would take awhile, and he planned to be there at her side. She hadn't yet decided whether that was the best of loyalty—or plain stupidity.

She stole another look at Parker, and thought she saw an expression intimating he was about to say something. She fancied he was about to reveal a secret of some sort. Something from his past— "baggage" he was loathing to reveal? Quickly, whatever she saw encompassing his face was gone. Undoubtedly, there were surprises ahead. She didn't think that a bad thing.

Parker remained silent, and she wondered if he would reach across the seat and take her hand.

After a moment, he said, "You're lucky to have someone like your aunt Margot. I know your father is close, but nothing like someone who loves you like a mother can."

For a second, she almost told him she thought Uncle Harvey was her actual father. It was a feeling she'd always had. But it really didn't matter, *now did it?* Of course she would never ask her aunt and father about it—too hurtful. As far as she was concerned, at this point in all their lives, *who cared?* At any rate, she thought this living-lie should be left alone. Far more convenient for all concerned. And definitely not something to share with Parker.

This was a big lie. But a lie worth preserving.

If they made it as a couple, she and Parker would create their own life-secrets. Her family's past indiscretions were not relevant to their future. And with that thought, Camille didn't wait for Parker to take her hand—instead she reached across and took his into hers.

Margot stood as close to her penthouse window expanse as her broad credenza-like windowsill allowed. She touched the glass— *cold*—as it always was, and on the street below she could see scraps of litter—trapped in mini-vortices of lake induced winds—whirling willy-nilly, with nowhere really to go. Just round and round, up and down, trapped in the city's unchangeable spiral of life, and from the twenty-second floor of The Salk, looking like wisps of tissue. *Metaphors for my life?* The trash would be picked up by the ever vigilant Department of Streets and Sanitation, or the Bureau of Street

Operations, then unceremoniously hauled off to an incinerator or land fill.

She remembered the eastward bound debris accumulated on so many NewTown chain linked fences, and she mused half-aloud, "Funny." Such different worlds—but with trash the great cross-cultural equalizer.

It was early Sunday, a uniquely quiet time on Michigan Avenue. She watched a lone jogger—in shorts and the top half of his body bundled-up against the wind's onslaught in a hooded sweat jacket—bravely make his way into Grant Park. Involuntarily, she shivered in empathy. Then remembering the horrendous dust storm that fateful day when she'd met Gusztáve, Margot wondered which was worse—frigid Chicago blasts, or blinding desert storms?

Like the trash, wind-hell on both ends of Route 66.

Fall had arrived, and Margot had done nothing all summer but think, remember, and take-in the experience of being alone once again. *Loneliness.* That was the toughest part.

Even this lovely morning, her mind imagined she *heard* George come up from behind her—like he had so many times in the past. *Smelled* his annoying Burberry Brit. *Felt* as if it were still real, him gently running his hand along her arm. He was capable of such comforting caresses. And like he'd done so many times in the past, she wished he was there to slip his hand into hers. And in return, as she had also always done in the past—she mentally closed her fingers around his. Without realizing, Margot closed her eyes, and once again felt his lips on her neck—on her mouth.

Funny game we played. And in the end, he'd disappointed so hurtfully—trying to imply he knew what Doctor Melon had wanted. He hadn't, and she knew it.

A game built upon a lie. George's lie this time. Convenient or otherwise, she didn't know. But for sure, she would never tell Camille about her "walk on the wild-side" with George—nor anyone else for that matter. Not that their affair had been the greatest lie of all, but it was indeed a "whopper."

Actually, who would care? The world had changed. *Had she? Maybe.*

Now, she would have to take care of herself. George may have been an untrue lover, but he'd always come through when she'd needed him—but he had a family to take care of. After the verbal reaming she delivered before sending him packing, maybe he'd treat his lovely wife and child as the blessing they were.

She sighed lightly, genteelly.

The jogger was gone, and the trails winding through the park were now all empty. The lakefront winds clearly had won the morning. She wondered if NewTown's winds were also wailing and battering Gusztáve's Quonset fortress? *Of course they are.* She half smiled, and almost tasted sand again.

Indeed, from the Mojave to Chicago—on the wings of the prevailing winds rumbling along Route 66—*life was being lived.* Yet here she stood, warm and comfortable in her cocoon of luxury—with only past memories to keep her mind and spirit occupied. With a long deep sigh of closure—*or*—she suddenly questioned, was it anticipation she was actually feeling? As was her habit, Margot straightened her neck, shoulders, and back—bringing herself to her full statuesque height. Her hands went to smooth the front of her thighs—*but she caught herself*—looked down at her hands poised in mid-air, and stopped moving for a moment. Then she took a long and deep breath and clasped her hands in front of her midriff. *Some old habits needed to die.*

"My, my," she said, and returned her attention to the panoramic view just above Michigan Avenue, out past Grant Park and farther, letting her eyes and heart finally rest on the flat far-horizon—blustering Lake Michigan itself—her old and comforting friend.

In that instant, without warning, and with crystal clarity, Margot knew without any doubt—change for her, was now.

M.M. Gornell can be visited at
http://www.mmgornell.com,
http://www.mmgornell.wordpress.com,
and emailed directly at mmgornell@earthlink.net.

www.ingramcontent.com/pod-product-compliance
Lightning Source LLC
Chambersburg PA
CBHW020942180626
46814CB00003B/899